In the Money With You

The Ladies Alpine Society
Book 2

Edie Cay

© Copyright 2024 by Edie Cay
Text by Edie Cay
Cover by Dar Albert

Dragonblade Publishing, Inc. is an imprint of Kathryn Le Veque Novels, Inc.
P.O. Box 23
Moreno Valley, CA 92556
ceo@dragonbladepublishing.com

Produced in the United States of America

First Edition November 2024
Trade Paperback Edition

Reproduction of any kind except where it pertains to short quotes in relation to advertising or promotion is strictly prohibited.

All Rights Reserved.

The characters and events portrayed in this book are fictitious. Any similarity to real persons, living or dead, is purely coincidental and not intended by the author.

ARE YOU SIGNED UP FOR DRAGONBLADE'S BLOG?

You'll get the latest news and information on exclusive giveaways, exclusive excerpts, coming releases, sales, free books, cover reveals and more.

Check out our complete list of authors, too!

No spam, no junk. That's a promise!

Sign Up Here
www.dragonbladepublishing.com

Dearest Reader;

Thank you for your support of a small press. At Dragonblade Publishing, we strive to bring you the highest quality Historical Romance from some of the best authors in the business. Without your support, there is no 'us', so we sincerely hope you adore these stories and find some new favorite authors along the way.

Happy Reading!

CEO, Dragonblade Publishing

Additional Dragonblade books by Author Edie Cay

The Ladies Alpine Society
In Knots Over You (Book 1)
In the Money With You (Book 2)

Chapter One

London, 1868

PRUDENCE CABOT SLIPPED her hands beneath her wool cape and pulled at her shirtwaist. Nerves were supposed to be a thing of the past, so why did she suddenly feel like her clothes didn't fit? The drizzle had left a fine mist on her woolen mittens, and likely her hat as well. It reminded her of the spring showers back home, but then, there were usually clear skies after that. Not this endless gray. The rain in Minnesota had the decency to start and then stop. London's was endless.

The door to the modest townhome swung open. A young man stood there, clearly a servant of some type. It still flustered her, which she hated. She'd grown up doing these sorts of duties for her family, and then after her marriage, they'd hired on people to care for the house. But there was something particular about the English servants that made her feel like she was being judged.

But who cared anymore? She was far from anyone whose opinion actually mattered.

"I'm here to see Mr. Moon." Prudence didn't bother trying to mask her American accent. She swallowed her vowels sounds and cooed the long double *o*'s in the man's name.

"And who shall I say is calling?" The young man kept his face aloof, but Prudence could see the interest flaring in his eyes. Young women were not supposed to call on single men.

However, Prudence was not a young woman, at least by her status. She was an American. She was a member of the Ladies' Alpine Society, and the real reason she could get away with visiting a bachelor was that she was a widow. "A Mrs. Prudence Cabot, of the Ladies' Alpine Society."

The flare suitably extinguished, the footman invited her into the foyer to wait while he informed Mr. Moon. Prudence looked down at her boots, still slightly muddy, on the polished hardwood floor. How did Londoners clean their boots? She didn't see any boot-rakers next to the door like she'd had growing up in Minnesota. And in New York, there were rugs everywhere.

In Spain, they hadn't needed them, and when she was climbing with the Ladies' Alpine Society in Scotland, no one worried about dirt. But she so wanted to make a good impression, and Mr. Moon and his mother had seemed so very proper when she'd met them before.

Suddenly, a housemaid came thundering down the steps. "Pardon me, Mrs. Cabot. Mrs. Moon invites you to the drawing room." The maid cleared her throat and glanced at the door where the footman had disappeared. "First."

Prudence tried not to raise her eyebrows and round her eyes, because she was tired of every Brit telling her she was too expressive. No doubt she did. But as soon as she nodded, the maid trotted down the steps to take her hat, cape, and gloves. She followed the maid up the stairs to Mrs. Moon's drawing room, unsure of what to expect.

Mrs. Moon seemed frail, an impression taken wholly from Mr. Moon's doting on her. She had sat during the one party they'd both attended. In truth, Prudence couldn't think of why Mrs. Moon would want to see her, other than she might be bored.

The drawing room was like a step back in time. The fashions were outdated, with baroque-looking gold frames around every picture, and dark, bold colors everywhere she looked. Inside the room, Mrs. Moon sat tall in a crushed velvet chair next to the fire.

It was April, a month that could hold either a promise of summer or the chill reminder of winter. The fire was roaring in any case.

"Daisy, tea." Mrs. Moon was erect, giving directions to the maid, and dismissing her with a hand. "Sit, please."

Prudence wasn't sure if she should curtsy or bow her head, but she certainly didn't get the impression that Mrs. Moon wasted time. So she did neither and sat in the chair opposite Mrs. Moon's, the heat of the fire already uncomfortably warming her leg.

"You are Mrs. Prudence Cabot." The old lady's ice blue eyes bored into hers. Her hair was silver white, like an illustration of an ice fairy in a children's picture book.

"I am." Prudence did her best not to fidget. She felt all of twelve again, being assessed by the schoolmaster to determine if she would be allowed to continue on in the one-room school.

"A member of that ladies' mountain group with Miss Ophelia Bridewell."

"That's correct." Prudence maintained polite eye contact.

"You smile too much."

Prudence blinked. "I wasn't aware that I was smiling." But now she couldn't help but smile. Since crossing the Atlantic, her pleasant facial features were seen as a pathological deficiency.

Mrs. Moon sneered at her expression. "If you think to catch my Leo, you'll have to be more subtle."

Prudence blinked again. Catch Leo? Was that the cat? She looked on either side of the chair. "I'm sorry, but wouldn't one of the maids be better suited?"

A flush swept up the woman's face. "How—"

"Is the cat—?" Prudence asked, concerned that she'd offended Mrs. Moon.

"What cat?" Mrs. Moon barked.

And then realization dawned. "Oh." She meant her son. Leo was Leopold Moon. Prudence did what came naturally to her— she tipped her head back and laughed. Which probably didn't help any.

"Close your mouth! I can practically see your breakfast."

But Prudence couldn't stop laughing. This woman thought she was there to capture her son, when she was here on Alpine Society business. And there wasn't a lost cat. All the nerves that had accosted her earlier washed away in the wave of her laughter. "What an utter delight. Thank you, Mrs. Moon." Prudence wiped her eyes.

"I certainly didn't—" Mrs. Moon sputtered, but Prudence had heard enough.

"—No need, Mrs. Moon." Prudence held up her hand. "I'm not after Mr. Moon for his money or his company. I'm here on Alpine Society business."

Mrs. Moon drew herself up, now offended on her son's behalf that she wasn't seeking his attentions. So Prudence thought she might have some fun. She was a widow after all.

"My Leo doesn't have time for silly women, Mrs. Cabot." Mrs. Moon scowled at her. "Nor will he fall for your act of disinterest."

"Then my excuses won't be of interest to you, so I'll be perfectly blunt. I married extremely young, to a much older man." Prudence might be mistaken, but she thought she detected sympathy in the woman's eyes. "After nursing Mr. Cabot for the last five years, I've come to Europe to find a lover. I have no need of fortune, or a man's name. But I would like to know what it would be like to find a completely inappropriate man to woo me. Mr. Moon doesn't seem the wooing type." Prudence leaned forward and patted the woman's hand. "He's quite safe with me."

Mrs. Moon looked positively shocked, or at least tongue-tied, which was enough. Prudence stood, feeling much better about her visit.

"If you'll excuse me, I should attend to my business and get on with my errands. Thank you ever so much for your company, Mrs. Moon. I quite enjoyed our conversation. Good day." Prudence passed the maid with a tea tray entering the room just as she was leaving it. She informed the maid of her plans and asked the way to Mr. Moon's study, but before she could leave to explore the house, the footman appeared to escort her.

She followed him back down the stairs, noting the fine polish on all the furniture. Even the muddy footprints she'd left in the foyer had already been mopped up. Behind the stairs was a hallway, which is where the footman opened up a door, eyes averted as she presented herself into the company of Leopold Moon.

In contrast to Mrs. Moon's gilded drawing room, Mr. Moon's study was utilitarian but comfortable. The wood floors were polished, but the rugs smaller, as if creating islands where furniture floated. The bookcases were enormous, stretching up to the ceiling, with a ladder to help fetch the loftier titles. He stood on the ground, fiddling with some kind of filing system that occupied the back wall, behind his desk. He switched out the labels, crushing one into a ball and crossing the room to throw it in the smoldering fire before acknowledging her presence.

"Mrs. Cabot," Mr. Moon greeted her.

She was of half a mind to greet him as Leo, given his mother's discussion, but she reined herself in. His steel-gray eyes did not invite frivolity. Indeed, the only thing they seemed to invite was a *get the hell out*, as the men in Minnesota might say. Well no, they wouldn't say that because they were far too nice for such a sentiment. But the river captains weren't.

"Mr. Moon, I do apologize for calling on you unannounced, but I was far too impatient to wait."

He didn't smile in acknowledgment or offer her a seat. He just stood there, waiting. The muscle in his square jaw pulsed.

"How do you do?" Prudence offered. She couldn't very well ask after his mother's health, as she had just seen the lady, but there had to be some kind of nicety to offer in conversation.

"Very well, thank you." He stared at her expectantly.

Prudence noticed he did not return the question. She cleared her throat. On to business, then. "As you know, we are preparing ourselves for our Matterhorn ascent. We will not be attempting our climb this summer, but rather, next summer, as you are likely aware."

"I am."

Prudence felt rather on the back foot. He wasn't giving her an inch. "As it is so close, Miss Bridewell has asked me to be the liaison with you in regard to fees to purchase equipment and travel expenses."

"I have not heard this." Mr. Moon turned on his heel and strode back to his desk where he sat down.

Prudence followed him, now standing in front of his desk. He'd sat down without offering her a seat. It made her feel . . . well, poorly thought of. She didn't think she had a bad reputation, but clearly Mr. Moon didn't see her favorably. She pulled out the letter from her purse. "I have here a note from Lord Rascomb. Both he and Miss Bridewell have signed it."

Mr. Moon reached for it as Prudence thrust it across the desk, their hands colliding as the paper fell onto the blotter. She pulled back at the tingle that shivered up her arm. It was merely the surprising warmth of his hand, she was sure. Her eyes met his—was that from awkwardness? She suddenly felt far too aware of herself. And aware of him.

She looked at him anew. He was thin, yes, but his shoulders were broad under his coat. His hands ink-stained and calloused. His expression closed, secretive, suspicious.

Was this a cultural difference, or had something happened to this family that made them so very unwelcoming?

He broke their connection first, scanning the letter.

"It's signed right there—" She leaned over to point to the signatures, but he waved her off.

She could almost feel the heat of his body coming off of him in waves. Like the summer sun shimmering across the hot stones of a quarry. How very peculiar a sensation. She'd never felt that before. There must have been some kind of static electricity in the room.

"It looks in order." Mr. Moon glanced up at her. "But how do

I know this is not a forgery?"

Was he accusing her of lying? Her cheeks went hot. There was one thing Prudence did not do, and that was lie. She might have her vices and her flaws, but she did not lie. "Because it is in his own hand. I assume you know what your client's handwriting looks like?"

That ruffled his feathers. He drew back, puffing his chest, just as a bird might. "Madam. This is not the frontier. There are procedures."

If this were the frontier, there would be a place for her to wipe her boots. She was nearly ready to cry an outraged *How dare you* or an *I beg your pardon* but resolved to be more level-headed than that. One thing she despised was when she was accused of being hysterical. She'd never been hysterical in her life. "Then proceed as you wish, so long as the job gets done." Just to add emphasis, she smiled one of her jaw-cracking American grins.

He narrowed his eyes at her. "I will contact Lord Rascomb personally to verify the veracity of this claim. Where might I find you?"

Oh, she was loath to tell him where she stayed, but fine. She jotted down her address—the Strawbridge Hotel, a small but luxurious inn she liked from her last sojourn in London—and returned the paper to him. "When might I expect your summons?"

"Summons?" he repeated, his voice very nearly mocking.

"Unless you want to be seen calling on a shocking American widow who might be forging the name of a Peer of the Realm." She used an exaggerated voice to say the last part. Just to show him how American she really was, and how that hierarchy didn't apply to her.

"Business is business," he said.

She chewed her lip, wondering if that were really true. That much was true in her experience—in New York. She helped her husband with his ledgers for years, and no one questioned when she showed up in offices with them, explaining how she'd taken over secretarial duties for him after his apoplexy. Why? Because business was business. But here, in London, they had this strange class order that mattered more than money. Reputations were made generations before, and could be lost in a moment.

To Prudence, all the bowing and scraping seemed exhausting. She liked the clean clear negotiations she'd conducted. She liked the agreements brokered not because they had a certain last name, but because they had the land or the money, or the need. In Minnesota, more than one woman owned her own establishment outright, since there weren't enough men to stick around and maintain the facilities needed. Though, such an establishment could be taken over at a moment's notice by a man, if she weren't careful.

"Business is business," she echoed. This was silly. She was wasting far too much time on a man who clearly thought she was beneath him. "I'll wait to hear from you then. Good day." She twirled on her heel and left the room, closing the door firmly behind her. Was it a slam? Not really. Enough that her mother wouldn't have yelled at her for it, but was it still too loud? Yes.

Did she regret slamming the door on Mr. Moon? Not one bit.

LEO LOWERED HIS forehead to his desk, letting the cool wood work against his hot skin. Bloody hell. He took a minute to breathe and calm the ache that had now spread to his entire lower body. He'd overheard the woman's conversation with his mother. The bit about looking for a man to woo her, to seduce her, and then seeing the honey-haired American beauty walk through his study door robbed him of all words and decency.

Normally he had so much self-control that there was an excess. Should he have been eavesdropping on his mother? Of course not. But he had never heard a woman so explicitly say she was looking for a lover her own age. Who said such things aloud?

But it wasn't the first time he'd had to fetch a visitor from his mother. The old woman made a habit of taking his callers, reducing them to tears or bringing them to blows, then foisting them off on him, saying the visitors had been the ones ill-behaved.

Leo would like to blame his mother for his trouble conducting himself this morning. And the sunlight, as well. For as Mrs. Cabot entered his room, the sun had clung to her, making her hair glimmer and shine in a way that dazzled. But could he blame the sun?

Perhaps he could blame it on Mrs. Cabot herself. For he'd never met a person—not a single one—who had *laughed* during a conversation with his mother. And for all his mother's rudeness, Mrs. Cabot kept her patience, her candor, and her calm demeanor. *I would like to know what it would be like to find a completely inappropriate man to woo me.*

What did she deem inappropriate? He'd hurried back to his study and sent his footman up to guide Mrs. Cabot wherever she cared to go—whether to finish her business with him or flee the premises. He would have understood either.

But then she came in here, as he was working very hard on not thinking about the open invitation to become this woman's lover. True, he'd not been invited specifically. In fact, she'd said that she didn't think he was the *wooing type*. Was anyone?

Breathe. There were plenty of things to do that didn't concern Mrs. Cabot and wooing. Or picturing her with a much older husband. He shuddered. How did young girls do it? He knew plenty of them did, for various reasons. Mostly obligation, it seemed.

He shook his head to clear the thoughts of Mrs. Cabot's bedroom habits. He was relabeling his file cabinets. Part of his dealings as a private banker was secrecy. He was trained in law, but specialized in money. Why? Because money was what made the world turn. A man could have social power, generational power, but the days of those were waning. Look at the Americans, for God's sake. It was money that brought the Confederacy to its knees. Starving soldiers couldn't fight.

But Leo didn't have the temperament for social power. He didn't have the family for generational power. His knack for numbers and the training of the law meant he could move mountains with capital, and that was where his power lay.

Which was precisely what Lord Rascomb asked him to do. Of course, when he'd initially agreed to keep the books for this enterprise, he'd agreed to do so *pro bono*. He'd thought this would be like many ladies' societies, where there might be a few fundraisers, then eventually the members would marry, the society would dissolve, the money might be donated to an orphanage or the women's hospital, and they would enter a life of domesticity. It required a few meetings a year, entered him into the good graces of a respected aristocrat, and was well worth the trouble.

Leo never expected Miss Bridewell to actually climb a mountain. But then, after the planning and budgeting, they had. The budget had predictably gone over. With so many wealthy women, it was surprising that the excess wasn't more. In his experience, the wealthy were prone to overspending because they weren't accustomed to the harsh realities of having nothing left over. Women even more so, given they were not often privy to the exact income of their husbands.

Mr. Tristan Bridewell had warned Leo early on not to underestimate his sister. Or her plans. So Leo dutifully attended the meetings with his ledger to keep them on track. Would he deny that he was instantly attracted to the American widow? No, of course not. He had eyes, after all. Was he taken by her accent? Of course. Shocked by the toothsome grins that appeared for no reason? Naturally.

But did it make London seem less gray when she was around? Also, yes.

Leo lifted his head, aware that he may have the desk's decorative edging imprinted on his forehead. The ache subsided. Work.

He had three appointments this afternoon to prepare for, and his file system had grown again. This was a good thing, as it meant business was continually growing.

Still, he used his Morse code system, disguised as floral artistry, to label the drawers of ledgers and contracts. While yes, one could just open a drawer and find what one needed eventually, this would require time. And the files were not in alphabetical order, but in birthdate order of his clientele, notated in an alphanumeric cypher. The client birthdates were listed in a ledger in a hidden compartment of his locked desk drawer.

After he finished his new labels and slid them into place on the drawer fronts, he pulled the Ladies' Alpine Society file. In it was the accounting ledger, pertinent documents, and most importantly, signatures. He compared them to the letter that Mrs. Cabot produced. They were identical. Still, he sent a note to Lord Rascomb, asking to call upon him at his earliest convenience.

One couldn't be too careful when money was involved. Disguises and trickery were employed often enough to smooth over outright theft. If anything, Leo's job was the security of his clients' funds.

He looked out his window at the sturdy oak tree. He clocked his seasons by that tree. Examined its gnarled bark. Watched its feathery and furred inhabitants year-round. He celebrated when eggs hatched. Laughed when a squirrel lost its footing, congratulated the rodent when it held an acorn in its jaws.

Today he stared through it. Tonight he could relieve himself of this burden. Give himself permission to picture Prudence Cabot as she might receive a lover her own age. Think of that honey-blonde hair wound about his fingers, silky and soft. About her laughter dissolving into quick pleasure-filled huffs.

Breathe. The tightening below his waist eased as he mentally chanted prime numbers. He ought to get out his monthly to-do list and do extra work today. Otherwise, his afternoon clients would not appreciate his lack of focus. Sighing, he returned his attention to his desk, banishing all thoughts having to do with Americans and with widows.

Chapter Two

"Sounds ghastly," Eleanor Bridewell, neé Piper, commented, taking a second scone. Prudence admired the woman's zest for food, even if she couldn't stomach any more jam. She'd never eaten so many sweets in her life. Even when she lived with her husband, they ate simply. Gregory's constitution was never suited to indulgence. She assumed hers wasn't either.

Prudence shrugged. Telling the story of Mrs. Moon's drawing room accusations had the other ladies roaring with laughter. Well, as much as the Brits roared. Eleanor and Ophelia tittered appreciatively, and Justine's outlandish sigh and blasphemous muttering of *For God's sake* helped make it feel like an accomplishment.

"What did you say after she accused you of designs on her son?" Ophelia's eyes danced with mischief.

Prudence laughed. "Why, the truth."

Eleanor's brows furrowed. "That you are here to climb the Matterhorn?"

"That I came to England—" Prudence explained, and if they didn't know, they'd soon find out, "—to take a lover."

Eleanor coughed swallowing her scone. Ophelia's eyes rounded in shock. Justine threw her head back, American-style, and guffawed as well as any frontier-born girl.

"I'd thought to go to France or Italy to take a lover, as those seemed better cultures for it," Prudence sighed, thinking through last year's dull enterprises before she fell in with this lot. "But while I know the best season to plant different breeds of corn, and have a fair estimate of how many tons a coal cart can hold, I can't speak French."

"I can help you with that," Ophelia said. The flaxen beauty was determined and able. Ophelia could likely teach a rock how to speak French.

"Thank you." Prudence had no intention of taking Ophelia up on the offer, though speaking French might be helpful. She simply didn't want to learn a new language. Climbing a dangerous mountain was enough of a task at any one time.

"Have you found any?" Justine asked, leaning forward.

Bad News indeed, thought Prudence. The nickname had been given to Justine by Ophelia's brother Tristan, now Eleanor's husband. But she was a mischievous girl with a buxom figure that could not be helped. She was cute as a button to boot, making her a magnet for every male in a fifty-mile radius. Prudence had watched Justine in a ballroom, and for every minute Justine protested that her reputation wasn't her fault, she watched as Justine laughed openly and sassed anyone she pleased. While that wouldn't have passed for anything remotely out of order where Prudence grew up, it was decidedly outside the normal behaviors of young ladies in London.

"Found any what?" Prudence asked Justine.

"Lovers."

Eleanor coughed again. Ophelia poured her another cup of tea to help her wash down the dry pastry.

She'd started with the unfiltered truth, so she may as well stay with it. "No. I found that I'm not as bold as I thought I would be. I thought with all my red dresses, I would make quite the splash. But I've slipped into the waters unnoticed, it seems."

"Your dresses aren't red," Justine protested.

"Of course they are," Prudence protested. She'd had them made specifically for the task of attracting a scoundrel. Or a *rakehell* as they might have once called such a man here in

London.

"They're burgundy. Mauve. Wine. If you want a red dress, find a Frenchwoman. They know red." Justine sat back in her chair and took up with her tea again.

"Is that why I can't find a lover? I'm too subtle for Englishmen?" Prudence teased.

"Likely," Ophelia chimed in. "Many need to be bashed over the head to realize the obvious."

"Well," Prudence sipped at her tea, trying not to wonder if Ophelia had ever needed to bash a man over the head with her beauty, "I was blunt enough with Mrs. Moon. I bet that will get the word out. By the next event, I suspect I shall be swarmed with all manner of disreputable men."

"Aren't you afraid of tarnishing your reputation?" Eleanor asked, glancing around each of them. "And tarnishing ours?"

Eleanor's observation took the wind out of her. She'd spent so long in Spain over the winter that she'd quite forgotten about the need to keep her activities quiet for the benefit of the other women in the Alpine Society.

In order to fund their journey—which was expensive indeed—they would need a hefty sum. Ophelia had already penned a few articles about their adventure on Ben Nevis, but had quite a time getting them published. Men's magazines didn't want them because she was a woman, and women's magazines didn't want them because the topic wasn't feminine. The London Alpine Society flat-out rejected women as climbers in general, and ignored Ophelia and Justine, hoping they might go away of their own accord. But neither woman ever just *went away*.

Ophelia looked down at her hands as she spoke. "Prudence, you know that I loathe telling people what to do—" The women snickered. Ophelia looked up, acknowledging her straight-faced humor. "—But I would ask you to deny this claim should it come out openly. I really do need respectability in order to achieve my goals. If we were men—"

"—If we were men, *everything* would be different." Justine

threw herself back in her chair, open disgust on her face.

Prudence felt as if she'd been kicked by a mule. "Of course," she assured Ophelia. "I wasn't thinking. I wanted to set the old lady back a bit, that's all."

Ophelia nodded her thanks, and Prudence suddenly felt old. She was only three years older than Ophelia and Justine, and a few months younger than Eleanor. But her life had been fuller, bigger, harder, than her companions'. She'd swaddled her younger siblings when her mother was busy with some other task long before she was tall enough to see over the kitchen table. She'd helped plow at harvesttime, driving the plow cart as straight as an arrow down the field. And then she'd married, without a courtship, without any trouble, on the suggestion of her parents. Which meant that she'd skipped over this part of life—the feeling of possibilities, of butterflies in her stomach, of having suitors and pretty, meaningless baubles. And despite her pragmatic nature, God help her, she wanted to feel those things.

"But that does bring me to a serious matter," Ophelia said, looking around at them. "Mr. Moon came round yesterday afternoon. It seems he didn't quite believe our Prudence would be handling the funds. But while he was there, he spoke about an uncertainty of budget. That there is a deficit that we may have to make up. Apparently, there are rumblings of a war between the French and the Prussians, and that has driven the market up on everything from leather goods to train tickets. And that's now. It could be worse next year. We might not be able to get to the Alps next spring."

Murmurs went around. Prudence's pride prickled. She had been assigned the task of looking over the ledgers for just this purpose. She did not like that Mr. Moon had gone over her head. As if she didn't know what she was after. As if she hadn't handled sums just as large as he did.

And she'd done so while wiping the bottom of the man whose name graced the bank account. To say her husband had been a railroad baron was to sully his name. He had been much,

much more than that. He'd taught her every one of his tricks, and the last year, she'd done all the banking and business deals as he wasted away in his bed. A fate neither of them wanted, but had little power to prevent. Prudence's fist tightened. She was tired of being underestimated. "I do apologize, Ophelia. I tried to get Mr. Moon to understand the situation."

Ophelia gave her a tight smile. "It's perfectly all right, Pru. It isn't your fault. Besides, Mr. Moon knows now to work with you. Especially since we will be holding a charity ball."

Justine frowned.

Eleanor cocked her head in confusion.

But Prudence couldn't help but reward her friends with an American-sized smile. "That sounds perfect, Ophelia. Give me the details."

"It won't be for some months—the closing of the Season. We'll have an ice theme, of course, since we're raising money for our trip to the Matterhorn."

The confusion on the other two women's faces cleared. "Oh, *we* are the charity," Eleanor said.

"Quite," Ophelia said, pouring another round of tea. "But, as my mother pointed out, sometimes one needs to spend money to make money. So this will be the talk of the season. Lavish. Extreme. The kind of party they threw in the 1700s with animals and newly dug lakes."

Prudence couldn't help but mentally tally the workload of such a party.

"You aren't really digging a new lake, are you?" Justine asked, skepticism underlining every word.

"Probably not," Ophelia admitted. "But I want you to think on that scale. Prudence, I know that you will find me the funds or the work-around for what we need."

"Of course." But all of her contacts were American. She'd need to start over if she expected some kind of discount for whatever amorphous desires Ophelia was dreaming up. And who would be coming up with the ideas?

"This seems like a poor gamble," Eleanor said, the line between her brows visible.

"It's better than Tristan visiting the gaming hells to raise the money," Ophelia said, referring to her brother and Eleanor's new husband. He often got distracted by socializing and forgot to pay attention to the game.

"Very true. But I guess then I could leg wrestle Francis into giving it back," Justine said, referring to her brother, Tristan's best friend and usual game winner.

"No one is leg wrestling anyone," Ophelia said. "Because we are *ladies*."

Justine gave out a disgruntled harrumph that made Prudence laugh. She felt lucky to have fallen in with this strange crowd. It was luck that she'd been spotted by Ophelia and Justine at a party last year. Had it only been a year? So much had happened that it felt as if she'd lived an entirely different life in that span. A life where she acted on behalf of herself, not her husband or her father. A life where she gave orders, rather than take them from her mother or her husband's physician. A life that was utterly hers.

And a life where she could have everything, from transacting her own business to feeling those butterflies in her stomach. As for the meaningless pretty baubles, she could buy those herself. Probably after the Matterhorn ascent. She wouldn't need them on an icy, Swiss mountaintop anyway.

"Mama and I have created a wish list of sorts, but I would appreciate everyone's opinions. I bow to your superior knowledge and experience of what is realistic, Prudence. Give me lavish, and I give you free rein of the purse strings." The pale afternoon light hit Ophelia through the drawing room window, and her golden hair glowed.

Oh, to have that beauty, thought Prudence. But she wasn't envious, she was admiring. Prudence wouldn't know what to do with that kind of face. She preferred her own. "I'm an American. I can only do extremes." Prudence smiled behind her teacup as

Justine roared with laughter.

LEO WAS NOT looking forward to his audience with Mrs. Cabot. He'd made an arse of himself by denying her claims on the Ladies' Alpine Society's funds. Last week he'd personally called upon Lord Rascomb, only to have the man look at him like he was the biggest idiot in the entirety of England and her territories. Which encompassed quite a lot.

Still, he'd brought the ledgers and gone over the accounts with him and his daughter, Miss Bridewell, so they had a starting place. But they both deemed the sum insufficient. Miss Bridewell had left the meeting, returning with a piece of paper, which she handed to her father. He'd glanced over it, nodded his approval and handed it back to her, whereupon she deigned to give it to Leo.

And then Miss Bridewell had gone on at length about Mrs. Cabot's history, her fortune that was entirely her own, and her vast capabilities and formidable mind. It had not helped Leo's situation at all. He'd gone to the Bridewells hoping to get rid of Mrs. Cabot. To banish her from his thoughts.

Instead, he had to concentrate to not recall the dreams he'd had every single night in which Mrs. Cabot had a starring role. Or the fantasies he'd indulged in while he was awake. None of them were the kind of thing a man should think about his client. But it was hard not to remember the visceral ache in the morning, the hardness so strong that he felt it throughout his body, the need that ran down into his thighs. As if he wouldn't be able to think again without finding a way to touch her.

Worst of all, the reason Lord Rascomb instructed Leo to deal with Mrs. Cabot was a budget for a party, of all ridiculous things. He couldn't believe that this silly girl would be the first woman up the Matterhorn. Miss Bridewell was truly frivolous if she believed throwing a party would make her money. But no, she and her mother were convinced that a lavish charity ball would be just the thing. And if Miss Bridewell were so silly, then it stood to reason Mrs. Cabot was as well.

He heard the front door open, and he looked up from his desk in his study, listening. Like clockwork, the maid dashed down the stairs from his mother's drawing room to discover the identity of the guest, so that his mother could shanghai the visitor before Leo could have his appointment. Two sets of footsteps trudged up the wooden stairs. He heard the telltale squeaks of the floorboards in his mother's drawing room. No matter how thick her carpeted rugs were, the wood still groaned in certain places.

He would wait ten minutes. Enough for his mother to bring Mrs. Cabot down a notch. She would be nicely malleable, and he could persuade her not to throw a charity ball, but rather invest the funds in bonds and delay the trip another year or two so the bonds could reach maturity. And by then, the girls would be married off, and all would be well. No one would die on that deadly mountain.

Ten minutes passed, and he hadn't heard any yelling. Nor any squeaking of floorboards to telegraph a departing guest. That was odd. He crept up the stairs, listening.

"He was forty years my senior," Prudence was saying.

Surely she was discussing her father, and not her husband. He frowned.

"He didn't look it, so don't feel sorry for me, Mrs. Moon. He was an attractive man until the end."

It sounded as if she were smiling. How could he know that? Well, she smiled like a daft idiot, so it tracked.

"Still, it isn't right." His mother sniffed in her imperious way. Normally that was a sign she was being dismissive of her company, but it sounded as if she were siding with Mrs. Cabot.

"Perhaps not, but here in England, it seems there are plenty of young women married off to much older men for the sake of a dynasty."

"A *title*, my dear. Nothing so petty as a dynasty."

"Minnesota doesn't have any titles. But we do have railroads. Once the Transcontinental Railroad is finished, the economic engine of the United States will change dramatically. No longer will the Pacific and the Atlantic be separate, but—"

"My dear. Please do not espouse the glory of a railroad at me. My constitution cannot bear it."

Leo could. He very much wanted to hear what Mrs. Cabot was about to say about the American economic prospects. That could very well affect his own investments. He'd assumed the Civil War had destroyed the foundations of domestic trade of their former colony, but perhaps he was wrong. The wealth of Mrs. Cabot would definitely signal a healthy American stock market.

He stepped into the drawing room before he could change his mind. Hands clasped behind his back, he cleared his throat.

Mrs. Cabot jumped, her ungloved hand flying to her chest. She looked at him with surprise in her gray eyes. "My goodness, you scared me."

His mother stared him down with a knowing glance.

"Mother, I have an appointment with Mrs. Cabot. I don't want to run behind."

"You'd rather I perish from loneliness? Keep me locked in a tower, unable to let my old eyes alight on the visage of youth?"

"You're very poetic for a prisoner." Leo was not fazed by his mother's feigned melancholy. She was a nasty piece of work when she wanted to be, and her while she had her outings to her favorite societies, there were whole groups that avoided her for that very reason.

"That's what happens to those craving human kindness." As if his mother wasn't as sharp as two people half her age.

Mrs. Cabot stood up, showing off the cinched waist of her pinstriped white-and-blue day dress and the wide flaring skirts. Her honeyed hair had been curled and styled in such a way that she had arcing tendrils artfully escaping their pins.

Swallowing his urge to ask to touch those curls, he gave her a tight grimace. "I believe you know where my study is."

"Indeed. Skulk off. I'll send her down directly," his mother said sourly.

"It seems our time is at an end," Mrs. Cabot said.

Leo descended the stairway, holding his breath so he could still hear the conversation in the drawing room. He would go arrange himself in his study, keep himself aloof and imposing.

But the women's words faded. As he entered his study, bell-like laughter rang out upstairs. It was a beautiful sound. A pleased sound. And it wasn't his mother.

HONESTLY, MR. MOON was infuriating. His mother, while caustic, was delightful. "I'll pop in early next time so we can have a proper visit," she assured Mrs. Moon as she left the drawing room. Unescorted this time, she could have explored the house as she was compelled to do, but she had been summoned. Time was part of his complaint. So fine, she would appear as requested.

She knocked on the door to his study and waited for his imperious call of "Enter." As if he didn't know who was on the other side of the door. Ninny.

He was ensconced behind his desk. This time, he stood and offered her the chair in front of it with a simple gesture of his elegant hands. She was more sure-footed this time, and it gave her an opportunity to look around the room. The bookshelves she'd noted last time. There were filing drawers behind the desk, labelled artfully. She squinted, trying to make out the drawings. Something with flowers? Unusual for a bachelor, wasn't it?

Her eyesight was not perfect, she would admit. All those late nights with a candle and Gregory's ledgers. But the labels reminded her of botanical drawings, greenery floating in mid-air with reddish-orange flowers in different stages of budding. It seemed so at odds with the rest of the spartan room. There was a baroque touch to the labels, more akin to what Mrs. Moon might want, as opposed to the heavy simplicity of the rest of Mr. Moon's study. The green vines laced about one another, and small red flowers intermixed with buds danced on the upper left corners and upper right corners. They were well-balanced, but her mind snagged on the design. There was something about them. Each label held a different number of buds versus flowers on each corner.

"Mrs. Cabot." He caught her attention.

"Yes, Mr. Moon. Here and accounted for." She gave him a wide, beaming smile. She would kill him with kindness. Smother him with niceness. And she would adore watching him squirm under the weight of her enduring cheerful temperament.

"I see that."

He assessed her. No doubt she was meant to squirm here, but she didn't care. His gaze was nowhere near as penetrating and painful as his mother's.

"I heard you met with Lord Rascomb and Miss Bridewell?" She pushed on. If he wouldn't begin the conversation, she would.

"I did. They were in agreement that you should have open access to the ledgers at all times."

She smiled smaller this time, not just in acknowledgment of what he said, but also of what he did not say. "And that I use the funds at my discretion."

"Naturally. But I retain my rights to oversee any purchases. I would hate for the money to be misused."

Prudence did her best to not clench her jaw or narrow her eyes, even though she desperately wished to do so. This man thought she was either a confidence artist or an idiot. And she'd bank on the latter rather than the former. So she smiled in her best empty-headed American way. "Did Miss Bridewell also inform you of the task I am dispensed with?"

Now Mr. Moon's steel-colored eyes narrowed.

Glee struck her. "Which I suppose, in turn, you are to help

with, since you must oversee my purchases." Oh, she would absolutely rope him into this because he would loathe it. He deserved it. "Miss Bridewell believes we must throw a fundraising ball. And not just any run-of-the-mill charity party. No, an epic, no-holds-barred wildly extravagant soiree to rival the ones of the eighteenth century."

Mr. Moon's jaw dropped open just slightly. Prudence would take that as a win.

"Now, I don't know what that last part means," she continued. "But I trust you can help me with that." His face flushed with color. She rather liked it.

"I am not a party planner," he said through gritted teeth.

She stood. "You are now, Mr. Moon." She held her hand out, inviting him to shake on it, like business partners. He slowly got to his feet and clasped her hand in his. He met her gaze gravely, and it felt as if he were building steel walls around her with the intensity. Instinctively, she looked away as her body flushed from her toes and stopped below her waist.

But, oh! All it took was her shift in perspective, from sitting to standing. The labels on the drawers were Morse code. They were numbers. Birthdates, judging by the continuity of the numbers. Her hand was still in his when she said, "Why have you labeled your files by birthdate? That doesn't seem very efficient." The words popped out of her mouth before she could stop herself.

"How would you know that?" He did not let go of her hand.

She gestured towards the labels with her free hand. "It's obviously Morse code. And with a repeated four digits on each label with numbers, that could only be years."

He closed his eyes for a moment and then let go of her hand. Puzzled, Prudence sank back down in her chair, her hand suddenly cold. "You are likely accustomed to being the smartest person in the room. How aggravating to find out that might not be true."

His expression was cold and smooth. She couldn't tell if he was angry or embarrassed or pleased or anything. "I would be interested to find out if that were true."

Prudence didn't know why, but she blushed. It had been a long time since the last time she blushed. "I am more than what you think I am."

"I have never doubted that for a second," he said, sounding as if he meant it.

She took her turn evaluating him. His thin frame was covered in neatly pressed tailored clothes. She liked the look of his broad hands, ink covered, with long, fine fingers. He had an angular face that wasn't exactly handsome, nor was he ugly. He was sharp edges and high cheekbones, with cold gray eyes that saw everything.

"Mrs. Cabot," he said, his voice suddenly low and quiet. But he didn't say anything after that. Just her name.

Her mouth was suddenly dry. She swallowed hard. "Yes, Mr. Moon?"

"I have a confession to make."

"Oh?" She could barely squeak out the word. Her mind ran faster than a pony on a wet track, sliding this way and that, trying to figure out what he might say.

"I did not mean to, but I found myself eavesdropping on you and my mother during your first visit here."

Prudence frowned. And? That was hardly something that needed to be confessed.

"To be very clear—" Mr. Moon cleared his throat. "I overheard you say that you were in search of a lover."

Her mind blanked. Her stomach clenched as if she were about to be chastised by her father—the absolute worst punishment she'd ever experienced.

"I would like to put myself forth as a candidate." His facial expression betrayed nothing.

Prudence wasn't sure her mouth wasn't hanging agape. "I beg your pardon?"

"I've done some inquiring about town. I understand that the Ladies' Alpine Society requires its members to be above reproach.

Even as a widow, you must be discreet for the benefit of your maiden members."

"Well, I certainly wasn't going to be going around letting my decolletage hang out of my gowns." Prudence felt strangely dizzy thinking about this. She was affronted. Definitely insulted.

Mr. Moon's eyes flicked to her bosom. He murmured something low and deep that she didn't hear. He cleared his throat and looked into her eyes. "My offer stands. A business agreement, if you wish. I've discovered you are quite the shrewd investor. You must know an advantageous deal when you see one."

Was he trying to flirt with her by praising her business acumen? Or was he after something else? He must be after her money or investment secrets. There was no way a man would just offer up his body as her lover. This was absurd. "I don't appreciate being mocked."

Mr. Moon relaxed his posture, and with it, his facial expression. An almost-smile toyed at his lips. "I offer no mockery. In my questioning about you, I learned that several men were taken with you last season, but you failed to reciprocate interest."

"What? Who?" she demanded. No such men existed.

"Lord Avendon, Mr. Nathaniel Ryksted, and Mr. Richard Reeves," he said, ticking them off his fingers.

Prudence sputtered her protests. Those men had paid her some attention, had danced with her, fetched her drinks, but they weren't interested in that way. "They were only being polite."

Now Mr. Moon smiled, and it seemed to transform his face into someone approachable. Someone kind. Someone, well, handsome. "Men don't make a habit of being polite. Especially powerful men. They were trying to get into your bed."

Prudence searched the room, mulling the information. Then, upon a realization, she turned her gaze back to him. "You aren't being polite."

"No, I'm not. Politeness didn't get those men anywhere. And since I'm not interested in taking a wife, as I have my mother to contend with, and I have no time to seek out a mistress who may be very expensive to maintain, I believe a proposal between the two of us makes a great deal of sense."

She frowned. "Why would your mother preclude a wife? She's perfectly lovely."

His sudden bark of laughter startled her. "My mother is anything but lovely. She's smart, she's insightful, but she suffers no fools."

She chewed her lip, thinking. It would solve her trouble of finding a lover. And they had every excuse to seek one another's company. But this didn't leave her with butterflies in her stomach. There was no poetry in this. There was no wooing. Was everything to be so dry? Would she even enjoy coupling with him?

To be utterly fair to Mr. Moon, he stayed silent as she thought, which she appreciated. He didn't pressure or cajole. Merely answered her questions when she posed them.

"This isn't what I had in mind," she said, finally.

"Am I not handsome enough?" It could have sounded pleading or whining, but it was not either. He was asking for her opinion.

"It isn't that," she said quickly. "I find you unconventionally handsome. You are fascinating to look at. But this seems so . . ."

"Business-like?" he suggested.

"Exactly. Yes. I was hoping to be wooed."

Mr. Moon nodded. "That can be arranged."

Prudence shook her head. "I shouldn't like prescriptive things. It isn't worth it. Please dismiss this entire conversation. I should go."

Feelings of disappointment whirled around her as she stood, making her way to the study door. She turned, thinking to mention that they hadn't even discussed their actual business, but he was right behind her.

Prudence was tall for a woman. But still Mr. Moon had inches and inches on her. And up close, he was not nearly as thin as he seemed to be. In fact, it seemed a trick of his tailored clothing.

The first sound of his name died on her lips. Lips that he was staring at quite intently. And she found herself looking at his.

No, she ought to be looking at his eyes. But those seemed to draw her in even further. His gray eyes were shot through with green and gold, as if they couldn't settle on a single color to accent the hard coldness of his gaze. She wanted to lean in further, pick apart the strands to make sense of him. But no, she couldn't be leaning in further to him. What was she thinking?

Oh, what would Gregory think? She felt suddenly foolish and utterly childish for trying to seek a lover.

He caught her cheek in his hand, cradling her face. He pulled at one of her curls. "I would very much like to kiss you, Mrs. Cabot."

"Oh," she said, because she honestly could not say anything more intelligent.

"I think it would be pleasurable for both of us. And if we don't suit, you may say so now, and we bypass any further embarrassment." He was so very close to her.

"Okay," she said.

"What does that mean? O and K?"

"Sorry, it means yes." She stared up at him dumbly, not wanting to be the ninny who waited for a man to take action, but also unable to make her limbs move. It was not how she envisaged herself as a widow. She had thought she would be the seductress. Except, she had no idea how.

"Excellent." He bent his head down, brushing his lips slightly against hers, and then pulling her in slowly as he deepened the kiss.

For her part, she felt as if she were falling. No kiss with Gregory had ever melted her knees. The taste of him was so different, the smell of him unlike the men she'd known. She reached up to pull him closer, finding the soft hair on the back of his neck. Softer than Gregory's. His entire touch was soft but scorching. As if she burned every place they connected.

He pulled away, leaving her breathless. "Goodbye, Mrs. Cabot," he said, his accent breaking apart each syllable as if cut by a diamond. "Please send word when you are ready for another appointment."

Prudence reached for the doorknob behind her, and fairly fell out of the study into the foyer. She closed the door behind her, feeling the cool air on her flushed cheeks. What had she just done? Who knew that a man as controlled as Mr. Moon had so much heat built up inside of him? The thought alone threatened to weaken her knees all over again.

No footman or maid appeared, so she gathered her bonnet and gloves herself and crept out of the house. She didn't want anyone to see her dazed and bewildered face. As she walked back to her hotel—not terribly far from where Mr. Moon kept his house—she wondered how to proceed. Did she want to kiss Mr. Moon again? Absolutely. It had been more than she thought a mere kiss could be. But what would Gregory think?

That was a silly thing to even consider. Gregory's approval was no longer needed, nor wanted, nor available. And she could be with any man she wanted now. Gregory had been her husband, but not her lover—not in the bigger sense that she'd wanted. She'd finally gotten to an age where she wanted romance, heart-stopping desire, and not the comfortable friendship she'd had with him.

Her hands felt cold, yet the rest of her felt hot. The sensations she'd felt in the span of mere minutes were shocking. As if she hadn't felt so much in her entire life, and then her emotions sped through her like a steam locomotive. The connection she'd felt with Mr. Moon, and then the phantom guilt and disapproval.

In Spain, she'd attempted to flirt, but never felt the sudden frenzy of emotion that she'd experienced just now with Mr. Moon. Perhaps it was because she'd never seriously believed in the man's interest or attraction. There had been games galore with those men, and it had felt more like she was playing pretend with her younger sisters than sussing out possible lovers.

Mr. Moon was different. That smoldering look in his steel

gray eyes was clear. Even she couldn't be so oblivious, as he had claimed she was with Lord Avendon and Mr. Ryksted and Mr. Reeves. But what made him so appealing? It couldn't merely be that kiss. Or maybe it could. She'd never been kissed so thoroughly in her life. And after all, kissing was a type of wooing.

Chapter Three

Leo read the same letter over and over again. His client, Mr. Philby III, wanted him to do a thing. But what was that thing? Dear God, Mrs. Cabot had positively ruined him. If the nights before he'd kissed her had been troublesome, the ones after had been excruciating. The dreams were in all manners—soft and loving, but also quick and hard—no. This was not the time or place to recall his illicit fantasies. He must focus on his actual work. Adjusting investment shares and confirming dividend payouts.

There was no magic to his work. It was merely tracking numbers, which required organization. It was his own nature that bent him toward secrecy. He glanced behind him at the botanical labels he'd used. The labels she had figured out with merely a glance. If only he could hire an assistant that astute. Should he redo his filing system? Any new label would still be obvious to her. He could use a code similar to semaphore. Or still use Morse code, but have a simple substitution code hidden inside that could be color-coded?

It didn't matter. Unless he changed how the clients were systemically identified, there was little point in redoing the labels. She knew how he organized his business. That irked him. He didn't like that she'd seen something in him that he hadn't allowed her to see. But the look in her eye after they'd kissed led him to believe she didn't remember much.

That, at least, was gratifying. His pride might be at the end of his priority list, but it still existed. Having a woman melt in one's arms definitely buoyed one's sense of self. He'd sent flowers the next day. Calla lilies. Not roses, not daisies. Nothing so obvious. There was the language of flowers that Society prattled on about, not that he cared one whit for it. He didn't. Nor did he know what calla lilies meant. What he did know was that they were rare and expensive. They didn't care for the constant damp of England.

He hoped she liked them. No note of thanks was delivered to his doorstep. Nor did she send a note regarding her availability for an appointment to discuss their actual business: the budget for the Ladies' Alpine Society's fundraiser. Still a ridiculous idea, but it wasn't his society, and they didn't want his ideas.

Still, he felt himself thinking about grand parties that had taken place in the affluent houses of his boarding school mates. There had even been descriptions of Mary Queen of Scots's three-day party, where an entire boat was sailed into the dining room to serve guests their fish course. Complete with the Greek gods and goddesses draping themselves about the rigging.

At least thinking about a silly party would get his mind off of Mrs. Cabot's honey-colored curls wrapped around his finger. The taste of sweetness on her lips. He needed to go for a walk before his body screamed for release. He stood, leaving a project undone, a letter unread, and his business scattered about his desk. So very unlike him. But he felt certain that if he could simply engage in this affair with Mrs. Cabot, his desire would fizzle over the course of the Season, she would leave on her asinine aspiration to climb that great Swiss hill, and he would get back to his regular routine.

This business was ideal for both of them, despite it costing him nearly every part of his moral decency to suggest. But he was glad he'd risked it, for both their sakes. He put on his hat and grabbed his walking stick. He didn't require a cane, but it was still handy in case of urchins or bounders. As he walked, he found himself wanting to whistle—a strange occurrence as well. He was not a man who whistled, drew attention to himself in any way, or was so oblivious to his surroundings.

He curtailed the urge, and instead listened intently as he strolled in Hyde Park, catching fragments of conversations. Old habits died hard, and vigilance had kept him and his mother safe for too long. Fortunately, all anyone seemed to be talked about was the upcoming Season, and the cost of silk.

"Leo! I say, Leopold Moon, you old devil." A man dismounted from a horse a few feet away as Leo turned to face him.

It took a moment to recognize the man, but it was Eyeball in the flesh. "Eyeball?"

The man laughed. His shoulders were twice the size they were the last time he'd seen his old school chum. Were they chums? Not really. Acquaintances. Fellow scholarship students and bullied outcasts. They'd both been scrawny things once upon a time. But Eyeball was the son of an impoverished viscount, who took up rowing. It broadened his shoulders. Suddenly, what the boys had all mocked him for—having one eye a different color than the other—became a siren song to older women. "In the flesh. As are you. I wondered what happened to you."

Leo ducked his head politely. He had not taken up rowing—not then and not now. He'd found his safety in doing other boys' work for a fee. He had the time, not to mention schoolwork was laughably easy. He'd been running gambling odds for his father for years. School had been simple. Except for the people part. "You're a viscount now, I believe."

Eyeball tried his best to look humble and sheepish, which he wasn't terribly good at. Leo had always been able to see right through him. His avarice, his desire for his title and respect.

Before they entered university, he bedded an older wealthy widow. She kitted him out in fine clothes, personal effects, and taught him about the finer things in life. The correct wines, the best hotels. He'd worked his way through several women, garnering wealth each time. His name was his own, but Leo found Eyeball's ways to be morally reprehensible. He used the women for their influence, money, and power.

"The old man finally departed. Poor fellow was infirm for longer than was polite." The sun caught his face through the dappled spring leaves, illuminating his one blue, one green eye.

The man wasn't good with words, so at least Leo could take comfort in that. "Are you in town to take your seat in the House of Lords?"

"Last month, yes. Decided to stay for the Season."

"Surely you don't need the Season to keep yourself company." How many women had he bedded by now? The count must be astronomical.

Eyeball chuckled. "Don't you understand, Leo? I'm a viscount now. And a lord is always in need of a wife. Carry on the lineage, all that."

Leo made a noncommittal noise. Lineage didn't matter if there was no money to go with it. It seemed to mean inheriting debt from poor investments, houses too old to be maintained, and herds of sheep and cattle.

"Speaking of, good friend. I hear you are associated with Drummonds?"

Leo shook his head. "No, I'm a private banker."

Eyeball gave him a sideways smile that Leo associated with con men. Mostly because his father had been one. "With which bank?"

Leo tipped his hat. "I must be off. Good day, my lord." He began walking before Eyeball could catch up. He didn't trust the man, and men he didn't trust didn't deserve his time.

"Wait now, Leo." The man trotted after him, his horse on a lead behind him. "What has you cagey? Are you doing illegitimate business?" He grinned, looking annoyingly like the boy who'd been his friend so long ago.

Leo stopped in his tracks, suppressing all the desire he had to sigh or squeeze his eyes shut in exasperation. He stared down Eyeball. Enough of Leo's life had been disreputable. He'd been disreputable since birth, and he was trying his best to make up for that. "Of course not."

"I hear that you are the man to know when building a fortune. I'd like to give you my business." Eyeball said, finally coming clean with his intent. "Legitimate or otherwise."

"So you ambushed me in the park instead of making an appointment?" Leo's palms were sweating, and he wasn't sure why.

"I'd heard you were very selective about your clientele, and I hoped our old school days connection would aid my appeal."

Leo shook his head. "Do you forget that we were both scholarship students? Your father hadn't two shillings, let alone enough for me to work with."

"Yes, well, times have changed." Eyeball glared back at him. "Don't be snobbish with me now, old chum."

Leo arranged his face in the politest expression he could muster. "I am not taking on new clients at the moment. My roster is full. Should you still be in need of assistance, you can check back with me next year." This time he gave a formal bow, one that could not be mistaken for anything but cold dismissal.

"I'm not even sure what you do, exactly, Leo. That's what I want to find out. So I can do it on my own." Eyeball called after him. "Just give me the basics, I'll catch on after that."

Leo turned on his heel. "If I gave away my secrets, my demand would fall. I think not. Good day."

⫸⫷

"GEORGIE, I'M GETTING you your own suite." Prudence had thought and thought and thought. She'd lain in her bed, soft and comfortable with a goose-down tick both above and below her, and thought. She'd breakfasted at the dining table, the pale-yellow walls accented with white chair railings and crown molding gleaming, while she took her coffee and toast and thought. She pretended to read the newspaper, seated in her lounge, the rich cream-colored damask glinting gold in the brilliant morning sun streaming through the large windows, while she thought.

If she were to embark on a tryst, a full-on affair, she had to sort a few things first. Namely, privacy and birth control. She couldn't be gossiped about, and she certainly could not become pregnant. Not for the scandal, and not for the mountain climb ahead of her.

Ophelia was demanding training days as a group be reinstated, which only made sense. They needed to see each other's strengths and weaknesses. Next year around this time, they'd be boarding a ship to France to begin what could be a month-long journey, given weather and political conditions. Any time with Mr. Moon would have to be built around those mandatory meetings.

But the biggest obstacle was Georgie, her paid companion. She could dismiss the woman entirely, true, but a companion was there to ensure her respectability. Dismissing her would signal either poverty or scandal.

Georgie, for her part, just blinked at Prudence. The young woman had many excellent qualities: Georgie could haul luggage like an ox, never believed anyone at face value, and was loyal to a fault.

"Why?" Georgie asked. She was pretty enough, with dark hair and large dark eyes.

"Don't you want your own space?" Prudence asked, hoping to distract her. But Georgie was tenacious.

"Is there something I've done wrong?" Georgie asked, a line forming between her two dark brows.

"Not at all," Prudence assured her. In fact, Georgie was far better as a companion than she ever could have hoped. She was the niece of the housekeeper they'd had in upstate New York. She was young, uninterested in marriage, and not terribly good at working in service. She didn't possess the ability to be obsequious, which apparently often bothered her employers.

Since Prudence didn't mind Georgie considering them equals, their travels had worked well. Georgie stayed in her room during social outings, slowly reading her novels or mending clothes. Which was to say, Georgie was slow, but she wasn't unintelligent. The opposite. But one could not make her go any faster than the pace she went.

"I'd like to give you some space," Prudence said. "To let you explore London and find your own society, and be a young woman in an exciting place. Your pay should be adequate to find some amusement somewhere."

"And I need my own room for this?" Georgie asked.

"You need to be untethered from me. I'll be busy with the alpine training at early hours of the morning. I shouldn't need to disturb you for that. You aren't my maid."

"I can close my door. I'm a heavy sleeper." Georgie slipped the bookmark into her novel and set it aside, giving Prudence her full attention, which was precisely what Prudence didn't want.

The two women stared at each other, a good-natured and generous stand-off that could not be ended until the truth was out. Georgie looked at her expectantly.

Finally Prudence caved. There was no other way around Georgie than the truth. "There's a man." Prudence confessed, her lips throbbing in memory of Mr. Moon's kiss.

Georgie gave a faint triumphant smile, but said nothing.

"I'm trying to be discreet." Because she wanted so much more than a kiss, if she were honest.

Georgie still said nothing, not offering judgement nor opinion.

"I'm not even sure I want to begin an affair, but this was the entire reason I came across the ocean. To have an affair with a man who wouldn't know me. Wouldn't know Gregory. Someone I wouldn't worry over, pine over—"

"Love?" Georgie suggested.

Prudence pointed at her as if she'd just said the most brilliant thing in the history of the world. "Exactly. A fling. An *affair de coeur.* The kind men have all the time with no consequences to their reputations and professional and business lives." Except, if all that were true, she would have an affair without putting it off by arranging rooms and appointments.

"That I understand." Georgie pulled her novel back onto her lap. "Tell me which room to move into, and I will pack my bags."

Her companion's statement left Prudence wondering about her—what was it that Georgie wanted that made her understand Prudence's desire for a love affair? Not that it mattered at the moment, anyway. She would find out later. Now, she had a room to rent, maids to notify, and then, when she was feeling bold enough, an appointment to make.

⋙⋘

LEO ARRANGED A luncheon for his mother. She would go to Verrey's for her meal, and then to Charbonnel et Walker's for drinking chocolate and truffles. Since she'd be on Bond Street, he also suggested treating herself to a new frock.

Mrs. Moon was no fool, unfortunately. She narrowed her eyes at him. "Why are you kicking me out of my own home? Do you have some kind of . . . strumpet coming?" She spat out the word with all the force of her disdain.

"No. Not at all, mother." Leo gave her the sternest look in his arsenal, which was nothing compared to his mother's. She didn't so much as bat an eye. "If you must know, I have a client arriving who demands secrecy. He doesn't wish anyone to know we are working together." With that one pronoun switch, he lied to his mother. He hadn't lied to his mother in decades.

"Who is this supposed client?" she demanded.

"If you must know, it's an old school acquaintance," Leo said, remembering his encounter with Eyeball in the park.

"No, absolutely not. Those blue-blooded nincompoops treated you terribly. I'll not let you alone here without anyone to defend you!"

"Mother. I'm no longer a schoolboy, instructed to not use my fists. I can handle this." Leo was surprised and even touched by his mother's vehemence. Decrepit in body now, she still had the vigor of the tigress she once was.

"Who? Which one is it? I'll write to their mothers if they abuse you." His mother shook her arthritic fist.

"For your information, it's Eyeball, so you needn't worry."

"Pah," she said, waving her hand. "He's fine, then. He understood money better than all the rest of them. What does he need of secrecy? Especially from me?"

"He is in search of a wife and doesn't want there to be talk of his former poverty."

"Ah," his mother said, nodding her approval. "There are quite enough other rumors going about of him anyway. He's never been a stranger to the ladies. That will no doubt help him secure a wife just as well as a flush pocket!"

"Mother!" Leo's stomach lurched. The idea of Eyeball being pursued by his mother was the most nauseating thought he'd ever heard of.

She shook her head. "The gossip is consistent, if nothing else. But fine, pass my regards along, while I go enjoy myself and spend all of your money. That'll show you."

Leo inclined his head, wincing. She would be extravagant just to spite him. No feather, no jewel, no imported wine would be too good for Mrs. Moon.

He practically pushed her out the door and into the waiting carriage. Two footmen would accompany her, both to carry her should her knees ache too badly, and also to handle any and all packages she might accrue. He had no doubt she would return with the riches of the Empire nestled in ribboned boxes.

He asked for a tea tray to be brought to his study and then gave the remaining servant, the maid, the rest of the day off. The cook was asked to prep a supper of cold meats and cheese, and then she too was dismissed. Both women were happy to oblige

Leo's unprecedented whim.

So at four o'clock, when there was a knock at the door, Leo himself opened it. For it was not Eyeball coming to call.

Mrs. Cabot seemed taken aback. "Good day, Mr. Moon."

"Mrs. Cabot." He ushered her inside. "May I take your hat?"

She looked lovely. Her honeyed hair was in the same style as last week, with single curls escaping her coif, waiting for his greedy hands. The color in her cheeks was high, and it might have been the walk that caused it, or perhaps her anticipation of their meeting? A man could hope.

She wore a pink and cream day dress, with a tailored bodice to resemble a man's coat. It should have had a masculine effect, but on her, there was no such thing as masculine. It emphasized her slim waist, her strong shoulders, and pert breasts. He needed to stop staring.

"I suppose I should visit your mother first," she said, not meeting his eye.

Was she nervous? "Then I ought to tell you my mother is out for the day." He waited for her to look up at him. Instead, she glanced up the stairs at the drawing room.

"What is she up to?"

"Dining at Verrey's, visiting the Queen's chocolatier, and perhaps ordering dresses with the intent to bankrupt me."

Her gray eyes finally met his, and she smiled. "From what I understand, that's a herculean task."

He raised his eyebrows, not bothering to keep his stoic mask in place. "Do you believe I am that wealthy?"

Her smile widened. Honestly, with teeth that perfect, it would be a shame not to show them. "Does the pope wear a funny hat?"

He sputtered, surprised. "I don't believe I've ever heard that expression."

"I hope I didn't offend."

He suspected that it was a test. Some way that she could see if he was tough enough to withstand her American manners. Her frontier spirit. "England is an Anglican nation. You'll have to go to Spain to offend the Catholics."

"Not what I meant."

"Shall we?" he asked, gesturing towards his study. He offered his arm. Any excuse to touch her. Strange as she was.

Almost hesitantly, she threaded her arm through his. He couldn't look at her. Not this close. Not with her gazing at him, as if waiting for him to explain a magic trick.

His heart sped, but he walked them slowly to his study. The sitting area, off in the corner of the room, was rarely used, but it was where the maid set up the tea tray. His intent was to start off casually, politely, then ease her into kissing and make plans for more. "Tea?" He steered them toward the chaise longue and chair.

She resisted, so he stopped. "Mr. Moon. We have business to attend."

Her words weren't sharp, but they were insistent. "I hoped we could discuss it over tea."

Color rushed to her cheeks. "Not *that* business. Though that too. I mean our business that we never spoke of during our last encounter. The fundraising ball."

He tried not to be disappointed, but he was. He dropped her arm and gestured to the other side of his room, where his desk sat. His desk, full of work. Full of demands. Full of numbers and columns and statistics and speculations. Definitely not full of a perfumed, honeyed woman who might melt in his arms, as if she were a lemon sweet.

"I'll not disappoint my friends, Mr. Moon," she said, sitting in the chair opposite his desk. She fished a paper out of her reticule and cleared her throat. "These are the numbers I'm currently anticipating. I'm not entirely sure what the party will entail, of course. Adjustments might need to be made."

"Perhaps you ought to call me Leo," he said, coming around his desk. He took the paper and opened the ledger for the Ladies' Alpine Society. He read the list. "You have an item here for wild animals?"

"Yes. Miss Brewer's idea. She thought wild animals would be a particular draw."

"And how much ice?" He was utterly confused. Were they throwing a party or putting together a circus?

"Miss Bridwell's idea. She wants the theme to be ice, since even though we will climb the Matterhorn next summer, it will still be covered in ice."

"And how will you display this ice?" Leo asked.

She smiled brightly. "Haven't the foggiest."

"I don't think I need to tell you that this is an . . . aspirational budget." He hoped she understood that the Ladies' Alpine Society could not handle this kind of expense. No one could. Not now. The global economy was not what it was a century ago when the rich were fabulously rich, and the poor had nothing but the clothes on their backs.

"I believe if we put a number on the budget, then it's a starting place. Once actual plans come into being, we will know where to whittle it down."

"Whittle it down?" Leo asked. It did occur to him that Mrs. Cabot was shifting in her chair as if she were agitated and also that she had not invited him to use her given name. Both circumstances were disappointing. "This is astronomical."

"It's not really your decision, is it?" Her tone sharpened. "You were very clear that you were not a party planner. You didn't want to be involved, so fine, it's my problem and my problem alone."

"That's not—"

"No, your priority is the math. And believe me, I understand. When the math works, the world is grand. When it doesn't, someone gets fired or worse."

"Where did you—"

"I've done my fair share of budgets, *Leo*."

Damn it all. This is not how today was supposed to go. "Why don't we calm down and—"

"—Do *not* tell me to calm down."

He watched blood pulse in her neck. It was strangely erotic. He was noticing every bit of her, and she grew more magnificent with every inch he noticed. Which was incredibly poor timing because it seemed she would rather throw things at his head.

"You *will* help me with this budget." Anything she said in that tone of voice made him want to comply instantaneously. Preferably without his clothes.

"Of course." He took a step back, wanting her to feel comfortable.

She looked away and shook her head, her jaw tensed and pulsing. "I shouldn't have come. I thought, well, it doesn't matter what I thought. You're just like the others."

That put a damper on his ardor. He straightened his spine and let his business mask fall into place. "If you would give me specifics, I should like to prove to you otherwise."

"You think that because I am a woman, I can't possibly understand a simple ledger."

He folded his hands on his desk. "It is my turn to insist that you do not tell me what I think."

"I don't have to, do I? It's evident in the way you treat me." She stood and paced behind her chair.

"Would you like to know what I am thinking?" Leo tried to smile at her, he really did. He was not known for the gesture, however, and it might have made things worse.

She shot him a look like he was the village idiot.

"I'm doing my best to not seduce you. I'm trying to focus on business, but I find it damnably hard to do so when I see your blood thrumming in your neck. I'm thinking of all the things I could do to make your blood pulse like that."

Her posture softened, and she licked her lips. It was what he'd hoped to see.

"I'm wondering if you taste like honey, and if it's anything like the honey color of your hair," he continued. "I want your fingers in my hair as I coax you to climax, and I want my fingers in yours when I do. So you see, I am unable to tell if your budget is worthwhile or not. I do not disrespect your mind, Mrs. Cabot. I find that your presence has eclipsed my capacity to do my work."

Her eyes burned into him. "Is this how you conduct your business?"

He kept his voice calm and even. "Only with you. I have not bedded a woman in several years. I don't believe in adultery, and I haven't the patience for a paid mistress."

She folded her arms across her chest, serving only to accentuate her mouth-watering breasts. He breathed through his nose slowly, maintaining his control. That thin veneer that kept him from leaping over the desk and taking her like a rutting animal. "You expect me to believe that?"

"It is the truth. I can't see why you wouldn't believe that. I have not shown myself to be dishonest in any way."

"Because I am not the sort of woman who inspires lust in a man. That's not who I am."

"As you so eloquently put it earlier, madame: do not tell me how to feel." He stood, painfully aware of the erection straining his trousers. If she needed proof, he was happy to let her explore it. "You are a smart, capable woman. I've done my due diligence and discovered that you made your fortune what it is. Your husband's money was nothing but a seed when you married him."

She shook her head. "It was timing—I merely—"

"Don't downplay your accomplishments Mrs. Cabot. You are a formidable businesswoman." He came around his desk, walking slowly toward her as if she were a deer that might leap away at the slightest scare. "You smile and smile, tricking your companions into thinking you're so amiable you must be empty-headed. I can see the gears working inside your mind right now. You have solutions three different ways for every problem. You are always prepared." He stopped in front of her. "Until this."

She looked away, the color again high in her cheeks. Her eyes closed, fluttering, as if she was protesting without words.

He could smell her. The scent of her rose-scented soap, the silky talcum powder on her skin, and underneath that, he could swear he smelled the scent of arousal. It made his eyes want to roll back into his head. "I am struggling, madame. We made an agreement to begin an affair. I could have kept these thoughts from my mind had you not heard my proposal. But I find that since you have not dismissed the idea, all I can think of is you."

Her breath hitched and came faster.

He did not touch her. No, not without permission. But he scented her, following the crux between her shoulder and her neck, up, up, teasing those honeyed curls, behind her ear, to her closed eyes. His throat was dry. "I can smell you," he growled. "I can smell your wanting."

"I—" she whispered, opening her eyes to look at him.

His gaze caught on hers. "Anything."

"You'll stop if I say stop?" she asked. "No matter when?"

"No. Matter. When." He met her eyes with every word, wanting her to know that his desire was loud, but her needs were louder. "Don't be afraid to stop me."

Their lips were millimeters from each other. The taste of her teased him. He remembered it from last time.

"Then, okay." Her voice trembled. She sounded uncertain, which he didn't like.

"I will only take the most enthusiastic encouragement or none at all. I have no interest in goading a woman into relations." He searched her eyes, her face. Dear God, he wanted her to say yes in the worst way.

She straightened her shoulders, looked him straight in the eye and said, "Give it your best shot, Mr. Moon. Make me scream your name or I don't want any more."

He grinned. "My pleasure." A second later, he'd pulled her face to his with both hands, kissing her greedily. She tasted better than anyone he'd ever kissed in his life. It was intoxication, lust, blindness to all other things. He'd never been so focused in his life. As he kissed her, he guided her to his desk.

Her hands roamed his chest and shoulders and hair, exploring him just as he did her. Damn it all, why were there so many clothes? He pushed her to sit on the desk, spreading her legs until the long skirt went taut.

"Tell me I can use your name," he panted, rucking up her skirts to her thighs. He marveled at the strong, shapely legs encased in white silk stockings. He stepped back, running his hands from her booted ankles to her mid-thigh. Just a handswidth from her cunny. So very close. He could smell her scent again, powerful this time.

"You may," she panted, watching him as he enjoyed her.

He licked his lips. There were so many things to do, to try, to experience with her. "Prudence," he whispered. "My dear, dear Prudence. What do you like?"

"I'm sorry?" she asked, an adorable crease between her eyebrows formed.

He let go of her ankle and leaned in to kiss that line, bracing his hands on the desk on either side of her. "What do you like? What makes you scream?"

"I don't know," she stammered. "I can't think of anything."

"Nothing makes you scream? Then I have my work cut out for me." He kissed her again, this time scooping up her thighs and pulling him flush against him. His hardness met softness and she gave a startled moan. He smiled against her mouth. "That seemed promising."

Their bodies pushing against each other, he freed his hands to work the buttons on her bodice. With three large buttons on her waistcoat, and a hidden secure button on the inside, he pulled the garment off her shoulders. She wore a white, sleeveless shift with a corset underneath. Her breasts were pushed up, encased in fine, ruffled linen. He traced his finger from her temple down her cheek, her chin, her neck, down to the middle of her chest, and into the dark well between her breasts. This was fast. Too fast maybe, but she hadn't stopped him. Hadn't protested the speed at which he took his liberties. "I think you would like being worshipped."

She let her head fall back. "Who wouldn't?"

He laughed and kissed his way down the line he'd just traced with his finger. He lapped at her breasts, cursing her corset, but careful not to dislodge it. Women's undergarments were tricky, and he didn't want her leaving his house looking like she'd done what they were doing now.

>>><<<

PRUDENCE WAS DIZZY with his attentions. No one had ever looked at her like this. Gregory had never traced her legs, looked at her as if she were somewhere between a chocolate mousse and a goddess. She let her head fall back as Leo kissed her neck, and then down to her breasts.

Somewhere inside her, she ached. She ached for having never experienced this kind of seduction before. She ached for all she had missed, and for wanting more. His hands were hot, tracing her corset, tugging at her thighs. His hardness pushed against the crux of her body. This wasn't like it had been with Gregory at all, who seemed at times embarrassed at his own stirrings. Still, he'd tried to have her enjoy his time with her, but he seemed so ashamed of it. Like he was doing something wrong. Which made Prudence wonder if she was somehow untoward.

But Mr. Moon. Leo. He was devouring her like a starving man, letting lose an animal that had scented blood.

"I want to touch your quim," Leo said in between kisses.

She made a noise in her throat. It was the best she could do.

His kisses slowed. "Prudence. I need to know you want me to. Say yes. Dear God, please say yes."

"Yes," she breathed, and his hand snaked between them, finding the slit in the linen bloomers she wore. She gasped when his fingers found her wetness.

His other hand came to her neck, and he slid up to cradle her head, bringing her to look at him. The fire in his eyes was new and strange. "I want to see it."

"See what?" she panted, as his fingers found the hard nub that sent pleasure shooting down to her toes. Her thighs tensed against his.

"I want to see your face when you come. You're so beautiful. Pretty, pretty Prudence." His fingers tightened in her hair. He leaned forward and nipped at her lips.

She no longer felt in control of her own body. She clutched at his biceps to keep her balance. He was pulled as taut as a piano wire, all steel and barely contained lust. He wanted her so badly, and that was heady in and of itself. He nudged her back, and she let him take her erect nipple into his mouth.

And suddenly, it was all too much. Her thighs flexed and her feet pointed straight until it hurt, and then pleasure flooded her and she cried out.

He lifted his head. "There we are," Leo breathed into her neck.

She shivered again, an echo of the first.

"My God, you're powerful," he said.

Prudence could barely lift her head to look at him. Every limb was full of warm lead, heavy and wonderful and thick. "I beg your pardon?"

He smiled. "Your legs. I thought you might crush me."

She snorted and leaned back on her elbows. "Ophelia has us running three days a week in the mornings, and climbing stairs on the off days."

"Poor thing," he murmured. "Perhaps you need a massage?" He took a step back and lifted her leg so he could knead her calf muscle.

"What about you?" she asked. In her experience, which was limited to Gregory, to be honest, he typically came right after she did, or right before.

"I am enjoying myself immensely," Leo assured her.

"But what about—you know." Why was it she could engage

in illicit behavior but couldn't talk about it?

"My orgasm?" he asked, smiling at her. "Oh, I don't need one right away. For if I do, this playing will end, and I'm not ready for it to be over."

Leo Moon was actually smiling at her. Prudence never thought she'd see the day. His fingers had also done some sort of magic in her nether parts, which was also unexpected. She hadn't known men to be so attentive. In fact, this was not how she'd imagined their tryst. It was far better.

"One of the amazing and wonderful things about women is that they don't have to pause between orgasms. Some do, but most don't."

Prudence frowned. "Really?"

His smile vanished. "Have you not explored that?"

"When would I explore that?" Prudence asked. She'd never had a bed to herself. She was either with her sisters or with Gregory. Well, until he got truly sick, but then the last thing she wanted to do was explore orgasming. It was exhausting taking care of him, even with the help they'd had.

"When you are on your own." He leaned and planted a kiss on her silk-clad calf.

"I'm rarely alone—and never before now."

"Do you want to explore it?" he asked.

"Is water wet?" she asked, using her father's expression.

"Yes, and so are you." Leo gently let her leg drop as he got to his knees. "Let me see how wet."

"What are you doing?" Prudence braced herself on the desk as he wrapped his arms around either thigh and pulled her to the very edge.

"Exploring," Leo said, and then he opened his mouth.

It was his tongue she felt. Soft and smooth and licking at her.

He hummed. "It does taste like honey."

With his head between her legs, she lost all shame and self-consciousness. She gripped his hair in one of her fists and bucked against his face. She gave an incoherent yell and saw stars. Actual stars. She'd thought Eleanor had made that up when she'd whispered it to her, wanting to share her wedding night experiences.

Leo chuckled and sat back, pulling his handkerchief from his pocket and wiping his mouth.

Prudence slumped back on the desk. "Witchcraft," she mumbled, closing her eyes.

"Sherry?" he asked.

"Got any bourbon?" she asked, still not opening her eyes. Her limbs felt like they were underwater. How did he make her feel so good so fast? It was uncanny.

"I have scotch," he said.

"That'll do." She sighed. The desk was quickly growing uncomfortable. She turned and looked over to the much plusher-looking chaise. Grunting, she sat up and straightened her skirts to find a pleasanter place to relax.

"You'll put your scent on all your clothes if you sit down there," Leo commented, pouring two tumblers.

"Pardon?" Her brain was not working correctly. What scent was he talking about?

"There are two things you could do. One is to use a rag and clean yourself. The other, which is what I would prefer, is that when you recline on the chaise, you hook one leg over the back and air yourself out."

"Am I laundry?"

He chuckled, following her with two glasses. "Will you allow me?"

Her limbs were full of sawdust and stars and she would let him put his hands on any part of her. He maneuvered her to a reclining position, making sure her skirts were up, and not wrinkling beneath her. He lifted one leg up over the crest of the chaise, and the other slightly bent with her foot resting on the floor. Her cunt was fully exposed.

Leo handed her the Scotch, and moved the chair over to the foot of the chaise. He settled in and smiled.

"Enjoying the view?" she asked. Normally she wouldn't have agreed to this. But she was more than aware that he had yet to take his pleasure, and that this afternoon was far from over. Seduction was quite intoxicating. The smoky Scotch burned her throat, and more drowsy pleasure flooded her.

"Immensely." He sipped at his own glass.

"Do you have anything you wish to talk about?" Was this part of his game? Pretending to have a polite conversation?

"Whatever you wish." His eyes darted between her face and her legs. There was something almost animal-like in his expression. As if the razor-sharp mind was not resident in his body at the moment. All of it was replaced by the man who'd licked her until she saw stars.

"What do you like?" she asked. "In bed, I mean."

"I like an enthusiastic partner." His eyes now stayed fixed between her legs.

"What else? Do you enjoy doing what you just did? Licking me?" She bit her lip. This was as bold as she'd ever been.

"I do, yes. Especially when you come from it. I know that I've done well."

"And reciprocated?" She'd never done it, though she knew from some of the books and pamphlets she'd found in Gregory's library that it was possible.

"Yes. As long as my partner enjoys doing it. Would you like to?"

A blush of all things stung Prudence's cheeks. "Perhaps next time?"

"Yes," Leo nodded. "Next time. Right now, I don't want to stop this."

"Are we doing something?"

"I am. I'm watching how wet you become with whatever we talk about. It is fascinating. And particularly educational for me." He sipped his scotch.

"I didn't realize." She started to close her legs, but he leaned forward and stopped her.

"Touch yourself," he said. "And I will, too. I want to come at the same time."

She frowned. "Don't men want to be inside a woman?"

"That is fun too. But today, let's do this." Leo said, unbuttoning his trousers. His cock sprang forth, hard and buoyant. It curved a bit to the left, and it was the same but altogether different from Gregory's.

Leo's cock was longer, a bit thinner, and paler. She wanted to touch it, just to see what it felt like. Would it feel the same?

"If you don't want to, say so," Leo croaked. "But if you want, put your fingers where you'll enjoy it most."

"Okay." She slid her fingers into the wetness between her legs. His eyes were on her hands, and as she moved slowly, he fisted his cock.

"Funny word," he said. "But at least I know what it means now."

She swirled her fingers around, finding a soft, easy rhythm. Leo pumped his cock at the same rate. His face grew flushed, and she watched his eyes change. His brows came together. And she felt hers reflect the same way.

Without realizing it, her hips bucked. Leo hissed as he watched.

"Leo," she panted. "I think—"

He kept pumping with one hand, and grabbed the kerchief he'd cleaned himself with earlier and wrapped it around his cock.

"Are you going to come?" she squeaked.

He nodded and closed his eyes. His hips bucked off the chair, the red kerchief pumping and catching his seed as he came.

She was there too, climaxing, her knee flexing against the chaise, causing the furniture to creak as she came harder than the other two times. When she opened her eyes, she saw Leo slumped in the chair, his head thrown back, his eyes closed. It was the most relaxed she'd ever seen him.

He was more handsome this way, if that were possible. With all those harsh planes of his face no longer pulled taut, he was softer. Kinder looking. Like he might tell a joke any moment. She wanted to know that Leo. Not to say the focused, elegant Leo who had coaxed her into three orgasms wasn't a lovely companion.

She picked up her scotch tumbler from the floor and sipped at it. She didn't care about her rumpled clothes or her likely mussed coiffure. This had been a revelation. The burn of the scotch her throat was perfect. She sighed, letting out yet another layer of tension. "Leo, you are magic."

He chuckled and lifted his head, opening one eye at her. "I should accuse you of the very same thing."

"I came three times. You only got one."

"Yes, but I thought I might lose my testicles in the force of it." He groaned as he cleaned himself and tucked himself back in. When he was done, he took a sip of his own scotch. Then he put his hand up. "I almost forgot."

He stood and went to his desk, procuring another rag. He crossed the room again and handed her the handkerchief.

"Such a gentleman."

He smiled. "Anything but, madame."

Prudence wiped herself clean and straightened her skirts, sitting up. "That was . . . more than I'd hoped for, actually."

Leo looked up at her, fixing her with that unsettling focus. "Stay longer, then, and I'll show you more."

Prudence shook her head. "Ophelia has us running early tomorrow. I can't. I need my legs to work."

"Then tomorrow night."

Prudence didn't want to be the one sneaking out of a house at odd hours. If she were stopped or recognized, it would be a disaster. But for Leo, no one would bat an eyelash at him skulking about at odd hours. Men's intimate lives were not to be questioned.

"I've sent my companion to another suite. I will be alone in mine now."

Leo's forehead creased in amusement. "Is that so?"

"I may have been putting things in place the last few days." Prudence sipped the last of her scotch.

"Is that what took so long?" Leo asked, crossing his legs.

He was such a picture of English elegance. It wasn't just the pose, the scotch, or even the clothes. There was something almost too perfect about it. Studied, even. It was like watching the difference between a woman born as a proper lady versus the middle-class women who elevated themselves with their strict mannerisms in imitation.

Leo's affect was intoxicating. And almost effortless. But it bothered her in some way. Like she knew this was a show for her benefit. Despite it, she still trusted him some way. This intimacy, the way he'd treated her, always making sure she wanted to continue the way he'd suggested, it felt real. He was taking care of her, in his own way.

"So tomorrow night then? A late supper?"

"If you like," Prudence felt suddenly shy. Her chest felt heavy with anticipation and nerves.

"I can bring wine. Or scotch, if you prefer."

"Or I can bring out the bourbon I have stashed away for special occasions." Prudence looked at the tea tray laid out on the table next to the chaise, forgotten and cold. He had tried to steer her in this direction, and she'd refused. She'd wanted to get business conducted, and had they even accomplished anything? Her mind was foggy about everything before he kissed her. She couldn't even remember how it started. What did this man do to her?

"I'd be honored." He threw back the last of his scotch, maintaining his eye contact with her. Something about his expression was different. A wryness, a crack of opening and familiarity in that face. She couldn't put her finger on it, but she liked it.

Chapter Four

"You seem more relaxed," Justine remarked, looking her up and down. They all stretched in Ophelia's extensive garden, wearing the old-fashioned jumps instead of corsets because they worked better for running. Their skirts were shorter than normal so they didn't trip. Their blouses were cotton and loose. They would sweat into them and it would be challenging to get the scent of hard work out.

Prudence certainly didn't want to tell Justine why she was more relaxed. So she gave her big Minnesota smile, which never fooled Bad News Brewer. "I slept very well last night." Which was true.

Eleanor, the only other married woman in the group, which likely meant the only other non-virgin, gave Prudence a conspiratorial smile. Eleanor would never judge or begrudge Prudence for finding a lover. But Prudence didn't feel like telling her either. This was her secret, for herself alone. She ducked her head and stretched out her calves. They were tight and threatening a spasm since yesterday's "exercise" in Leo's study.

"Remember, it isn't about the speed," Ophelia said, walking across their group.

"It's the distance," the rest of them chimed in.

Prudence liked being in a group again. It reminded her of being with her sisters, a part of something bigger than herself.

"How did the meeting with Mr. Moon go yesterday?" Ophelia asked as they all started a slow jog.

"Fine," Prudence said. They hadn't figured out any real numbers or suggestions or a budget. So basically, they'd yelled at one another and then became as intimate as Prudence had ever been with a man. More, really, despite the fact that the ending act was not one of insertion. She'd never seen a man's face when he finished. It was exciting. Eye-opening, really.

"I can't believe he went over your head to Ophelia's father." Justine made a face of disgust.

"It's fine," Prudence insisted. And, now, it seemed like it probably was.

"It isn't," Eleanor insisted. "You're the smartest person I've ever met. You had, what was that called? When you looked at our monies after Ben Nevis, to see how much we might need for the Matterhorn?"

"A post-mortem."

Justine made a face.

"Ghastly word," Ophelia said.

"My brother is a doctor. That was what they called opening a dead body to see what killed them."

"Bleh," Eleanor said. "I'm glad this was just numbers."

"It's the only term I can think of that's appropriate. We stayed close to our budget for the Ben Nevis climb. That's good. We want that information, as it helps our projections for this next bigger adventure."

"Speaking of which," Ophelia said, "we will be needing a hefty sum from the fundraising ball. They just increased ticket prices for the French-Swiss railway line. We could try another, but it saves us weeks of overland travel. It's the most direct route."

"Anything could go wrong trying to go south through the Alps." Eleanor would know about things going wrong. Out of all of them on the Ben Nevis excursion, she was the only one who was hurt. She and Tristan, Ophelia's brother, fell through a snow cornice and ended up spending the night on the mountain. The rest of them had been sick with worry, but knew they would be of no help if they hurt themselves too. They'd hurried down the mountain and alerted local guides to help mount a search, but it was too late. A storm came through and everyone hunkered down until the next day.

Prudence had listened to the Scottish wind howl across the windows of their small inn, worried that Eleanor and Tristan would be frozen solid when they recovered them the next morning. But in a miracle, they found their way down the mountain on their own the next morning, finding Tristan's mother camped at the base of the mountain, waiting. Prudence wasn't surprised when a wedding was announced a few months later. Their mutual longing glances had not gone wholly unnoticed by the rest of the Society.

Still, if anyone would be cautious about accidents, that was Eleanor. And she had a point: the longer they traveled, the more chances there were to be derailed from their goal. Getting to Zermatt and the mountain was already difficult enough.

"How much are we short?" Prudence asked. A firm number would help her figure out exactly what they required.

Ophelia stared at the ground as she jogged. All of them looked at her, their leader, their instigator, their organizer, their friend. "Two thousand pounds."

Prudence stopped short, feeling like she'd been punched in the chest. She braced her hands on her knees. "You must be joking."

"How could we be so wildly short?" Eleanor asked. "I thought we were close."

"We were close," Ophelia said, circling back to where Prudence hunched over. "But our guides have been up on a failed climb on the Matterhorn recently, and have increased their rates due to the dangers they saw and experienced."

"By that much?" Prudence asked.

"Well, that, and they insisted we have cash set aside in reserve in case of emergency. If they need to transport one of us out of Zermatt because of injury. And they have been seeing what happened to the guide for Lord Douglas."

"The court cases?" Eleanor asked.

Justine stepped up at this. "Are they still blaming him? It wasn't his fault that the ropes failed."

"But that won't alleviate his lawyers' fees." Prudence stood up. Now she understood. It wasn't really that they needed the money to get to the Matterhorn, it was that they needed it to ensure they had knowledgeable guides to help them get to the top. Extra hands that knew the terrain. Which meant there was some wiggle room with that number. Money that they could ask to be fronted by investors, if need be. "Let's keep going."

The women started their slow introductory jog in silence. Prudence didn't know what the others thought about, but her mind was churning over the budget for the fundraising ball. What would give them the most return? What would make it seem luxurious while not being all that expensive?

"Justine, what animals were you thinking needed to be at the ball?" Prudence asked.

Justine shrugged, not out of breath at all. She was a machine. "I don't know. But every party that gets written down has some kind of exotic animal sodding about."

Prudence wasn't sure what "sodding" meant, but she was fairly certain it was a rude way to say "wandering." "What if we cut that part of the budget in half, and use it for something like peacock feathers, or something equally showy?"

Justine gave her a disappointed look but rolled her eyes in acquiescence. "Peacock feathers inside are bad luck, don't you know that? Means we will all be spinsters for life."

"Too late," Eleanor said with a smile.

"So no peacocks at all, then. Ophelia, do you have any more solid ideas for the ice theme?" Prudence asked.

"The only thing I've come up with is ice sculptures and sugar sculptures." Ophelia answered.

"Ice sculptures are not too practical even at the end of summer," Eleanor pointed out. "We could serve several courses of ices instead?"

"I like your thinking, Eleanor," Justine said. Her sweet tooth was notorious and exceeded the capacity of anyone Prudence had ever known, including small children.

"So we have a dinner with ice cream between every course?" Prudence asked.

"Ices," Ophelia corrected. "In England, they are ices."

"Of course," Prudence said. "My mistake."

"Time to pick up the pace!" Justine said, as they rounded the large oak tree in the spacious gardens of Rascomb house. The four of them all sped up, with Justine in the lead. For being so short, the woman could really run.

It was a start. Sugar paste sculptures and ices served between every course at dinner. That was becoming downright affordable. But what would be the meal? She wasn't a party planner, and did not possess the eye for this sort of extravagance.

She needed help. Though the women of the Ladies' Alpine Society would help, no question, none of them had an eye for this sort of thing either. But she knew who did.

Mrs. Moon.

⟫⟫⟪⟪

LEO RETURNED FROM his walk in the park. It was a daily exercise he required, but the moment he saw the Eyeball on his massive horse, he hid behind a tree. The man would make a convenient cover for his indiscretions with Prudence, but Leo couldn't forgive him for who he'd become. They'd once been comrades in their boyhood ostracization, but Eyeball moved on. Leo had only been able to turn his once-distasteful academic prowess into a successful cash flow.

As he handed off his hat and walking stick to the footman, he heard his mother talking up in her drawing room. The woman's voice could carry across whole neighborhoods once out of doors. "Who is Mother speaking to?" Leo asked the footman.

"Mrs. Cabot is here," the footman said before excusing himself to tidy away Leo's possessions.

Leo frowned. Prudence wasn't supposed to be here. Their appointment was for tonight, at her suite. He crept up the stairs, but he forgot to avoid the telltale creak of the fourth step.

"Leo is home. Leo!" His mother called. "You may join us."

He winced. The last thing he wanted to do was pretend indifference to Prudence in front of his mother, who knew every single small tell he had. He took a grudging breath, the kind of heavy sigh he knew she would hear. This was acting, and hadn't he played so many roles in his short life? His father would have him be anything from a penniless orphan to a rich boy lost in the woods. Whatever it took to lure in unsuspecting and unscrupulous wealthy travelers. He imagined he was about to have tea with Eyeball. That ought to do it.

He entered the drawing room, his feet heavy with dread.

Prudence was stunning. She wore a peach day dress, the sleeves stopping at her elbows and flaring with short ruffles of cream-colored lace. The collar at her neck—where he'd lavished kisses just yesterday—was high, brushing those escaped tendrils of hair. When she turned to look at him she smiled her American smile, the one he'd resented when first they met.

But he understood it now. Just as his steel façade was his armor against the world, so was her wide smile. It kept people at bay, making them not want to ask questions or dig any deeper. Implied that the person beneath it was one-dimensional and not worth the effort. But he knew Prudence was anything but boring or vapid, despite that Atlantic Ocean–sized smile.

"Mr. Moon," she said, from her perch in his mother's damask chair. "It's so wonderful you could join us."

His mother fairly beamed at him. Prudence—no, he must call her Mrs. Cabot, even in his mind. Mrs. Cabot was working some kind of wiles on his mother. He sat next to his mother on the matching damask couch.

"Daisy, fetch another cup!" his mother shouted to the maid downstairs. He flinched, her voice ringing in his ears.

"Mother. That is what the bellpull is for."

"My knee hurts. I refuse to stand."

"I could get you a bell to ring from here. A pretty silver one. Wouldn't that be better?"

She grumbled. "You always have a solution, don't you?" It was a question, but it didn't sound like a question.

He didn't want to bicker with his mother in front of Prudence, but he couldn't resist one last barb. "Only when there is a problem." He turned to face their guest. There was intricate cream-colored stitching down the front of the bodice that trailed onto her skirts. He swallowed hard, banished the thoughts of his hand following the stitching like a guide in the dark to find her petticoats.

He coughed. "Mrs. Cabot. What brings you here today? I don't believe we have an appointment."

"Daisy! A cup! Mr. Moon's throat is dry!" his mother yelled.

Leo looked up at the ceiling, wishing to be anywhere else but there.

Prudence—no, Mrs. Cabot, damn it all. Mrs. Cabot looked at him with the same polite distance that he had addressed her with. "No, I came only to see your mother. I need advice."

He narrowed his eyes. "On what?"

Oh, his mother could give advice, but none of it on topics Prudence should need. Well, that wasn't quite true. His mother had an encyclopedic knowledge of stain-removal techniques.

"How to make a lavish party appear more lavish."

He shook his head. "And why would she be the person you would go to for this?"

Mrs. Cabot raised her arms, gesturing to the drawing room. "I've been a guest in some of the most lavish drawing rooms in London. I've seen the rooms of a duchess. But none *feel* as rich as this one. Why?"

Leo looked around, trying to see it not as his mother's haven, but as a room unconnected to her. He shook his head. "I haven't the foggiest."

His mother preened next to him. She patted his leg. "Exactly."

"She'd promised to tell me her secrets." Prudence—Mrs. Cabot smiled conspiratorially and winked.

His stomach twisted. His mother could not tell all her secrets, for her secrets were his as well. Slowly, with control, he looked at his mother, who returned his gaze, confidence in her eyes. They'd been co-conspirators, secret keepers, for so long, it was what had bonded them so permanently together. Mothers and sons were always bonded, true, but not like them. And the best way to keep a secret was to never tell a soul.

⤳⤶

HE WAS LATE. Her clock chimed, and she couldn't help but glance at it. Prudence paced her suite, not wanting to sit and wrinkle her skirts. She wore a silk dress that had easy clasps in the front. The kind of thing made for a tryst. Or a husband. Which is why she had it, though Gregory had not been the kind of husband who would have wanted it. Or needed it.

Dinner was ready on plates at the table, under silver domes. She didn't want the hotel staff to suspect anything, so she ordered what she normally did for her and Georgie. As a favor, she also told Georgie to go out for dinner and handed her an extra stipend to do so.

Prudence cracked her knuckles. She knew it shouldn't, but her heart felt strange, and her head felt light. Old habits were soothing, even if they were bad ideas. Once all her knuckles were cracked, she snapped her fingers. *Please come, Leo,* she begged in her thoughts. She rested her head against one of the pillars that separated the dining area and the lounge area. The cool marble felt calming against her face.

Had she ruined everything by visiting his mother? Or was she too much trouble? What if she was bad at being intimate? Had she been too selfish? She'd let him guide her, and was that not appropriate? She wouldn't know. This was all new to her. Surely he would give her some grace for that.

Her lip was raw from where she'd chewed at it all day. The only time she'd been composed at all was sitting with Mrs. Moon. The older woman had been very helpful, and had thankfully not taken offense at what Prudence had implied—that she had come from very little money and could keep up appearances through creativity instead of cost.

And she'd had good ideas—draping cloth that pooled in places made a room appear more sumptuous. Rich colors might not be as fashionable, but they didn't wash out in the evenings when light was low. That candlelight still made everyone appear more elegant than gas lamps. Brass will shine—if polished well enough—and used sparingly. No one will notice the difference.

All helpful tips, even if she wasn't sure how they might incorporate to the party.

A soft knock at the door. Finally!

She cleared her throat for no reason whatsoever and went to the door. Her heart galloped like a stray dog after the butcher. Composing oneself was not an easy task. She opened the door, and there he stood, a bottle of wine in his hand.

He looked up at her from the brim of his gray hat, a color that matched his eyes. The well-tailored suit accented his slender build and his wide shoulders. The strong jaw set as if his teeth were clenched was the focal point of his gray-on-gray appearance.

"Come in," she said, her voice barely above a whisper.

He glanced at her, at the room beyond, his expression unchanging. Prudence felt a tingle in her body as he returned his gaze to her, flicking his eyes from her feet to her hair. He stalked past her, and she caught his ink and bergamot scent.

A tremble went through her entire body. It felt like . . . butterflies! This was butterflies! She'd done it. Or rather, Leo had.

"Good evening, Prudence," he said, taking off his hat. She took it from him and stowed it in the small closet next to the door.

"Good evening, Leo." She stared at him, unable to break away from whatever this was, this feeling like a giggle, but in her bones.

"Your gown is beautiful, but you are stunning." His voice was lower than normal.

Heat radiated through her. Blushing? Here? Now? "Thank you." She willed the heat to die down. "You look rather dashing yourself."

He gave one of his rare smiles to her, and she felt like she'd been rewarded.

"Dinner is ready on the table." She gestured into the other room.

At the table, he lifted the silver dome left in place by the staff to keep it warm. Unfortunately, it also often made things soggier than necessary.

"Fish," he said.

Prudence lifted her dome and stared at it. Normally, it was perfectly respectable, but after sitting for so long, a grayish cast had come over the scaled filet. "It looks much more appetizing when they bring it fresh."

She saw Leo wince.

"Oh, no! No, I wasn't subtly chastising you for tardiness. No, I'm not as clever as all that." She didn't want him to feel bad. Yes, she'd been anxious for him to arrive, but she wasn't angry. She was honestly grateful he arrived at all.

"You deserve an apology for my tardiness, Prudence." He replaced the dome and looked about for the drink cart. He stowed the bottle of wine on it and searched for the wine key. He looked up at her once he had it in hand. "I'm sorry that I am late. I had misgivings."

Prudence frowned.

"I was . . . surprised by your visit to my mother today."

She started to shake her head. "You and your mother are not connected."

Leo chuckled and opened the wine. The cork popped dramatically. He stepped back over to the table and poured them each an ample serving of dark red wine. "Tragically, I am connected quite closely with my mother."

"I meant, in my head. I wasn't thinking of you when I went to your mother. I was thinking of the fundraising ball."

Leo nodded, not looking at her. He stared into his wine. "We have to keep this . . . separate."

"Separate?"

Now he looked up at her. "You have no intention of marrying again."

"Goodness, no." It came out of her mouth before she could think. Marriage for her meant loss of her autonomy. Loss of her wealth. Upon marrying a man, it would become his.

"Nor do I. There is no room in my life for a bride. I mean no offense."

"Neither do I." Prudence was baffled. Why was he bringing marriage into this conversation?

Leo nodded, his chin jutting out more than usual. As if this somehow displeased him, even though she agreed with him.

"I'm sorry, I don't understand why we are discussing this? Are we not here for more enjoyable things?" Prudence felt heat rush to her cheeks again. She absolutely was the worst at talking about this.

Leo swirled the wine in his glass and took a sip. "Absolutely correct. Why are we talking about this?"

Prudence picked up her glass and sniffed. The boozy smell of it was still wafting away. This encounter didn't feel right. She turned away from him, unsure. "If you aren't hungry, perhaps we can talk instead."

The lounge area was set with two sofas in an ell shape. They were well stuffed and comfortable. She'd napped on them plenty of times—proof of their softness. She settled herself in the sofa, right at the corner that connected the two pieces of furniture. Leo followed her and sat on the adjacent sofa, closest to her.

"What would you like to talk about?" he asked.

She watched him a moment, observing. His shoes were polished to a high shine. His trousers were perfectly tailored. His coat revealed the exact amount of shirt sleeve at the cuff. His waistcoat was tailored, adorned with the gold chain of a pocket watch. Even the burgundy pocket square of his coat was ironed into conformity. As his mother had proven with her acuity of projecting wealth, this was also a façade. This was a barrier. While he'd managed to step around it yesterday in his office, today it was back firmly in place. "I'd like to talk about you."

His eyebrows raised, wrinkling his forehead. "You wish to die of boredom?"

She sniffed her wine. It smelled full and ripe, and when she sipped, the taste of black cherries and earth exploded in her mouth. This was a very good wine. "I doubt that would be the case." She held his gaze. "If you told the truth."

"Why don't you tell me the truth about you?" he countered.

"I thought you had researched me. You know everything there is to know. If one would like to die of boredom."

"I know facts. I know dates and events. I don't know you." Leo leaned back into the sofa, relaxing for the first time.

"I don't even know facts about you, Mr. Moon. I'd like to know some." Prudence smiled at him, but a genuine one. Dare she say, a flirtatious one? Was she successfully flirting? She hoped so.

"Facts. I can give you facts. You've met my mother. My father died some years ago. I attended an elite boarding school on scholarship where I honed my skills at taking money from aristocratic classmates. Repeat *ad nauseum*. Here we are." He gestured with his hands wide, as if to encompass the world.

But there was something about his face, his tone, that made her think that he wasn't telling the whole truth. Not that he was lying *per se*, but that something in his very brief accounting of his life wasn't accurate. But she'd conducted enough deals to know that there was a price of doing business. And the price here was not questioning Leo about this. There was something he didn't want to talk about.

She'd seen his face that afternoon when Mrs. Moon had said she would reveal her "secrets." Leo had gone rigid and pale. There was a secret he needed kept. That was fine. After all, they weren't starting an *affair de coeur*, this was . . . a different sort of business. An affair of the body, not the heart.

"I see. Your life story was very brief and to the point," Prudence said.

"You asked for facts," Leo reminded her.

"How did you take your classmates' money?"

"I did their homework for them. They paid me."

"That's not really *taking* their money. That's earning their money."

"You don't know what I charged." Leo gave a hint of a smile, which Prudence considered success.

"I'll give you that point," she said, unwilling to argue further.

"Those are the facts. Tell me something about you now," he urged.

She sipped at the wine, it was so juicy and full she could down it in a gulp and be happy. "What area would you like to know about?"

"What makes you so pragmatic?" He echoed her gesture of drinking wine. "You might be the most prudent person I've ever met, living up to your name."

He wasn't the first person who'd told her that. She sighed. "I'm the oldest daughter of seven brothers and sisters, all born very close together. My father had not just the railroad business, but also a farm. He did his best to hire an assistant manager for his railroad needs, because he preferred farming. But at harvest, we all helped. As the oldest, I drove the horses for the initial reaping. It was slow and kind of tedious. Needing to keep the rows straight, the horses on an easy walk. But I was good at it. Even when I got bigger and could help with the other work, my siblings couldn't manage the horses, so it was always my job."

"But not for long. Because you married young."

She nodded. "At seventeen. Which wasn't really that young."

"It is for London standards."

"Well, I was in Minneapolis. Not London. And my father's business partner needed a bride. He wanted a child to inherit his fortunes, and marrying me would solidify the partnership. Once the Transcontinental Railroad completed, of which both of them had a stake, it would be beneficial to have their interest combined in the form of one child."

"So you were the sacrificial lamb?" Leo challenged. There was something hard glinting in his eye.

"I didn't see it that way. Marrying Gregory meant I would move to New York state, which was exciting, since I'd never traveled. And being with him meant I wouldn't have to care for my siblings, I'd have a legion of maids. Which I did for a short while anyway. Turns out that I dislike sitting around."

"So it didn't matter that you had to marry an old troll?"

Prudence reared back. They might not have had a love match, but Gregory was not a troll. "That is not the way it was at all. Gregory was much older, yes, but he was handsome. He was weary of trying to find a wife amongst his social class, and he needed a bride who would be willing and able to have children, which I was. Why would I not marry a rich, handsome man who could sweep me away from constant hard work? It sounds like a French fairy tale, doesn't it? Of course I accepted. I was flattered. I was honored to be his bride."

"He was the one who should have been flattered and honored." Leo's voice was flat. Was he angry about this?

"I think he was, in his way. And he taught me everything I know about business. There is no better teacher than sitting at the feet of a master."

Leo looked away, clearly trying to hide his disgust.

"It wasn't like that," she insisted. "Gregory was a good man."

"Perhaps, but you sacrificed your girlhood to him. You went from being a servant in your own home to being an old man's bride. Where was the time for you? When did you get to be a child? A girl? A young woman?"

"Now," Prudence said, looking him in the eye. "Now is my time. Otherwise, you wouldn't be here, alone, in my suite."

Leo froze, hearing her admonishment. Good. She needed to impress upon him that her life had been not just acceptable, but appropriate, even if it hadn't been conventional or fun.

She continued, softer now. "It's the reason I have no intention of marrying again. Gregory had health issues, and I became his nursemaid. But it meant I had full control of the companies, and conducted business in his name. It's why I know Morse code. Gregory had a telegraph installed in the house upstate, so he could continue his business while in a place of respite. His associates didn't know if he was the one behind the messages or if I was. And making deals, changing our investments, especially during the turbulent times of the war, it kept me sane. I'd been a nursemaid to my siblings, and then to my husband."

"And you needed freedom from that constant caretaking."

She caught his eye. "Exactly. Which I have a suspicion you do for your mother."

Leo looked away. "We aren't talking about me."

"We could be." Prudence leveled her gaze at him. Challenging him. Asking him.

Leo let out a sigh that didn't sound as frustrated as she expected. More resigned than anything.

"My mother and I have been through some troubles together. I would never abandon her to a dowager house or even to a house where she wouldn't be in control. She's earned her place, and I will do all I can to keep her there. Hence, why I have no intentions of marrying."

Prudence inclined her head and raised her glass, acknowledging his reasons, and making clear that she had no matrimonial designs on him.

"My father was not a . . . good man. He was not good to me, nor to her. When he died, we left, set up here in London. I promised to take care of her, so that she would never have to endure a life like that ever again."

"It's amazing how you tell a story with absolutely no particulars," Prudence teased.

When Leo's gaze flicked up at her, his eyes were nothing but steel. "There are things I will not share with anyone. Anyone, Prudence. Not you. Not anyone."

It felt a bit like a slap. She'd shared so much of her past. Why would he not share his? Other than what was clearly a horrible situation. Leo intimated some kind of horridness, but that was tragically not uncommon. There must have been something more to it. But she willed her mind to stop picking apart the puzzle that was Leo Moon. It wasn't her place. It wasn't what she wanted from him anyway. There was no point. So she put her curiosity aside.

"Fine, if you won't talk about your mother, how about your schoolmates? Tell me something specific. A recounting of something not sordid, so that I cannot pity your upbringing as you have pitied mine."

His expression softened. "Fine." He was quiet, then looked around the room, as if he might find something hidden up in a corner.

"Having trouble thinking of something?"

"Frankly, yes. None of my stories that are happy cast me in a terribly respectable light. Most of them entail swindling my betters. Of course, my motivation was retribution for beatings they'd given me years before."

"Ah. So you hold a grudge, do you?"

"Tragically, yes. It might be what I do best, actually." He leaned forward, bracing himself on his knees. "I know it isn't my place, and despite your protest, I will always hold a grudge against your husband, even though he is dead and cannot defend himself. You were too young to know what you needed, and he clearly didn't let you learn how to be you. He only continued what you had already known: how to care for others. How to be of service. And I cannot forgive him that."

She hadn't thought of it in that way before. That she had existed in service to others. It had been her obligation, her joy, to take care of her family and then her husband. It had never occurred to her to protest or see inequity there. There had simply been a need, and she filled it. Yes, it had been at the expense of herself, but now she'd gotten the chance to do what she wanted. And look at what she was doing! She had a lover and a plan to climb the Matterhorn! How could she complain? "He got me to where I am today. So I will always be grateful to him."

Leo looked up. "*You* got you to where you are today. The American war bankrupted most everyone. Yet, you came through smelling like a rose. That was you. You did that."

"With his name and his money," she amended.

"His name only mattered because men are twats."

Her laughter rang out like a burst bubble. "I've never heard you speak like that."

He shrugged, another layer of armor shedding. "I'm not wrong."

She shook her head. "No, you're not wrong at all."

He put down his glass and rose, finding a new seat on her couch beside her. "I want you to know that I admire you, and not just desire you."

"That rhymes, so you know it's true."

Leo chuckled and played with one of the tendrils of hair she'd so carefully curled earlier that evening. "I hope you feel the same about me."

"I do." Her mind went fuzzy. His nearness triggered some kind of drug in her body, and she felt the sensation flood her entire body. She was almost drowsy with desire.

He smiled at her, a real one, not a polite grimace. "Good." He lifted her hand to his mouth and kissed it. Then turned her hand over, palm up, and kissed the sensitive spot on the inside of her wrist.

The fire that was already ignited between her legs surged. She swallowed hard. "I'm glad we talked," she managed.

"May I kiss you now?" he asked.

She nodded, and he began slowly, as if playing with her. But she wasn't in the mood for playing. The anticipation for this had been too stressful, the need now too big. He moved to her neck, as he'd done the day before. "I have a French letter," she whispered.

"Excellent," he said between kisses. "I didn't want to be presumptuous."

"I invited you to my private suite at night, after a discussion of becoming lovers. After what happened yesterday at your office, how could you not presume this?"

"You talk too much," he said, taking her mouth with his.

She didn't mind at all.

⇶⇷

HE WAS A weak man. Before Prudence, Leo had believed himself to have nerves of iron. He was merciless in his decisions, never looked back, never regretted an action taken. And while he'd struggled with the idea of not seeing Prudence at all tonight, he'd determined on the walk over that he'd not go to bed with her. It was better for both of them to stop before certain lines were crossed.

Her involvement with his mother made it impossible for them to have a physical relationship. His mother was caustic, hard to get along with, and yet, here was Prudence, slicing through his mother's thick exterior like a hot knife through butter. The American widow would get too close, too fast, and his mother would tell her everything.

And that would place them in jeopardy. He didn't care about

it for himself, not at all. But he would not risk his mother's life—her fortune—on what was nothing more than a natural expression of bodily needs.

But Prudence was painfully, ethereally beautiful, like the women of a Millais painting, and as soon as she'd opened the door, he could tell she'd dressed for him. She was expecting a seduction. Except, as he uncorked the wine bottle, and she challenged him at every turn, he wasn't sure who was seducing whom.

Talking was certain to be an antidote for him, it always had in the past. But tonight it served only to draw him in more. When she told him the specifics of her life—one of servitude, not unlike his own mother, really—his rage had gotten the better of him. Leo had meant it when he said that he'd hate her husband, this Gregory, who hadn't deserved the pedestal she placed him on. Who'd left her desiring. Who'd left her feeling wanting. That somehow, she wasn't beautiful or fascinating, that she wasn't the exact fucking object of every fantasy he'd ever entertained. Perhaps he hadn't known the face to put on those imaginary women, but once he'd met Prudence, the fantasy had come to life. And he wasn't prepared for that. Didn't know how to fight it.

He wound a finger around the honey-colored tendril she'd curled for him. He kissed her neck below her ear. Her breathing was his measure of her excitement. She hadn't the words to tell him how she felt, and he wouldn't pressure her to be more explicit—not yet. And he could hold both ideas in one moment—that this was a terrible idea and he placed his entire world at risk *and* the only thing he wanted in this life was to hear what Prudence desired from his mouth, his hands, his cock.

She pulled his hand that had cradled her cheek to her mouth, kissing his palm. The wetness of her mouth, the promise of her tongue, made the building tension in his groin grow taut. He hadn't come prepared for lovemaking, but here he was, and while conflicted, it was a curse he blessed.

He turned and took her mouth. In return, she guided his

hands down to the front of the silk bodice. He thought she meant to turn his attention to her breasts, only to discover she was showing him the hook and eye front closure of her extraordinary gown. And then he cursed his stupidity that she was wearing lingerie for him. This was no day dress nor elaborate evening gown. He groaned.

How dare she make this easy for him? To guide him into wine-soaked pleasure? He deftly unhooked the widely spaced closures, peeling the silk layer from her shoulders. She wasn't wearing a corset at all. She was nude, wearing only her silk stockings with ornate forest-green clocking design snaking up the side of her lovely calves. She looked like a frontispiece for an erotic novel.

"Prudence," he said through gritted teeth, taking her in. "I do not deserve such preparations." And he meant it. She was so beautiful, curved and muscled in all the right places. Slender but not brittle, tall but perfectly proportioned. He could not have imagined a woman better.

"I do what I want." Prudence looked at him with a ferocity that surprised him and aroused him all at once. "And what I want is you. Tonight."

He leaned her back over the arm of the sofa, her back arching, her breasts on display. "At your service," he said, taking one breast into his palm and the other his mouth. She let out a moan of pleasure, and he growled. He hadn't meant to, it was a primal sound, a sound that he didn't know he could make. Time shifted in ways he couldn't perceive. His focus narrowed to this woman, this sofa, and all the combinations those things could do.

Her silk robe laid out beneath her, he lifted his head so that he could remove the pins from her hair. He wanted to see it. When she realized that's what he wanted, she took over, removing pins as his hand slid lower, between her legs. She gasped, which brought him an unexpected satisfaction. She was slick with want already.

Honeyed hair tumbled down over her shoulders, longer than

he'd realized, wavy with touches of auburn, until it settled over her breasts. He was stunned. Then she looked at him with her gray eyes, gripped his shoulder hard, and came, grinding into his hand.

"Fuck," he whispered in awe, and somewhere in his chest, something ripped open.

"Your turn," she said, her cheeks glowing, her eyes bright. "Shirt off. Now."

He licked his lips in the face of this goddess. There was no arguing with her, reclined on her sofa, draped with hair and silk. His fingers somehow found the buttons on his cuffs. He threw off his coat and unbuttoned his waistcoat, shrugging it off, careful to place it on the floor as it contained his pocket watch. Next he pulled off the braces, then ripped away his collar and worked his shirt as quickly as possible. Finally, he sat before her bare chested, awaiting her judgement.

Her eyes flicked all over him, as If evaluating him, finding every freckle, discoloration, birthmark, and scar. With a single light finger, she touched the scars she found. The round cigar burn, about the size of a shilling, just under his collarbone. But her touch was like an anointment with oil. A sacred exploration.

The jagged scar from a rock that he'd failed to land on top of that should have been stitched, but he didn't want to worry his mother, so he said nothing instead. The strange indentation on his side from another fall, this one out of a tree, that never healed, but rather knotted up, leaving a misshapen lump under his skin.

But Prudence asked no questions. She finished her assessment. "Take off your trousers."

He stood while she reclined back, her head propped on her hand, as if he were about to give a lecture and not undress. She was unnerving, this woman. But Leo had prided himself on his self-possession. Ah yes, the very pride that had failed him earlier in the evening was now making him take off his trousers. Irony, that.

She bit her lip as he cast away his shoes, socks, and then his trousers. Finally, there was nothing between them but air. And that air was thick and humid and charged. But he dared not make a move, despite what his waving cockstand might demand.

"Is this agreeable?" he asked, his own challenge to her.

A teasing smile flitted past her swollen red lips. "Most agreeable."

"Do you have another command for me?"

Her eyes went dark with desire as it sparked something in her imagination. The depth of her intelligence was not yet clear to him, and his cold heart sped as he anticipated her imagination.

"I want you to do what you did yesterday, with your mouth. But I want to be able to touch you while you do it."

He raised his eyebrows, pleased. To be asked for encore performance was always a good sign. But he wasn't going to let her get away with the request so easily. "I did a great many things with my mouth yesterday. To which are you referring?"

"Your mouth, between my legs. Where you lapped at my pearl." Her cheeks didn't flush, which surprised him. She was deadly serious, and if he did anything well, her second orgasm would not take long.

"As you command." He knelt, pushing her legs apart.

"No," she said, not forcefully, but he froze in place. "I said so that I may touch you as well."

He relaxed. "Then we should adjourn to the bed." Standing, he held his hand out to help her off the sofa. She passed by him, her soft skin brushing his arm, her silky hair teasing him. Watching her naked body move fascinated him. He'd never seen a naked woman so well-muscled, so sleekly formed. It made her arse a damned work of art.

Prudence reclined on the bed, while Leo positioned himself perpendicular. He was still able to accommodate his tongue on her pearl, as she called it, and her hand worked his blazing hard cock. It was a potent mix for him, making it difficult to concentrate on his ministrations. When she shuddered beneath him, clamping her thighs around his head, he nearly came in her hand.

But as he prepared to slip from her and take himself in hand, she all but took a handful of his arse cheek. Her eyes were furiously dark, intense in a way he had never seen in another person, her pupils blown wide with pleasure. "I want you inside me, Leo. Now."

Dumbly, he could do nothing but nod, nothing but maneuver himself between her legs, the anticipation of her wet heat pulling him in. In his fog, he heard her say, "Wait."

He blinked, breathing hard through his mouth to make himself stay his body.

"The French letter," she said, and her hand pointed.

It took him some moments to realize what the words meant, why her hand was outstretched. Ah, yes. Prevention. Yes. He stumbled over to the drawer she indicated and pulled out the small square envelope. He opened it, clumsily pulling on the thin membrane over his cock. He looked up at Prudence, reclined on the bed, watching him, her lips cherry red, her face flush with pleasure and desire.

He didn't wait for instruction. This time, he could figure out himself how to resume his position between her legs. His cock nudged at the slick entrance. "Yes?" he asked, so desperate he thought he might gnaw his own lip off with the amount of control he exerted.

"Yes," she said, the word almost a sigh of relief.

And he pushed in, and she cried out. It wasn't in pain, thank God, but in pleasure. He tried to be slow, to make their joining one of seduction and not rutting. But she pulled her legs up, and reached down to grasp his arse, pulling him in deeper. He groaned at her need. Faster he pumped, thrusting deep every time, watching her face, her chin tipped back, her dark lashes fluttering on her cheek.

"Leo," she groaned. "Faster."

He grunted his assent, his own pleasure very nearly mastering his body, but he obeyed. Faster he went, blind with need and tension and maddening friction. But there it was, his own orgasm, no longer willing to wait. No longer capable of waiting. "I'm going to—" He gritted his teeth, hoping to give her time.

She let go of his arse and grabbed him at his ear, met his eye, and demanded, "Come."

He obeyed. And she came with him, shuddering together, his hips unable to stop immediately, his bollocks pushing him to continue just a little more. He shuddered one last time and did his best not to collapse on her.

They both sweated, and where they were joined it was slick and sticky. He knew he should pull out. He should absolutely not give her his weight. This was business. But oh God, what blissful business. He wanted to kiss her nose, her eyelids, the space beneath her ear, as a lover would. Could.

But she held onto him, her arms curled around his back, her legs cradling him. As if she were giving tacit permission for him to cross those lines. To kiss her nose. To fall into her as he desperately wanted to. He lowered to his elbows.

"Prudence," he whispered.

She opened her eyes to meet his gaze. Tears slipped from her eyes.

Horrified, he scrambled up to sitting. "Oh no, I didn't—"

She smiled at him, open and warm. "It's not tears of pain or regret, Leo. It's tears of . . . pent-up frustration. It's at last getting what I wanted."

"Oh," he said, still very uneasy that she may have not wanted him to do what she had very clearly instructed him to do. "Are you sure?"

Another smile. "Leo. My only other lover was my husband who clearly felt shame every time he bedded me—which only happened for the sole purpose of begetting an heir. And that didn't happen. I always dreamed of being vocal, of getting exactly what I wanted, rather than lying there like a . . ." she searched for the word, "a wayward nun."

He laughed, and that shake finally pulled his now-shrunken cock from her entrance. Fortunately, he was quick enough to catch the French letter before it slipped off and spilled. "I'd like to think I take instruction well."

She smiled and bit her lip. "So far."

"Towels?" Leo asked.

Prudence pointed to a closed door. "In the bathing room. There's even plumbing, if you can believe it."

"With warm water?" Leo asked. The new invention was the talk of every circle. Hauling hot water was a burden, and running cold water was nice, but to have indoor plumbing with heat was revolutionary.

Prudence nodded. "I'll soap your back if you soap mine."

⇾⇉⇇⇠

DAWN FAST APPROACHED as Leo finally slipped into his shoes. "I'm famished," he said as he kissed her again.

She rather enjoyed his kisses. In fact, the whole night had been more than she could have ever dreamed. "Me too, but I can't very well order for two up here."

Leo grinned. "Can you imagine the look on their faces?"

"No!" she said, relishing the thought of scandalizing the hotel staff. Scandalizing anyone would be a first for her. But she couldn't. She wouldn't jeopardize her friends and the opportunity to climb the Matterhorn. "But I can stop by this afternoon to talk party business."

He groaned, and it wasn't the sexy one he'd emitted several times during the course of the last eight hours. "It's ridiculous."

"It's necessary, so you might as well get on board. The theme is 'ice.'"

"You might as well have a theme called 'weather' for all the good it will do you." Leo shrugged into his overcoat and put on his hat. He really was going to leave her.

Of course, he should leave. It was nearly morning, and he couldn't very well be seen leaving her room. His best bet was a sleepy doorman downstairs.

"Then you ought to help me so that things don't get out of

hand. And I'm taking you to Bond Street."

He reared back. "Why?"

"Because the best way to make a party look fancier than it actually is while still on a budget is cloth. And where is the cloth? Bond Street."

"Cloth is not budget friendly."

"It is compared to fresh flowers." She stepped forward and rebuttoned his waistcoat, where he'd inadvertently mismatched the closure. "And if you won't believe me, look into it yourself."

He gave a heavy sigh. "You're never going to let me live down calling on Lord Rascomb to see if you were telling the truth."

Prudence smiled, somehow, the hurt of his initial insult no longer stinging. "Nope." She went up to her tiptoes and kissed his nose. "Now shoo. Go on, git."

He turned and went to the door, but before he opened it, he turned back. "Prudence, I know I can't send you flowers tomorrow, or rather, later today, without spurring gossip. So I'd like to say now that I rather enjoyed myself last night."

"I should think so," she said. "I rather did myself as well."

"And I hope we might do it again."

Her body went suddenly languid and hot, as it had all those hours on the couch, in her bed, and in the bathing room. "I do too."

Leo smiled at her—a real, genuine expression of happiness. And then he left.

Prudence listened to his footsteps disappear down the hall before she ran giggling through her rooms to her bed. She flung herself on the mussed comforter and laughed. She had done it! She had a lover! And it was so good. Far better than anticipated. And she liked him too. She actually liked Leo Moon, which was somewhat surprising after their first encounters.

And despite the coolness of the room, and the peek of sunlight encroaching through the windows, Prudence fell into a deep, satisfied sleep.

Chapter Five

"Here are the swatches," Prudence said, presenting the cloth squares to Ophelia. The other women leaned over to peer at them.

"I like the dark blue paired with the light, almost silvery blue. It reminds me of the depths of the sea," Eleanor said.

"It isn't about the sea," Justine argued, pointing at the green-blue cloth instead. "I like that color."

"But is that really a color of ice?" Ophelia asked.

"Does it matter?" Justine countered.

"It should if you dismiss Eleanor's suggestions of the sea," Prudence said, wanting to stick up for Eleanor.

They all sagged back into the silk cushioned chairs of Ophelia's mother's drawing room. They'd run again this morning, bathed, dressed, and had refreshments. Now it was time to finally get some business done.

"How did you even come up with this, Prudence?" Justine asked. "It's brilliant, but I just wouldn't have thought of it."

Prudence wondered if she should reveal her source as Mrs. Moon. It would strengthen her tie to Leo, which she wasn't sure she could afford. But well, why not? Theoretically, her visits with Mrs. Moon would excuse her excessive time in his company.

"It was Mrs. Moon's idea, actually."

The normally placid and even-tempered Ophelia made a dreadful face. "Mr. Moon's mother?"

"Yes, I quite like her," Prudence said. "And she certainly knows her way around a penny."

"But she's wretched," Justine said. "The only things I have ever heard her say have been mortifying insults."

Prudence shrugged. "We get along. Maybe it's because we're both widows."

Eleanor's posture noticeably softened. As a newlywed, the idea of losing her husband was unthinkable. But Prudence's life with Gregory bore no resemblance to the bliss Eleanor had with Tristan. Prudence put her hand over Eleanor's and squeezed it, an acknowledgment of her friend's sympathy.

"If we are interested, I also got quotes from a shop where we could have snowflakes embroidered on the cloth banners in silver thread."

Justine gasped. "That would be gorgeous!"

"Especially if we use candlelight," Ophelia said, her eyes distant. No doubt calculating costs and returns on her investments. "How wide are these banners you are proposing?"

"Four feet wide," Prudence said, double-checking her notes. Her notes, scrawled in Leo's hand.

She had imperiously picked up both him and his mother and taken them both on her trip to Bond Street. His mother had plenty of opinions of which shops were worthy of their business, but often stayed in the carriage, complaining of pain in her knees.

It had been a thrilling outing, not looking at Leo as she remembered his kisses, his mouth suckling her pearl, his palms covering each breast. She had to keep cold and aloof, as did he.

She thought she'd done a fair job, as Mrs. Moon neither commented nor shot her warning looks. After all, their very first conversation was all about how Mrs. Moon wouldn't allow Prudence anywhere near her son.

As an aspiring American hussy, Prudence had vowed to stay away. But, well, things happened. She had been trying very hard to be furious with him, as a matter of fact. It was merely that the chemistry between them had been too obvious, too heady for her to resist. No doubt that would soon fade, and when it did, their time would be over. Which was what they both wanted and agreed upon.

"Prudence?" Ophelia asked.

"Pru?" Justine prodded.

She shook her head and smiled at her friends. "Sorry. Head in the clouds." Even Eleanor looked at her strangely. "The run tired me out."

Eleanor kept examining her, a situation she didn't care for. Eleanor could be quite observant when she wanted to be. As the group's slowest athlete, Eleanor should be the one complaining, not Prudence.

Ophelia produced a sketchbook and a charcoal pencil. She flipped open to a page they'd examined last time. She held it up so they could all get a good look. "This was our last thought. But now . . ."

Ophelia turned the page and sketched her parents' ballroom again, this time with the cloth banners.

"Would we alternate the colors?" asked Eleanor.

"And how many colors are we choosing?" asked Prudence.

Justine frowned at the swatches, and then arranged them in order, from light to dark. "What if we did this?" She pointed at the one so light blue it was almost white. "When you first enter the ballroom, it is like the top of the ice, and then the deeper you go, the darker it gets."

"Like falling into a crevasse?" Eleanor asked.

Ophelia pulled a face.

"Exactly!" Justine said.

"Sounds like courting bad luck," Prudence said, glancing over at Ophelia.

"Nonsense," Justine said, "it's just a party. It'll be fun."

"Can we ring for more tea?" Prudence asked.

Ophelia nodded and rose to ring the bellpull. Justine took the sketchbook and added shading to emphasize her point. Prudence could see it. "What about if we made some kind of mountain

They both looked up to see Justine poking aggressively at the sketchbook paper as Ophelia made adjustments. Prudence and Eleanor giggled, which made Justine look up.

"I beg your pardon," Justine demanded.

Eleanor shook her head and Prudence kept laughing, her heart fuller and fuller. "I admire you Justine, more than you know."

At that, the girl smiled back, her dimples deep and becoming. She might not be in Minnesota, or even on the American continent, but she had family. These women would take her in no matter what she did, and there was comfort in that. She would do the same for them in a heartbeat.

⇢⇢⇢⇠⇠⇠

THE WEEKS WITH Prudence had turned into months, and still he could not break his obsession with her. All morning he'd been in a lather trying to forget Prudence for at least one minute. Her taste, her smell, her skin had been occupying his mind on a loop—an obsession he couldn't shake. Finally, he'd taken himself in hand, almost rubbed himself raw, coming quickly into a rag. A poor substitute for what his mind had suggested.

"An 'Eyeball' here to see you, sir," the footman announced without blinking.

Leo gritted his teeth. He was just now able to focus. And now here was this idiot coming to waste his time.

Leo threw his pen down. "Fine. Show him in." Leo stood, straightening his waistcoat. He was behind in his work thanks to his errant brain.

Not long after, the bulky form of Eyeball occupied the space in front of him.

"Leo," he said, tipping his head in gracious acknowledgment.

"Eyeball. To what do I owe this honor?" Leo gestured to the seat across from his desk, and both men sat.

"I heard the strangest thing at the club last night. You'll never guess."

Leo waited, as patient as he could feign.

"Guess."

"You just told me that I would never, so I won't, thank you." Leo gave a pinched grimace, the best he could do for a polite smile.

"You have absolutely lost all your interest in fun, Leo. It's positively depressing."

Leo raised his eyebrows, hoping to urge the man to continue.

"I was told that I had come in secret to your house for those investing lessons I'd asked you for."

Drat his mother for being such a gossip.

"And here I was, assuming you'd brushed me off completely. But no, there's at least a rumor connecting our names over the very topic I had hoped we might engage in." Eyeball bit his lip, showing off the top row of straight white teeth. "Of course, I would want to inquire as to why this untruth was abound, but rather than that, I thought I owed it to you to come here and tell you the gossip of the day."

"Is that all?" Leo asked. He was angry now, but it was his own fault, his own stupidity. His mother could keep secrets if she needed to—but he had not been explicit about this being a secret. So she'd told. Or perhaps one of their servants had overheard and mentioned it somewhere. It didn't really matter who the culprit was. The deed was done.

Eyeball gave him a wink, flashing that one green eye. "Of course not. I will gladly keep my mouth shut and not deny these charges on one condition."

"Do you feel that you are in a position to blackmail me?" Leo frowned. Truthfully, he could be in that position. Leo didn't want to contemplate a second intricate lie he would have to construct to cover up this one. And the quintessential axiom about lying is to keep it close to the truth.

"Blackmail?" Eyeball scoffed. "No. Both of us getting what we want. I get investment advice, and you get whatever it was that you needed by telling people we'd met up in secret."

Leo stared at him, not moving. He was thinking.

"Why did we meet up in secret?" Eyeball asked, scooting to the edge of his seat. When Leo made no move to answer, Eyeball waved him off. "Not important. I have time today and well, let's be honest, every day, to meet. Whenever you'd like to start those lessons."

Leo blinked. He did not want Eyeball to take up any of his precious time. He'd been a pain in the arse in school, and he was a pain in the arse now. He was just bigger. Reluctantly, he dug out his datebook. "Tomorrow," he said.

Eyeball slapped his hands on the arms of the chair. "Splendid!"

"Ten a.m. sharp." Leo looked up as the man stood.

"So early." Eyeball winced. "Could we not do a more civilized time? Say, two in the afternoon?"

Leo glanced at his datebook. Prudence would be coming by to see his mother. He'd come up with her own code for his diary. A collection of dots along the page, that could be excused as mere pen marks. "Fine. Two. Tomorrow. But I will not tolerate lateness."

Eyeball gave him a grin that no doubt would win his mother over. Leo gritted his teeth but stood out of politeness and respect for rank.

⁂

"You must be Mrs. Cabot, the American widow." A man's booming voice came from behind her.

Prudence jumped. She gripped the warm stone banister on the front steps of the Moon residence for balance. Her lace-gloved hand flew to her heaving chest.

"My apologies for startling you." A man came into focus. A

massive man, whose broad shoulders nearly blocked out the sun.

Prudence swallowed and composed herself. He was handsome, holding his hand outstretched. She didn't know if he was offering it as a gentleman or as a handshake. Unsure, she shook it. She was an American businesswoman, after all. What did he expect her to do? "Nice to meet you," she said. "I'm at the disadvantage. And you are?"

"Terribly rude and impertinent, I'm afraid," he said, with a wide winning smile. "But I saw you going in to visit, and having just come from there, I was wondering who you were here to see."

Prudence blinked. "That is terribly rude and impertinent."

He laughed, which was in itself disarming. If the weather had not been warm and pleasant, causing everyone in London to be kinder and more genial, she might have turned on her heel and walked away from him. Was that not what she was supposed to do? Truthfully, she wasn't sure anymore.

But Prudence had experience with men like this in New York, while she did business on her husband's behalf. They were slick like wet otter pelts. He waited for her charming response, and when it did not come, he had to continue the conversation on his own.

"I'm an old school chum of Leo's. I was wondering if you were his . . . *amor.*"

"I beg your pardon. You haven't told me who you are and why my business is your business." Prudence's hackles rose. She knew what he was asking. And she didn't like it one bit.

"Lord Grabe, at your service." He bowed fully, a show of respect in gesture he had not given in conversation. But it allowed her to see that he had a full head of thick, dark hair, barely tamed curls, and that his hat was made of the finest (most likely American if not Canadian) beaver skin. She wondered if the luxurious hat was not too hot for him, or if it was a way to flaunt his wealth that could not be foregone just because of the weather.

"Mrs. Prudence Cabot," she said, not bothering to curtsy or

bow. She was an American, and he was rude. He would get no genuflection from her.

His smile was wide, and his cheek dimpled in response. Normally she would sigh over such a man, but he was... nothing but awful to her.

"Not that it's your business, but I'm here to see Mrs. Moon. Widows have much to discuss."

"I don't doubt it." He whisked his hat back on his head. "If you are not here for Leo, then may I make up my absolutely insolent manner toward you, and ask you to go to the opera on Tuesday evening?"

Prudence took a step back, only to find it was a step up. She didn't even have the wherewithal to stammer.

"Do you have another engagement?" he pressed.

"No," she said, truthfully.

"If you are involved with someone else and would rather decline, I must confess that I understand." He took a step forward.

Was he baiting her? What did he know? Prudence swallowed. "I am not."

"I see no other obstacle," he said with another genial grin.

She narrowed her eyes. "I do not know you, sir."

"My lord," he corrected. "In England, you see—"

"I know very well where I am," she snapped. Instead of her rudeness putting him off, it seemed to enliven him.

"Then I shall meet you at the front entrance at 7:30. If I don't see you, I have a box that an attendant can direct you toward. But I do enjoy catching the full entertainment, so I don't like to be late."

She wanted to say something withering, but she hadn't said no to him, and there was something deep in her Minnesotan soul that couldn't abide being mean. Or late. "I will meet you at the front entrance."

"Excellent." He turned to leave her there, but something still bothered her.

"Lord Grabe?" she asked.

"Hm?" He turned back to face her.

"How did you know it was me?" Prudence pulled herself up to a startlingly stiff posture.

"The stand-offish American widow who has resisted wooing for a Season and a half? My dear, you are famous in my circles." He gave another disarming grin—one that sunk under the surface of her tough exterior this time.

※

THE WEEK WAS gone in an instant. Leo had tutored Eyeball, who was not as dim as Leo remembered. For that much, he was grateful. His nights were full of Prudence. It was rare now, to spend a night apart, but Prudence still had parties and events to attend as a member of Society's adjunct amusement. And she was obligated to go, Leo knew, to help spread the word of the Ladies' Alpine Society's fundraising ball at the end of the Season.

Ticket sales were mediocre. But that could change in a moment. Only one of them needed to become that Season's object of desire, and they would be sold out in a matter of hours. And then they would . . . go to Switzerland. Which was such a strange thing to think. Prudence's body was one that had worked. It was evident in the way she moved, not to mention the sleek rounding of her bare calves and thighs and biceps. He loved running his hands along her tautness, her power that she put away just for him.

And through some miracle, Leo was glad when neither of them suggested coming together Tuesday night. Both he and his mother loved the opera. Opening nights especially. There was something about the energy of the performers—practiced, yes, but somehow raw and new. They would either give the best performances, or the worst. And it was part of the thrill.

Of course, the epic music was the highlight of the opera, but

Leo also enjoyed the entire spectacle of the audience. And, though no one believed him, he enjoyed taking his mother. She was remarkably insightful about people they encountered, the audience scanning the crowd with their opera glasses. Even some of the performers. She was excellent at reading body language and facial expressions. It was her insights that allowed him to practice a reserve that broached no entry.

Her small, gold-rimmed spectacles hung on a spider-silk-thin gold chain that tinkled against whatever heavy, jewel-studded necklace adorned her that evening. For his mother never went anywhere without some marker of their wealth and status. She'd lived too long without them, and she wouldn't suffer the disrespect again.

Which begged the question of whether her observations of others were cruel. They were blunt and heavy-handed, yes. But these perceptions weren't meant for anyone other than him. Now that she was losing her hearing, she seemed to believe Leo was as well, which had inspired some humiliating moments during the last few performances here.

They settled into their box. Their usual wine was punctual. His mother plucked her glass from the waiter's outstretched tray without so much as a glance. Leo slipped a few coins for gratuity onto the tray as he gathered his glass. Champagne. Always champagne to start.

"Oh, there she is," his mother clucked. Putting down her glass, she scooped up her opera glasses and glanced across the way at another box.

"Where is who?" Leo asked, scanning the crowd down at the bottom. He liked looking at the clothing everyone wore. The feathers on the women, the pops of color from the men. He could never get over the extravagant colors the wealthy wore. He loved them, even if he despised wearing them himself.

"That girl. Prudence." His mother gave a low chuckle.

She rarely chuckled. And the hair on the back of Leo's neck stood on edge. Chuckling was reserved for a bold individual.

Someone daring.

"Oh?" Leo managed, trying so very hard to sound uninterested.

"Across the way there," his mother said, handing him her opera glasses. "In Lord Grabe's box."

He snatched up the opera glasses, causing his mother to topple into his shoulder. "So sorry, Mother," he managed. Lord Grabe. Eyeball.

The man was a walking venereal disease. Finally the people came into focus. Broad-shouldered, impeccably dressed, staring at Prudence as if she were the most captivating woman alive. Which she was, of course, but a rube like Eyeball would never be smart enough to pick up on it. No, he was courting her for one reason only: her money. Despite what he'd said about his estate being perfectly solvent, men like him always wanted more. And with the estate and title in his hand, he would be looking to make costly improvements to his land. Which meant he would need ready capital. Which meant Prudence.

His mother pried the opera glasses from him. "Shall we go over there?" His mother asked, her voice tinged with an inflection he couldn't quite parse. His mind was wholly focused on Prudence with Eyeball.

"Of course," Leo said, springing to his feet. He offered his mother his arm, and they toddled over to the other box, nodding their heads to acquaintances they passed. Though he and his mother were not of this world, they swam in it with the wealthy and titled. He winced, remembering that Eyeball had never said a cross word to him, even though Leo was teased constantly for being there on scholarship. Which Eyeball was as well. But Leo had the added taunt that he was not of blue blood. That he was like a two-headed sheep—an oddity. Smart for a servant's son.

But as he drew the curtains aside to enter the box, and he saw how close Eyeball's hand drifted to Prudence's perfectly muscled derriere, all his feelings of guilt and remorse evaporated. The man was not fit company for any woman. Let alone one as naïve and trusting as Prudence.

"Lord Grabe," his mother announced for him. "Too much drink will rob you of your impeccable balance." As if Grabe's hand was straying so far because he was about to topple over, and not to manhandle Prudence.

Grabe turned, his face not registering shame or surprise. "Mrs. Moon, what a delight."

Prudence turned, and upon seeing them, smiled. Inexplicably. And it wasn't one of those tight polite ones, but true delight. The kind that made his stiff exterior soften just a bit. Which was not what was required to save a damsel in distress. Nor was she drowning in guilt. Which he had expected her to, somehow. It stung.

They were not exclusive, nor were they lovers in the true sense of the word. They had a . . . business deal. One that was flesh-based, but business all the same. It was an agreement that didn't involve feelings.

And now Leo was having them. Feelings. Which was preposterous, and he needed to get a hold of himself.

"Mrs. Moon! Mr. Moon. What an utterly delicious surprise!" Prudence took two steps forward to grasp his mother's hands. Pearlescent beads swayed upon her bodice as she walked. It was distracting to say the least. He felt as if one of those charlatan hypnotists were practicing their arts upon him.

"We saw you across the way, and I insisted to Leo that we come say hello."

"How kind," Prudence said, an expression that was far too malleable, as if she'd just seen a baby animal she wanted to hold.

Leo scowled. No one in their right mind should be so emotional. Let alone him.

"Not for me, ol' chum?" Grabe said, catching Leo's eye.

"That's right! You two are friendly," Prudence said, as if the sheer joy of acquaintances thrilled her to her toes.

Leo would not say *friendly*. He would not use that word at all at the moment, since he was currently wondering if Eyeball would survive a fall off the balcony.

"Went to school together," Grabe answered. "Leo was the smartest; I was another one."

"I'm sure you had talents as well," Prudence said, smiling up into Grabe's stupid multi-colored eyes.

"Undoubtedly," Leo said. But Leo wouldn't be so crass as to innumerate the talents Eyeball had bragged about in their later school years. The sort of vulgar tell-all that no one outside of a boys' hall should speak of. Despite Eyeball's vociferous rants on the subject.

Instead of the warning glance that Leo expected from Grabe, the viscount gave an amused chuckle. "Indeed. When we entered school, I was no bigger than a tadpole. Tiny, scrawny, terrified."

"I don't believe you were ever terrified," Leo countered. At least he'd had a title to hide behind. Leo had only his wits and experience. No title. No height or breadth.

"You would be appropriately horrified to hear of the hazings we went through, Pru."

Pru? Grabe's usage of a nickname clanged in his head like a hateful bell. She didn't like nicknames. Very few of her friends used them with her, and the ones that did had special dispensation.

"Animals," Leo's mother interjected. "There isn't anything wilder than a group of boys without supervision."

"I wouldn't know," Prudence said. "Most of my siblings were sisters. Enough that my brothers always had feminine company."

"Even in the wilds of Minnesota?" Grabe asked.

Her eyes twinkled as she raked that gaze across all of them. "Unsupervised girls, of course, are not much better behaved."

"Do tell," growled Grabe.

Leo wanted to punch him in the mouth. But he kept his iron façade in place.

"Mud pies, unexpected haircuts, death-defying falls from haylofts, learning to spit from the fieldhands during harvest."

His mother laughed. "That sounds like an excellent childhood."

Prudence gave a shy glance over. "It wasn't much, but I enjoyed it."

"Wasn't much?" Grabe asked. "Look at where you stand, madame. In an opera box in the center of the world, wearing a dress dripping with pearls."

There was a flinch before Prudence's smile erupted. Leo remembered that reaction from when he told her that she had amassed her own fortune, as she tried to hand the credit to her dead husband. She didn't like the credit she was due. Didn't want the attention that such capabilities wrought. "I am a fortunate woman, Lord Grabe. I shan't forget it."

"Grabe. Mrs. Cabot. Very nice to see you both." Leo bowed his head to them. He couldn't warn her of Eyeball's intention to use her for her money. He offered his arm to his mother.

"Mrs. Cabot. I expect to see you in my drawing room tomorrow. I should be very put out if you forego our visit." His mother tutted and hooked her arm lightly with the handle of her cane.

Leo did his best to keep his brow smooth. Yes, he would be very interested to see her tomorrow as well. To see if he could smell Eyeball on her. If she had that relaxed, satisfied look about her that she did after their lovemaking. He could feel acid from his stomach traveling up his windpipe.

"Of course, Mrs. Moon. I won't forget." Prudence gave a fond glance to his mother and gently unhooked the cane, letting her take it back.

They excused themselves and as they toddled back to their own opera box, his mother leaned in. "She isn't a stupid woman, Leo. Have some faith in her."

"It's Grabe, Mother. The man has seduced more women than hoop skirts."

"Be that as it may, Mrs. Cabot isn't as wild as she pretends to be. I'd wager she hasn't taken many men other than her husband to bed. She'll be skittish to bare herself again."

"Mother!" He hissed. Honestly, the woman couldn't keep her

own counsel sometimes. But at least she didn't know about his nights absconding from their house to meet Prudence at her hotel.

His mother pinched the inside of his elbow. Fortunately, he couldn't feel it through his coat, despite her intentions. "I agree that Grabe is no boon to her or her devilish cause. But now is not the time to rescue her. Whatever damage she does to her reputation and that of her climbing girls is done, but she will be forgiven for the fact that she is an American."

"So you'll set her straight on appropriate men tomorrow afternoon?"

"Heavens, no." They arrived at their own box, and he helped his mother into her seat. "I'll merely tell her that if she takes up with Lord Grabe, she'll be expecting the pox soon after."

Chapter Six

Prudence woke up alone. The bed was luxurious, but she hated to say it, she longed for the simple life again. The kind she had as a child, or even with Gregory, when they let go of most of their serving staff. To be pampered and waited upon was fun for a while, but truthfully, she just wanted to be alone. Truly alone.

No lady's maid, no paid companion, no footmen, no maids, not even Leo. To sit in the morning as the sun rose, listening to the birds welcoming the day. Even as a child, she'd had that. Her family was not made for early mornings, but Prudence was, as was her father. While both she and her father were early to bed, early to rise sorts, he was off to his office near the rail station, and Prudence was free to sit, unencumbered. She still had this habit, regardless of months of late-night suppers, dances, and operas.

Here, with the luxurious bed, she should be able to sleep in. To not lay and listen for the maid to enter and light a fire. But there were all sorts of things she thought she wanted, but when faced with the actual choice, she didn't. Like Lord Grabe.

He'd been kind enough and too charming by half. He'd told her amusing stories about people in the high society whose names she knew. He whispered in her ear during the performance so that the flesh on the back of her neck prickled. He'd let her see how his eyes trailed down to her bosom. His intentions were obvious, which was helpful, as that had been her intention as well. But when it came to the end of the night, she was too tired. Her stomach hadn't fluttered as it had when anticipating Leo's touch. He invited her to his place, which she declined, and then he tried to invite himself into hers. Which she declined as she stifled a yawn. That seemed to have made her refusal understood.

He was attractive yes, with broad shoulders and enchanting multi-hued eyes. But he was rather boring. And obvious. And it seemed like the idea of bedding him was farcical at best. As if she might laugh as he took off his cravat. Or worse. Laugh when he slipped out of his trousers. Oh dear, that would be unforgiveable.

She was not meant for this kind of wild life. Or the attentions of handsome, titled men. She needed someone simpler than a man whose skill in bedsport came so highly touted. No less than a half a dozen ladies had recommended him after she'd visited a London Gardening Society for Widows meeting that Mrs. Moon had recommended.

It was less gardening and more gossip than Prudence had anticipated.

But he wasn't Leo. He wasn't teasing then taciturn, aloof and then intimate. Lord Grabe was never *there* with her. It was as if he were playing a role with her, as the seducer. And she didn't feel like playing a role. She liked being herself. And she liked herself when she was with Leo. Where she asked and received what she wanted. Where they could debate and scheme and laugh and tease.

Even if Leo still had that hidden room inside himself where he kept his secrets. He thought he was so clever about it, as if those secrets weren't a glaring sign to her every time he spoke. But it didn't matter. They had fun together.

She was truly surprised when Leo had arrived in Lord Grabe's box with his mother. But she assumed they were there because Mrs. Moon wanted to be friendly. Perhaps even throw her respected and ferocious reputation out there to protect Prudence from any gossip. But Leo's placid expression belied a steely undercurrent of outrage. But that was precisely why she was there with a peacock of a man like Lord Grabe. She was *trying* to live her dream. Her outrageous free widowhood. One where she could sample men like sherries. And didn't he remember that was their deal? Except she didn't think she was the sort. Not with the failed flirtations in Spain, and not with the very handsome, charming Lord Grabe.

Besides, regardless of what she did in her bed, being seen with Lord Grabe would throw all suspicion off of any dalliance with Leo. It kept them safe and discreet, as both of them preferred.

The door clicked open, and soft footsteps padded to the fire. Prudence listened as the hotel chambermaid set the fire, relieved that it was finally time to start her day. She had, after all, a party to plan. A party to end all parties. Which she wouldn't know if it hit her in the face. Why ask an American to throw a party that rivaled extravaganzas of bygone eras? But that was fine—the other women were caught up with logistics and letters, finding money in other pots. The least she could do was throw a party.

Indeed, she'd mentioned their plans to Lord Grabe, detailing the lengths they had to go to, including the faux mountain and the cloth banners symbolizing deep ice. He had generously offered her the use of his library to help her gain ideas. If he wasn't too sore at her for not going to bed with him, she'd take him up on it.

⇶⇷

LEO'S HAND SHOOK with rage. He rarely raged at his mother, but this was an exception. "You told her what?"

His mother noticed his rage, he knew that. But she dismissed it. "I told her that she might expect the pox, but why shouldn't she let a handsome man flatter her? The girl deserves some admiration, after all she has been through." Mrs. Moon waved her hand as if dismissing him.

He wanted to slap it away, but he checked himself. He would never, ever raise a hand to his mother. Or any other woman. He'd watched as his father had done so, and there would never be a chance he would follow in those footsteps. His molars ground even as he willed his jaw to unclench.

"And what, pray tell, has she been through that Lord Grabe could assuage?"

His mother looked at him with absolute pity. "Leo, darling. If you don't know, I certainly won't be the one to explain it to you. You're far too old to hear it from me."

Leo took a steadying breath and cracked his neck from side to side. He hadn't spoken to Prudence for days. When she'd come to call on his mother, he'd made a point to be out. The loathing he felt for her at the moment wasn't gentlemanly, and he hated himself for falling into a schoolboy crush. "I fail to see how bedsport would cure anything for Mrs. Cabot."

"It isn't only the bedsport. It's the wooing, the seduction. A girl like her has never been admired the way she ought to be. It's high time she has the chance to have a handsome lad like Lord Grabe—"

"He's an arse."

His mother gave him an arch look. She leaned back in her chair, the closest she would ever come to folding her arms at him. "If you are jealous of the time Grabe spends with her, perhaps you ought to do something about it."

The words conjured up Grabe wrapping his stupidly big arms around the slender Prudence Cabot in a heated embrace. Leo turned on his heel, thundering down the stairs, snatching his hat and coat from the closet, not waiting for any member of his staff to anticipate his need.

"Where are you going?" his mother called after him.

He shoved on his hat, folding the great coat over his arm, not wanting to spend the time to put it on. "Out," he yelled over his shoulder. He couldn't think. If he found Prudence in dishabille with that shit, he'd call Eyeball out to pistols at dawn.

"I CANNOT TELL you how much I appreciate this," Prudence said, giving her most earnest smile to Lord Grabe. "I'm afraid my frontier culture is not one of excess."

A low chuckle came from the man's broad chest. He really was impressively broad. She admired him a moment, but it felt like admiring a statue. He was very pretty. Elegant, even. She desperately wanted to be attracted to him. How perfect he was! That chuckle should have tingled in her legs, but yet . . . it didn't.

"If there is anyone who can help you find excess, it is me. But alas, I think you are looking more for the kind of excess reserved for the very wealthy in the past centuries."

Grabe guided her through his townhouse. It was a lovely home, modest by some standards, but every detail precise and clean. His hand at her waist, he ushered her into the library. It wasn't a large room, smaller than Mrs. Moon's drawing room, but it had fine wooden bookcases with neatly lined tomes.

"My father was a fan of royal histories. He'd lost a great deal of them during his lifetime, having to sell his books to pay off land debts."

Prudence murmured her condolences. She'd learned a great deal about the kind of money troubles that came to English landlords in the past centuries, when land became secondary to production. It was a learning opportunity for her own portfolio. She knew that while the bulk of her money was in railroads, and would be for a long while, diversifying one's wealth was the key to keeping it intact.

"I've made it my mission to buy back my father's works. Much easier now, since mass printings. His books are nowhere near as expensive as they were fifty years ago."

"That's very sweet of you," Prudence said, hoping that his expression might make her feel a twinge of attraction.

"Thank you. Please, have a seat here. Tea shall arrive shortly, and in the meantime, let me bring you the books that I think will help." Grabe gallantly ushered her to a comfortable-looking blue-velvet sofa.

Prudence sat and took out her notebook and pencil from her valise. She was very good at research. Party planning was not all that different from researching stocks and company futures. There were still returns on investment, risk assessment, and costs of doing business to consider. Unfortunately, some of those she didn't know how to calculate. The returns would come from attendance, which would be calculated from tickets purchased. But also from public support, which had no numerical value.

She hoped her friends were having better luck at attracting ticketholders. They needed the ball to be a triumph in order to raise enough money to get to Switzerland, and to stay there long enough to have good weather in climbing the Matterhorn.

In fact, her calves still ached from the stair-climbing exercises Ophelia had put them through that morning. Too bad Leo wasn't around to massage out any tension. Her cheeks suddenly heated as her mind drifted to last week's nocturnal activities. Thank goodness Lord Grabe had his back turned. She wouldn't want him thinking he'd caused her blush.

Prudence cleared her throat. "Have you been to a party like the kind I'm describing?"

Grabe turned and grinned at her, his athletic form once again reminding her of a statue. "Do you think I would admit it if I had?"

Prudence frowned. "Yes?"

Grabe turned fully and leaned against the bookcase. "I think you and I might not have the same ideas of a lavish party."

"I've been given strict instructions. 'Lavish party like they had in the eighteenth century.'" Prudence read from her notes. "The theme is ice, there will be blue cloth banners embroidered with silver thread to catch the candlelight, and a faux mountain to climb at the far end of the dance floor."

Lord Grabe leaned against his bookcase. "You know what

always brings out the wealthier patrons?"

"Do tell," Prudence said, her pencil poised.

"Masks."

"Masks?"

"Yes, a masked ball. A party where naughty behavior can go unaccused. Where mistaken identities are used for titillating purpose."

Prudence frowned but wrote down his suggestion. And while he chose a stack of books for her, she thought about it. A masquerade wouldn't be a terrible idea, especially if it attracted sales. There could even be some unmasking moments that could be auctioned off, again, for raising more money. The more she thought about Grabe's idea, the more she liked it. She would have to tell Ophelia.

A footman entered the room, pausing the conversation. "A caller, my lord."

"Excuse me," Grabe said, striding across the room to her. "I shall return shortly. Feel free to explore the library at your leisure." He kissed her hand and left.

Prudence pulled her shoulders up, squinting her eyes closed. Why could she not be a normal woman and find him irresistible? She sighed and dropped her shoulders. Because she didn't want to be a woman of many. She didn't want to be one more in a line waiting for a vacancy in his bed. Because she didn't give a fig for aristocracy and money. One she didn't understand, and the other she had plenty of herself.

Then why not want the man he was underneath the trappings? Because he was . . . dull. Predictable. Practiced. Because at the end of dinners with other investors, she and Gregory would pull men like him apart, discussing and debating them until their suitabilities as investing partners were obvious and clear.

She stood and wandered to where Grabe had stood. She read the faded spines, finding titles to be utterly uninspiring. *English Agriculture 1749-1800. Economic Ramifications of the Corn Laws in Scotland and Ireland.*

Was Grabe lying to her? Did he really have anything that would make a decent resource? How utterly disappointing if he were. She stepped to the next bookcase. Perhaps there was a cultural difference in how books were titled?

She heard shouting in the corridor. Apparently the visitor was not a pleasant one. Hopefully it wasn't some disgruntled husband. Or debt collector. Either way, she wanted nothing to do with that.

Turning her attention back onto the bookcases, there was a ladder to help her peer to the top shelf. She climbed up, scanning the titles. Leaning all the way over to read the very last title, she kicked her foot out to keep her balance. No tougher than walking across the beams of a barn loft.

The door burst open.

Prudence clutched the ladder, startled. Her foot slipped off the rung. Her feet paddled the air as she slid down the ladder in inches, finally gaining her purchase on the next rung.

"So you are here!" a man shouted.

Dear Lord, why was anyone screaming at her? She peeked over her shoulder to find a fiery-eyed Leo Moon. The initial terror she felt at being yelled at abated. She took a calming breath and climbed down the ladder.

"Hello, Mr. Moon." She gave her largest, most hospitable smile. As if she were the hostess here. Which she most definitely was not. She almost called him Leo. Which, in front of Grabe, would have been a mistake. As his shouting at her was a mistake. Surely, he could see this wasn't helping?

"I told you she was here," Grabe said, rounding the door frame.

"Who doesn't like a good library?" Prudence asked.

"You don't understand what this means," Leo spat at her. "What he's up to."

Prudence raised her eyebrows, opening her eyes as wide as any painting of an innocent. She was irritated enough that she wanted to poke at him. "That I might borrow a book from Lord

Grabe?"

"Young women do not visit unmarried men! Not without talk, not without speculation, and especially with a sod like Eyeball."

"Eyeball?" Prudence asked.

Grabe burst out laughing. "They used to call me that at school. On account of my different colored eyes."

Prudence smiled. "They are very charming. Your eyeballs."

"Don't compliment him, Prudence." Leo gave a scathing glance over his shoulder at his rival.

"Whyever not? It's nice to compliment someone. I like compliments. Do you not like compliments, Lord Grabe?"

"I do indeed," he rumbled.

"Mr. Moon, are you the particular sort of person that cannot abide a compliment?"

He ignored her. "If you do this, you will ruin your reputation, and the reputation of the entire Ladies' Alpine Society."

Her spine stiffened. Was that a threat? There were all sorts of missteps she would forgive, all kinds of rudeness she would ignore, but threatening her friends, with whom she'd been through so much, she could not abide. "You dare threaten me?"

"I'm not threatening, merely showing you consequences that you might not realize."

Did he not see what he was doing by making a scene in front of a member of the *ton*? A man who could easily walk to the nearest men's club and ruin not just her reputation, but her friends', and their chance to accomplish a feat no other woman had ever done?

"Lord Grabe, would you please—" The tongue-lashing she was about to dish out should not be observed. This was intolerable. Her hands trembled as fury snaked through her.

Grabe was already leaving, closing the door. "Take as long as you need. You won't be disturbed."

Leo strode across the carpet, his long legs eating up the space. "You don't know what you are about."

"I have a duty to fulfill, and I am doing so!" Prudence stood her ground. She would not be bullied by men who could use their height to intimidate.

"At the expense of the reputation? You think to help the Society, but yet you sully it? By sullying yourself?"

She stomped her foot. "Sully myself! How dare you! I went to the opera, as did you!"

"And all of London saw you with that seducer. You think his reputation is secret?" Leo stood inches from her now. His outrage obvious not just by the volume of his voice, but by the color in his high, perfect cheekbones.

"I know his reputation. In fact, he came highly recommended." Prudence watched with satisfaction as Leo's face went from patronizing outrage to shocked and scandalized. Prudence didn't want to mention their chance encounter on his doorstep. And that if it was anyone's fault they ended up at the opera together, it was his. It gave Leo too much credit. And right now, she'd much rather shock him.

"You knew?" he spat.

"Of course. Your mother expressly—"

"—My mother?"

"Your mother," she confirmed, putting her hands on her hips like a petulant child. "Warned me the day after what to expect from a man like him. Not to mention the other widows from her gardening society. After all, widows know what other widows want."

He pushed her up against the bookcase, his arms caging her in. "And what do widows want?" he growled.

She blinked, still determined to not be cowed. Men thought they could use physical force to bend her to their will? That she was some innocent, unknowing of the world? Unknowing of men? She tipped her head up to meet his gaze. "I cannot speak for any other widow. But this one wants pleasure."

As she said the words, she could see that he was trembling. That his mouth was so very close to hers. His eyes were expressive, and desire was clear in his gaze. "And you are not satisfied with what you have found?"

It was that growl that sent chills across her flesh. His low tone that echoed in her belly and between her legs. She dared not lie to him here. "I am. More than I ever expected."

His breath hitched. His eyes slid to her lips. Shifting his weight, his hand came to her face, hovering over her as if he would cup her face, then perhaps stroke her lips. She swallowed hard, anticipating his quicksilver touch.

There was absolute fire between them. Prudence felt drunk at his nearness, ready to fall into whatever spell he would weave. She straightened, closing the distance of their lips. She breathed him in, pulling him towards her, wanting.

"Then expect me tonight. I promise you'll forget any other man," he growled. Then he was gone.

The abruptness of his departure left her panting. Cold air covered her as the library flung open and slammed shut behind him, leaving Prudence stunned and alone.

Her hand fluttered to her chest. Grabe appeared in the doorway.

"Are you all right?"

Her whole body trembled with unquenched desire, need pulsing strong and hot. "Fine."

"Did he threaten you?" Grabe entered the room, seeming genuine.

"No, of course not." Prudence collected herself. "I'm sorry, I should really go. Mr. Moon reiterated the rules of society of which I was ignorant."

Grabe grimaced. "Ah, yes. My reputation."

Prudence smiled at him, genuinely sorry. "Yes. Well earned, so I've heard."

Grabe barked out a laugh. "Who told you that?"

"The Ladies' Garden Society. You came very well recommended." Prudence might as well be honest. Compliments should always be freely given. "I'd heard of you from them prior to bumping into you in front of the Moon residence."

"Ah. Hence your reticence." He had the decency to look sheepish. "A lad had to learn somewhere."

"Rest assured, you are considered an excellent student. And now, an excellent teacher." Prudence shoved her notebook and pencil back in her valise.

"But not for you," he guessed.

She nodded. "Not for me."

"Because of Leo?" Grabe guessed.

Prudence gave him a smile that she hoped he would interpret any number of ways except the one he'd already guessed. "Mr. Moon reminded me that I cannot afford a misstep when a larger goal is in mind."

"The Matterhorn, is that correct?" Grabe was all distant politeness now.

"It is. We've already conquered Ben Nevis without too much issue."

Grabe chuckled. "The issue being the marriage between Miss Piper and Mr. Bridewell?"

Prudence grinned. "Exactly. But at least a marriage didn't ruin our reputation. It only solidified it as being respectable. Which is, I think, how I'm going to make this event a success."

"I do feel badly for causing you strife." Grabe shoved his hands in his pockets. "May I write to you? I'll look through the library and if I can find anything, I'll let you know. Big parties, over-the-top celebrations, royal functions, that sort of thing."

Gratitude spilled out of her. "That would be lovely. I cannot thank you enough for that gesture of generosity."

"Just reserve a ticket for me. I am happy to pay full price. Especially if it is a masquerade." He gave her a sleepy, impish grin that would have turned any other woman liquid.

"Of course. And I will bring your suggestion to Miss Bridewell. A masquerade might be just the thing to entice London."

"Oh, well, if I get credit for the masquerade idea, then I request a dance as well. A naughty one."

Prudence laughed. "You enjoy your reputation, don't you?"

"I have to give the Ladies' Gardening Society something to discuss, do I not?" Grabe opened his arms. "Let me walk you out."

⇉⇉⇉⇇⇇⇇

THERE WERE, OF course, the top three idiotic things Leo had done in his life. One had been thinking he could trust his father in a con. They'd been fast-talking a brutish-looking fellow in a freshly-tailored coat—typically a good mark. They'd been doing the sick child pickpocket routine, but the pockets on that coat were nowhere big enough for anyone's hand. Leo suspected that was the point—a lure to find pickpockets and then beat them to a pulp. Instead, his father kept pressing the point, and Leo wanted to call off the job. But his father was already drunk and wasn't picking up Leo's cues.

He'd escaped with the brute's cigar burn on his collar for his troubles, and his father had received only growls about controlling his boy. It had smarted, being blamed for his father's misdeeds, and it made Leo resolve to never follow his father's ploys again. Fortunately, his father had left shortly after, so at least the cigar burn earned Leo's mother and him some peace.

The second most idiotic thing Leo had done was taking money for doing other boys' homework. It had given him money when he'd had none, of course. But in the end, it gave the rich boys better marks. This led to them believing they were smarter than they actually were, and finding prestigious positions after school. Even Eyeball had taken his hard-earned money and given it to Leo for his brains. Now, Eyeball was wealthier, and a viscount. He had power, position, and good looks. Enough to woo a woman like Prudence into his sphere of influence.

The third most idiotic thing Leo had ever done was walking into Eyeball's house and seeing her. But it was Eyeball who'd goaded him into it. Implying their relationship was already an intimate one. When he'd said she was "relaxing" in his library, Leo saw red. It was all he could do to keep his fists at his sides. But like an idiot, he'd flown to the room, needing to see the proof of it himself. But her hair was in perfect repair, her clothes unrumpled. Her notebook was out, for God's sake. And he'd been a perfect fool.

She'd melted in his arms. Desire seeping from her pores, and he'd been tempted to take her right there. But even he wasn't that stupid.

Leo looked down at his paper, full of scribbles of ridiculous verse. Odes to the curve of her neck, the grace of her capable hand, her confident stride as she faced down Eyeball, himself, even his mother. That perfect color of her honey-blonde hair as it shone in the light of the sun. How it looked twined in his fingers in the pale dawn light.

It was damned embarrassing. He was smitten like a schoolboy, frigging himself furiously all week, hoping that his fantasies of her would rid him of her image. It only made it worse. He woke up this morning hard as mahogany.

And then running to Eyeball's townhome like a jealous husband, making a scene. If he thought logically—which he hadn't since she'd sat down across from him and handily solved his filing code—he could see how her going out to such a public place as the opera was a good idea. That it threw off any suspicion of their involvement. That it heightened the appeal of the ball at the end of the Season. God, he'd been so stupid and jealous and he hated that he'd done it. That his temper had taken over in a way it hadn't since he was barely out of leading strings.

When he was a boy, there was a maid at school who had captured his esteem, and he'd felt the same way about her that he did about Prudence. But he was a grown man now, with a business, money, and people who depended on him. He couldn't be such a complete moppet about this whole thing. Men could admire women from afar and not lose their wits. Look at all the chivalric poetry of the thirteenth century, for example. It was utterly possible.

And if he weren't completely daft, he'd be able to do so as well. Keep his mind and his cock separate. For that was what had driven him to this edge. Definitely not his heart—that organ was cold and shriveled and dead.

Then he heard the front door open, and Prudence's voice. Leo stood, straightening his jacket and checking his collar. Was it starched enough? It felt strange. Perhaps a quick check in the mirror—the creaking of the front door stopped him in his tracks. Was she coming for him or his mother?

Cold sweat broke out under his arms. He needed water. And a new collar. This one was far too tight. No, this was simply undignified. He shook his head. It felt as if he were still in a dream, his mind clouded with the idea of her. The only reasonable thing to do was to go about his day as usual. If he felt like changing his attire, he would do so. But only to make himself more comfortable, and not because of her visit.

He threw open the door of his study. She was on the stairs, startled at the sudden movement. Her bare fingers gripped the railing, knuckles white. His mind immediately went to picturing bed linens fisted in hand. He gritted his teeth. That wouldn't do. She stared down at him, her expression grim. Ah, so she was as disturbed about his appearance at Eyeball's house as he was.

But he couldn't tear his gaze from her. They stood deadlocked. There was no muscle in his body that could move. He was lucky that his heart managed to beat. It was his mother that broke their stand-off.

"Prudence Cabot, is that you?" his mother called from her drawing room.

Her attention pulled away, and he felt the absence as clearly as a hand on his arm. She finished the climb up the stairs. "Coming, Mrs. Moon," she called.

He exhaled. When Jeffrey came back from stowing her bonnet and gloves, Leo requested a luncheon to be brought to his office. Still, Leo went to his dressing room to splash water on his face. Control was all he needed. Control. He braced himself against the chest of drawers. He'd done difficult things before. This was just one more. Control.

And then he'd go to her tonight and shed every inhibition. Show her pleasure, show her how little she needed anyone but him.

⇾⇾⇾⇽⇽⇽

"So, my dear." Mrs. Moon's face was lit up like a child's.

Prudence shook off the intensity of Leo's eyes on her. That moment kept flashing in her mind—his lips a fraction of an inch from hers. Her back pressed against the bookshelf. His arms caging her in. The scent of him, clean soap and ink, filling her senses, the almost feral look in his eyes calling to something so basic inside of her. She shook her head to clear her thoughts of him. She smiled, pulling herself back into the cheerful Minnesotan she truly was. "Yes."

"I'm very glad you have called, but I must ask why. I've seen you more often than I've seen my maid this week."

Prudence laughed at the older woman's directness. "And here I thought the English prided themselves on etiquette and circumspection."

Mrs. Moon snorted. "The only good thing about becoming old is being forgiven for ignoring the rules we once enforced. I can barely walk, my arthritis burns through my hands like liquid fire, and I can barely see past four o'clock in the evening. Give me the grace to not waste time."

Prudence smiled, this time because she genuinely liked Mrs. Moon. "Were you younger or I older, I think we would have been pals."

Mrs. Moon looked baffled. "Why can we not be 'pals' now?"

"Absolutely correct, Mrs. Moon. I am so sorry." Prudence

glanced over her shoulder when she heard someone enter the room, but it was only the footman, bringing a tea tray. Her heart had skipped, hoping that it had been Mr. Moon. "We could—"

"I didn't order tea!" Mrs. Moon barked at the footman.

The footman froze mid-step. "My apologies, ma'am. Er—"

"Jeffrey! Down here," a masculine voice called.

Funny how even his voice made her breath leave her body.

"He can wait," Mrs. Moon muttered, fluttering her hand at the idea of her son in his study. Waiting for her. "Now. Tell me why you've come."

Because she couldn't stop thinking about Leo. Because his rage and jealousy had been so foreign and intoxicating that she wanted to be near him as much as she could, even though he'd promised to come to her that evening.

Because she was afraid that he would dive back into whatever sulking he'd been doing every night in the past week where he'd ignored her and kept his distance.

"I wanted to check with you about an etiquette question before I brought a suggestion to Miss Bridewell for the party."

There was a brief flash of disappointment on the woman's face, but it quickly ebbed into an almost professorial interest. She gestured for Prudence to continue with her question.

"Are masquerades thrown by young ladies considered . . . respectable?" Prudence floundered in her question. She didn't really know what to ask. Her mind was no longer rational. All function had been taken over by the hot growing need between her legs. Oh God, she was a mess. Night could not come fast enough for her.

"First of all," Mrs. Moon said, looking at Prudence like she were a complete imbecile. Which, she did in fact feel like. "Young ladies do not throw any party of any kind. It is *not* Miss Bridewell's party."

Prudence's attention caught. "It isn't?" But Ophelia was making every decision, down to the budget. Well, with Prudence's and Leo's help.

"No. It is her mother and father who are throwing this party. Lord and Lady Rascomb are well-known to have a *penchant* for the unusual. And Lady Rascomb's . . ." Mrs. Moon's hand flipped as she searched for a word to describe the viscountess's permanent leg injury, ". . . limp is excuse enough to hold a masquerade. The poor dear can no longer dance, so a masked ball would be perfectly excusable."

Now her logical thoughts appeared, hiding as they'd seemed to be earlier. "But having a pronounced limp would make her easily identifiable even with a mask. How would that be a reason to hold a masquerade?"

"Because," Mrs. Moon said, leaning forward, "it isn't about other people being unable to guess her identity, it is about her fun guessing the identities of other people."

"Ah," Prudence said, finally comprehending. "Then I might bring this to them without fear of insulting them?"

"I think you are safe there, girl." Mrs. Moon leaned back in her chair. "Now, where did Jeffrey go with the tea tray? Must I do everything myself?"

Chapter Seven

LEO DIDN'T REMEMBER walking to Prudence's hotel. Didn't remember the cadence the soles of his shoes beat upon the road. But suddenly, he was in the passageway, knocking on her door.

She flung the door open, her hair unbound, but still in her day dress. She was in the middle of preparations for his arrival. They stared at each other. Blood thrummed in his ears, in his fingers, and then, only in his cock.

Already drunk on her, he passed the threshold and took her into his arms, kissing her as desperately as a drowning man gulped for air. He closed the door with his foot and guided her slowly backwards until she hit the wall of the foyer, missing the doorway he'd aimed for. It didn't matter. She hooked a leg around his arse, and he was so very glad that she was tall, and so very glad she was flexible.

The wrought iron hooks, intended to hold hats and woolen coats, were above her, and he guided her hands up to grasp them, meaning that he wanted her there, wanted to bare her body to his ministrations. Instead, she grasped them, hitching herself higher, until both of her legs were clasped around his waist.

He could feel the slit of her drawers open against his trouser front. As he couldn't remember how he'd arrived at her hotel, he didn't remember fumbling with buttons, but in moments he was seating his cock at her wetness, nipping at her lips as she panted into his mouth. It was ecstasy, it was necessary, it was life itself. And he plunged in, and she moaned his name, and nothing existed outside of them.

The two of them were one and the same, two halves incomplete without the other, and he was no longer sure if he was fucking her or if she was fucking him, and they were together in this rhythm, building and creating, straining and wanting. Her pace quickened, and he pulled back to look her in the eye, wanting to see her fall apart. Needing her to see that it was him that did it.

Her gray eyes met his and the thread that bound them knotted, pulling them closer. And she came, staring into him, and he came, shaking and pushing and turned inside out.

There had been no other time in his life where his mind had been so occupied. Where the very depths of his inner self had been explored. Not like this. And not by anyone but her.

He pulled out gently, and her legs relaxed, and she slid down, her feet on the floor. Their foreheads pressed together, both of them out of breath and unsure. He touched her cheek with his thumb, and she looked up at him, this time, aware and in control.

"We didn't use protection," she whispered.

The shock of his lack of control hit in waves of disbelief. How could he be so careless? "I'm sorry. I am so sorry—"

"It isn't only your fault. I'm just as much to blame. I couldn't think—"

Leo shook his head. "—Neither could I. Normally—"

Prudence nodded. "Normally."

He mirrored her gesture and nodded, unable to say any more. Not needing to say any more.

"Kentucky bourbon?"

"Please," he said, noting that his hands shook. Why was he trembling as if he were cold? He was warm. Too warm. And his body was both overtaxed and wanting. He felt like a walking paradox.

Prudence led him into the drawing room, and he adjusted his

clothes along the way, sticky and messy as he was. He was looking forward to the warm indoor plumbing here in this suite. She poured them both two fingers of brown liquor and handed him the heavy cut-glass tumbler.

He couldn't think of a toast, but she said nothing as she clinked the bottom of her glass to his and took a long swallow. She shook her head as the burn no doubt made its way down her throat. He was so foregone that he couldn't even drink his own, instead watching her, almost jealous of the whiskey that made its way inside her. He was a full-blown lunatic. Find him Bedlam, because he needed to be locked up. He indulged in his own drink while she collapsed into the sofa.

"I suppose we should talk about it," she said.

Leo fortified himself with the remainder of his drink. He didn't want to talk about the possibility of a child, or what it would entail. Of course, he was an honorable man, and though neither of them wanted to marry, he could see coming to some kind of arrangement—

"You can't be following me around London every time you see me with another man." Prudence's voice was tired, as if she didn't really want to say the words she'd just uttered.

Leo's mind stopped, skidding like a horse at a cliff. "I beg your pardon?" Had he really been entertaining scenarios of marriage, and she was worried about his behavior in front of Eyeball?

"Yes. If we are going to keep our affair discreet, you can't be charging after me like a jealous husband."

Leo's mouth opened and closed. He had not been prepared for this discussion. Nor did he think it entirely necessary. His reaction had been . . . instinctive. "I find," he said, wishing they were never having this conversation, "it difficult to keep control when you are concerned."

Her brows went up, and by the languid smile that came over her face, he could tell she was both entertained and very flattered by this information. Information that made him very uncomfortable. At his very core, he was in control. He had to be that way, it was molded by his character, by his circumstance, and now by his career. To be caught up in—whatever this feeling was—stretched the very limits of himself. And he didn't like it.

"I would very much like to avail myself of your bathing suite."

Prudence knocked back the remainder of her drink. "May I join you?"

The flavor of honey was left in his mouth from the Kentucky bourbon, and the sound of her voice echoed that dark sweetness. He nodded, still feeling bewitched and unsettled, and very, very willing. He wanted to see her nude, he wanted to glide his hands over the softness of her skin, watch her damp curls dry while his fingers coaxed them.

For the first time in his life, he thought, *I would die for you*, and he didn't mean his mother.

⇛⇚

"You're late," Ophelia said, her voice cold and precise, but without blame or ire.

"My apologies," Prudence said, out of breath from walking as quickly as she could. "I overslept."

"You missed a training run," Ophelia said. "You can make it up this evening."

Prudence winced. Of course Ophelia would insist on her not missing her exercise.

"I wouldn't say she's *missing* anything, Ophelia," Justine said.

Eleanor groaned.

"Oh please, it was funny," Justine insisted.

They sat down for tea in the drawing room. Prudence couldn't keep herself from eating everything in sight. She was famished. It was the first time Leo had stayed past dawn. They were both exhausted from the multiple rounds of lovemaking. There was water tracking all over her suite from the bathing room, and wet towels were still moldering in her bed. But she didn't care. Something was bursting inside her like sunshine through a bank of storm clouds. She was glowing, and she didn't care. Of course she was glowing. Leo was... Leo was... *hers*. And she liked it.

"I have something of a delicate nature to bring up," Ophelia said, after everyone's plates and cups were filled.

Eleanor glanced over at Prudence, a questioning look on her face. Prudence smiled back, but Eleanor didn't smile. She looked concerned. Oh. Oh dear. Eleanor *knew*. She might not know *who*, but she knew the look of a woman who'd stayed up all night having too much fun. *That* kind of fun.

But Prudence was a widow. She could very well do as she wished. And they had been discreet. Mostly. That was what she needed to talk to Leo about, and he hadn't so much as apologized, but explained. And that was enough. She would do her best not to rub any of her time with other men in his face. But she had to if they were going to keep things quiet. Didn't she?

Or maybe not? After all, Lord Grabe had called her aloof, or standoffish. Something like that. She could continue with that, and keep Leo in her bed, and all would be well. Next March they would be off to Switzerland, and that would be that.

"What could be so delicate?" Justine asked. "We already openly discuss our need for monthly rags."

"Justine," Eleanor complained.

"We do," she insisted.

"I know, but must you be so vulgar as to say it?" Eleanor asked.

"I beg your pardon, but rags? What's wrong with rags? Every person in this room requires them," Justine challenged.

"Quite." Ophelia cut both Justine and Eleanor off in the middle of their argument. "Which is adjacent to what we need to discuss."

All of them quieted. Not even Prudence nibbled at her scone.

"We are entering the last two months that you may get...

pregnant—" Ophelia struggled over the word. "Before our attempt."

There was nothing but silence in the room. None of them even breathed.

"It is now July, and if you conceive—" again Ophelia's voice strangled at the word, "—if you conceive this month, you will be in labor at the end of March. When we will be leaving for Switzerland. We may, depending on weather reports, leave earlier, if the journey seems arduous. We cannot miss the window for our ascent, and we must have adequate time to prepare."

Prudence suddenly felt as if the scene was stuck in the back of her throat. She had dismissed their lack of use of a French letter. And the two subsequent times that night. Suddenly, the ramifications of her nights with Leo loomed large. Her involvement with him was a threat to them all.

She looked to Eleanor, who had gone pale. Ophelia and Justine looked to her, as the only married woman of the group. But then Ophelia shifted her gaze to Prudence, apologetic but thorough. "While this is of most concern to Eleanor, I must address this concern to you as well, Prudence. I know not, nor do I want to know of your dealings with the ... other sex ... but I would be remiss if I did not address this concern with you as well."

"Naturally," Prudence said, trying to sound more confident than she was.

"I know that some women claim that a situation—" Ophelia stumbled. "A pregnancy, I should clarify, helps them with physical activities. However, no woman can be certain what it will do to their bodies. Because of this, I would respectfully ask that neither of you become with child in the next months."

The silence was broken by Justine biting into a crispy gingersnap.

"Of course," Prudence said quickly, burying her face in the now lukewarm cup of tea.

Next to her, Eleanor nodded effusively. "I wouldn't do anything to jeopardize this expedition, you all must know that."

Ophelia looked relieved. Whether from their agreement or for not having to say the word "pregnant" anymore, Prudence didn't know.

The group chattered on about the impending masked ball. Who they would dress as, the possibilities of auctioning items, any honored guests they might convince to come. Prudence was taken from her reverie as Ophelia pointedly asked, "Are you not going to write this down?"

She put down her very full plate and teacup to dig out her pen and notepad. She was suddenly not hungry.

⋙⋘

"I'LL BE GONE a fortnight. I hope you can survive." His mother sat in her bedroom as Daisy packed her trunks.

"I think I'll manage," Leo said. This was the first time his mother had gone to a country retreat in years. "Where will you be again?"

"With my dear friend, the Countess Gelfirdon. We've known each other for a very long time."

"A very, very long time?" Leo asked. Was this one of her networks of friends from when his mother had been a housekeeper, or was that later?

"From when we first came to London, you fool. What would a countess be doing in Thornridge?" his mother snapped.

Leo didn't like her tone. "Exactly. Are you not going to Thornridge now?"

"We are going to the country! Not that part," his mother said through gritted teeth.

He'd got her going now. She would be prickly to everyone for at least the rest of the day. He silently apologized to Daisy. He kissed his mother on the top of her head. "I'm glad you will be going to be with your friends."

"You're insufferable. I'm glad to be away. Dour one moment, patronizing the next!" His mother screeched at him as he walked away, whistling. "And now you dare to whistle in my presence?!"

He gently laughed and closed her door behind him. He suddenly had much to do.

Two days later, he presented his plans to Prudence. He'd made his excuses the previous night, knowing that he would be unable to keep his surprise to himself, and not wanting to spoil it without incomplete details.

They were attempting a night without immediately falling into bed. Leo had taken the opportunity for his cook to pack a cold dinner for two and bring it to Prudence's hotel, not wanting to order a hot meal for two and alert any suspicions belowstairs.

But he had to be honest. The bellman recognized him now and subtly looked away after Leo had slipped him a pound or two over the course of the last few months. They both pretended not to be there as Leo left early in the morning. So would ordering a dinner for two really be endangering Prudence's reputation that much?

Perhaps they were being ridiculous. Even so. Prudence picked at the cold mince pie and mostly drank the champagne he'd brought. Should he ask her what was wrong, or should he barrel on with his plan as he'd intended?

Paralyzed with this internal debate, Prudence solved it for him.

"I need to tell you something." Prudence couldn't look him in the eye.

His breath stopped. Fear that he'd never known took over his mind and body.

"If I become." She cleared her throat. "If I become with child, I cannot climb the Matterhorn."

Leo nodded. That was a given. Why was she only now thinking of this? He'd been worried about it for weeks.

"The other night we—" Here she finally looked at him, finally giving him what he'd hoped to see. She wasn't calling their affair off, she was merely instating boundaries that he would have agreed to instantly. "We were careless, not using the French letter. We need to be vigilant."

"Of course."

Relief flooded her expression. "Really?"

"I always was a proponent of it. You know that. If neither of us want to marry, then it goes without saying that neither of us want children."

She frowned. "I think I do. Someday? Maybe. I'm not sure."

His stomach twisted. Perhaps the pie was not as well cooked as he'd thought. "Well, it does nothing to talk about it now, does it?"

She shook her head, eyes cast down again. "No, I suppose it doesn't."

He brightened his tone, not willing to be morose when he had such a surprise for her. "I've arranged something for us. A reprieve from London."

Her champagne glass stopped in midair. "A reprieve?"

"A cottage in the North, where it's a bit cooler. A place for just the two of us. No servants, no staff, just us. What do you think?"

She bit her lip, which was not the reaction he'd anticipated. He'd envisioned her being overjoyed, coming and sitting in his lap while he told her the details. "But I have my training regime to follow."

"And you can. Just, in a different location."

"I'm not sure Ophelia—"

"Ophelia isn't coming," Leo said firmly. "Let's do something we can rarely afford to do here in London. Wake up together."

Finally Prudence's ever-present smile emerged. He reached forward and pulled a pin from her coiffure, and a tendril escaped.

"I want to see your hair in the morning sun."

"Better now than later, I suppose." Prudence sipped her champagne, the mood of the evening turning.

"Precisely," he said, grateful that the evening turned the way he'd hoped. He pulled her into his lap, poured her more champagne, kissing her throat as she drank it down. One of his hands held her firmly in place, while the other hunted the rest of her hair pins. Honeyed curls fell around his wrist, the most exquisite binding he'd ever seen.

"I fear you make me think poorly," she said.

"I fear you make me cease thinking at all," he said, his hand now attempting to undo the small pearl buttons on the back of her day dress. His other hand roved up to her breast as his mouth found her earlobe. She melted in his arms, and any troubles he might have had about their conversation were left at the dining table.

⟫⟫⟩✕⟨⟪⟪

The rest of the Society was not happy about Prudence's week-long London defection, but the more Leo talked about the seven days of country living, the more Prudence wanted to go. She could have her time of no maids, no servants, no noise. She could have Leo all night, waking up in the morning intertwined, instead of rushing him out the door in a purpled dawn panic.

"But the ball—" Eleanor had protested.

"Isn't for another four weeks," Prudence said. All the orders were in. Seamstresses were embroidering the banners, orders were in for extra ice to be delivered. Even the wines had already been accounted for.

Ophelia had been the only one to support her sojourn. "Prudence will return to us refreshed and ready. She has been hard at work, and doubtless needs a break from London."

Justine folded her arms and stared Prudence down. Had the girl any more experience with men, Prudence believed Justine could have seen right through her. As it was, Prudence excused herself and went back to her hotel to pack.

"And what am I to do?" Georgie asked her from the sofa.

Prudence's trunk was packed. It was a relief to not have to pack her gowns and silk shoes and retrieve jewels from the Strawbridge Hotel's safe. The trunk was barely half full of light dresses, comfortable shoes, and a parasol. She didn't so much freckle as other ladies did, but rather turned the color of a Maine lobster.

"You can do whatever you like," Prudence said, her own cheeks coloring. She couldn't bear telling Georgie what she was really up to, for this was somehow worse than asking for privacy—hiding away with a lover for a week-long orgasmic love cuddle—so she'd told her she was taking a watercolor course in the country. Prudence. Watercolors. It was absurd.

"Perhaps I'd like to sign up for some watercolors," Georgie suggested, her face not betraying anything.

"You can't," Prudence said quickly. "The class is already full. Very exclusive."

Georgie stood up slowly—because she had only one speed, and that was that of a tortoise—and said, "Mrs. Cabot, I would not hear an unkind word said against you. And you are my employer. Please do not lie to me."

Prudence trembled. She was horrific at lying. She couldn't abide deceit, and it had been ingrained in her that deceit was the worst sin—far worse than fornication, for example—so that even her lies of omission to her friends made her ache. To lie straight to Georgie, who had laced her into gowns, helped her with her hair, made travel arrangements, and stood by her side on boats, on trains, and even in unfriendly ballrooms, it was like lying to her own mother.

Whom she also had not written to about Leo. Or her sisters. Or her brothers. Because what would she say? *I'm overcome? For a man with whom I cannot consider a future?*

Prudence felt the shame coursing through her. "You are right, Georgie. I apologize."

Georgie opened her mouth, as if she were about to say something, but then closed it. Prudence had plenty of time to watch her change her mind.

"Georgie, please, speak your mind. You've more than earned the right. I cannot be mad at you when I'm the one who is in the wrong."

Georgie nodded and said, "Don't be ashamed of who you love."

The sentiment hit Prudence as hard as a physical blow. Georgie was already leaving Prudence's suite, no doubt to read or do something more productive than listen to Prudence flit about spreading untruths. Prudence took a steady breath, her stomach churning. "Thank you, Georgie."

There was something to be said for it, to hold one's head high and refuse to be shamed. She wasn't ashamed of being involved with Leo. She just didn't want any shame to come to her friends as a result of her deeds.

So should she do this? Or should she not? Prudence squeezed her eyes shut, suddenly wishing for Gregory's even-tempered mind. He was so good in a crisis. Especially an ethical one. He would ask, *Is this for the greater good?*

Prudence being naked with Leo? No. There was no greater good. It was inherently selfish on both of their parts. Neither of them had any intention of marrying, uniting their families, creating something greater than themselves. This was about the pursuit of pleasure.

Gregory would ask, *Is it hurting anyone?*

No, of course not. Leo enjoyed it, she enjoyed it, there was no harm befalling anyone. Well, unless they were found out. Both Leo and Prudence would weather the storm just fine. But would the Ladies' Alpine Society? Would they weather it?

Prudence looked at her open trunk, with the pretty yellow and white dresses. The pink parasol with white ruffles. She could practically feel the sun on her shoulders—something she hadn't felt since before she was seventeen. Since before Gregory.

But if she didn't get on the train—he had already left for the cottage—how would he know she had decided to not go? How would she tell him? A letter? But how quickly would it reach him?

What if . . . she bargained with herself. What if she only went for a day? She didn't spend the night. She just went for one day and then came straight back to London? Well, she would have to spend one night because of the train schedules. But surely that would be enough to satisfy Leo and assuage her guilt about going in the first place?

Yes. That's what she'd do. She'd still get on the eight p.m. train—her tickets were already purchased. And Leo would pick her up at the train station. And then she would come home the following evening. It would be perfectly simple to take a cab back to the hotel, and she didn't need Georgie at all. And then she could still make all of Ophelia's training courses that she'd planned.

Yes, Prudence wrung her hands. One night. That was it.

Chapter Eight

ONE NIGHT IN Thornridge was not enough.
Nor was two.
On the third morning, she awoke to what seemed like a dream. The cottage Leo had procured was small but lovely: one large room, with an enclosed stove and a ready supply of coal (which they did not need nor use), and east-west facing windows that let in beautiful amounts of long-summer light. There was a pasture nearby, not close enough for them to smell the sweet scent of manure or compost, but near enough to hear the light tinkling of bells around the animals' necks. Whether they were on cows or sheep, Prudence didn't know or care.

Hampers of food were delivered to a nearby tree stump, pre-arranged by Leo, which gave them utmost privacy.

While the bells were tinkling in the distance, the sun from the opened window heated her shoulder, and the cotton sheets slid soft and smooth across her naked skin. She slept on her stomach when Leo wasn't in bed. And his side was cool and emptied. But she could see his shoulder from the window, sitting in one of the garden chairs.

There was not another house for miles. The thick trees of the forest made it impossible for anyone to see them unless they were explicitly spied upon. Prudence loved it. She felt free and unwatched and relaxed. The mattress was nowhere as nice as the one in her Strawbridge Hotel room, but she preferred this cottage, because it was next to the open fresh air, and it was a way to live unencumbered in the fantasy of Leo.

She wrapped herself in her white silk kimono—all the rage in London—and wandered outside in search of her lover. Her Leo. He was different here too. His shoulders weren't tensed up to his ears, for one. He was better at making jokes, for two. And in a shocking turn of events, he kissed her freely, for no reason at all, for three. She'd never seen nor experienced that level of affection. It was strange. Welcome, but strange.

"Your tea, madame," Leo said, holding up a slender thermos. It came in the morning hampers, and it was prepared just as Prudence preferred if she were drinking tea and not coffee: scalding hot with a strong brew and a touch of honey. She drank her coffee black, but she found here in England it was easier to drink tea. They still hadn't gotten the whole coffee roasting quite right, and more often than not, she found herself with a burnt cup of lukewarm sludge. But switching to tea made her British friends more at ease, and Prudence didn't mind.

Leo didn't look up at her, his eyes on his sketchbook. Prudence peered over his shoulder to see a bird on his paper, matching the very bird sitting on the low stone wall surrounding the garden.

She sat in the chair next to his and sipped at her tea, still warm, thank goodness. The morning was almost gone, but Prudence didn't care. The only thing she could think of was the sun on her face and the incredible contentment she felt.

Oh, she'd been satisfied before. Happy before. But not content like this. She'd been satisfied when she'd bought out some of the burgeoning railroad barons. She'd been happy at the top of Ben Nevis when she and the women around her crested its treacherous peak and screamed their accomplishment into the Scottish winds.

But here, with Leo, in a garden hosting the last of the summer blooms, a bird exploring the remaining bits of grains scattered on the stone wall, she felt content. Easy. Perfectly balanced in a world that was always tipping one way or another.

"If you weren't concentrating so hard, I'd kiss you good morning," she said softly, not wanting to disturb the bird.

She knew nothing of birds. It was brown and a bit speckled. She could tell you that. Or did they call that marbling? No, that was meat that was marbled. Well, and rock. Her knowledge of animals was less than stellar, but she would bet money on that creature being a bird, considering it had wings.

"I'll take a kiss," Leo said, hands still sketching. He moved his cheek over, making it available for a kiss.

She obliged. "What have you been up to all morning?"

Leo was an early riser. And Prudence typically was, but here . . . here it was as if she were catching up on a hundred years' worth of missed sleep.

"Revisiting a lost love," he said.

Her stomach clutched until he continued.

"Sketching." He looked away from his paper for the first time, kissing her forehead. "I'd forgotten how much I enjoyed it." He offered her the sketchpad.

She started from the beginning, seeing the one room of their cottage on the first page. The garden on the next. Then there were a few figures and practice shapes on the next few pages. Then came a wine glass in the sun, shaded and textured such that she felt like she could pick it up from the pages. On the next was her sleeping form.

"Leo," she gasped. The woman in the figure was undoubtedly her, but she looked so beautiful, so peaceful. There was no way this was drawn without some kind of artistic license.

"I hope it doesn't make you uncomfortable, but I couldn't help but watch you in the mornings. The light catching your hair . . ." He took a wayward strand of hers between his fingers, playing with it in the sunlight. "I can't do it justice."

"I look so beautiful here." Her cheeks grew hot.

"It's because you are beautiful, Prudence. Perhaps you don't know it well, and you need to buy more looking glasses."

There was something else in this drawing. Something she couldn't name—more than just her sleeping form, and the bunches of blanket near her elbow. There was feeling and motion to this sketch. She could almost taste the feeling of waking after a deep sleep.

"Do you like it?" He sounded nervous—an emotion she hadn't really heard in his voice before. As if her opinion mattered to him a great deal.

"It's incredible, Leo. I'm flattered." She stared at it some more, tears welling in her eyes. She felt . . . *loved*. And even if that wasn't a word Leo would use, or her for that matter, she felt it all the same. Or perhaps it was that she felt loveable for the first time in ages. She sniffed away the blossoming tears. "You can do this, and you became an *accountant*?"

Leo chuckled. "I'm much more than an accountant."

"Well, you'll always be an accountant to me," she said sweetly, holding the sketchpad to her chest. He reached for the sketchpad, but she clung to it, so he succeeded only in dragging her onto his lap. Which might have been his goal all along.

He kissed her long and soft. She touched her forehead to his when he was done. "Good morning," he rumbled.

"Good morning."

"Shall we go back to bed?" he asked.

"Please."

He stood, doing his very best not to groan as he picked her up and carried her into their one-room cottage, closing the door behind him with his foot. Prudence clung to him, her arms laced around his neck, and her eyes on his face. This was the life she never wanted to end. Here, in this cottage, with a relaxed Leo Moon, for the rest of her life.

⇶⇇

LEO FELT AS if he'd lost his mind—in a good way. Yes, he was back in the very county he'd sworn never to return to. But the Thornridge cottage was in perfect condition, and he'd thank Mr. Brushworth for his excellent work. Leo hadn't thought of all his usual worries since Prudence arrived. The hampers kept their dining options simple—he didn't want to risk going into the village and having anyone recognize him, not that they would. He'd been a boy here, and no one had ever heard his voice as it was now.

Mr. Brushworth hadn't come to the county until after Leo and his mother had left, so there was no worry that he might recognize Leo. And for all Leo knew, the men he'd wanted to avoid were likely dead. One didn't become a highwayman for its career longevity. And so he relaxed his mind, let down his ever-vigilant guard, and enjoyed himself.

He enjoyed the wine in the hamper from Mrs. Brushworth. He enjoyed the morning sun—it was the hottest summer anyone could remember, and Leo was happy to make the most of the cool mornings. He adored watching Prudence sleep. The deep sighs she'd make when she shifted position, the way her head burrowed into the crook of her arm as she slept contentedly on her stomach.

And he got reacquainted with his sketchbook. He'd packed it on a whim, but he was so glad he'd done so. The play of sunlight off the trees, the low stone garden wall, the freshly pruned hedges, it was a treat to take time to study them. Now he understood why men allowed themselves leisure once a fortune was amassed. This was delightful, and far more enjoyable than his days in his dark study, comparing columns and figuring percentages.

But most of all, kissing Prudence's sweet lips whenever he desired was the best part of this sojourn. That he could lean over while she read a book and he sketched, and kiss her. Sometimes a small peck satisfied him. Sometimes, he kissed her until she dropped the book on the ground and climbed into his lap. He liked those times. Every man had his pride, and that bolstered his.

They spent the afternoon kissing slowly, letting fingers drift slowly, and then finally, he put on the sheepskin sheath and gently entered her body. Her fingers clutched at his arms as he did so, her body rocking in time with his, their gazes locked. This was more than a business arrangement, he could admit that. Prudence was an incredible woman all around. Not just her honey-colored hair, not just her funny American accent. She was intelligent and insightful. They talked for hours as they walked through the woods, both of them entertained and entertaining.

"Prudence," he whispered, thrusting with the most control he'd ever exerted in his life. He didn't know what else he would say but that. There felt like something more he ought to say, but his body took over, and while her back arched under him, her fingernails digging into his forearms, all speech was lost as he climaxed along with her, lost in the sleepy afternoon sun.

Later, after cleaning up and putting on clothes, Leo suggested another walk in the woods.

"I haven't been keeping up with Ophelia's training regime, so I could use a long walk," Prudence said, making a face.

Leo recalculated the route in his head. "We could climb Hooper's Hill and watch the sunset from there."

Prudence agreed, as he knew she would. Leo led the way, the hill not being too far.

"Why do you think they call it Hooper's Hill?" Prudence asked.

"The village kids would make hoops out of green sticks and roll them down the hill during the May Day festivals." He had many fond memories of those games. He was never the winner, but he was not last either. Always solidly in the middle.

"I didn't realize you knew the area," Prudence said, though her tone made it clear she'd like to know more.

Leo couldn't tell her much more; at least, he felt awkward doing so. In order to make everything comprehensible, he'd have to start the story far too early, and he wasn't prepared to do that. "I do."

"Did you ever do such a thing? Roll a hoop down a hill?"

Leo smiled, glad she was willing not to pry too much. "I did, as a matter of fact. You?"

"We made the hoops, but no hills where I'm from. We would throw things through the hoop as someone rolled it past, or we would race them."

"Ah, gentle childhood," he said, folding her arm into his.

"Maybe for you. My brothers were competitive. If they didn't win, they were more than happy to try to sabotage your hoop, and barring that, jump on you and lay on you until you agreed to give them your hoop."

Leo chuckled. "Sounds treacherous."

"It was like a Shakespeare play, having brothers like that."

"You must miss them," he said, realizing that they hadn't spoken much about their families. Their mouths had been busy with other things.

"I do," she said with a heavy sigh. "My family and I write weekly. I admit my letters have been rather empty and remiss lately."

"Why?" Leo asked.

She slugged his shoulder with a playful punch. "You! All my letter-writing time is going to you! I haven't the time to sit and write long descriptions of London's fashionable quarters, or what a countess wore to the opera, or what kind of meat they served at the hotel that night."

"Sounds like riveting and important documentation," Leo said drily.

"They'll likely never cross the ocean," Prudence said. "So to them, yes, it is."

He hugged her close to himself as they crossed the meadow. The summer had already burned hot enough to dry up flowers, but the grass was happy and green. The day was cooling, and butterflies and ladybirds flitted amongst them, attracted to Prudence's pink and yellow skirts. The shadow of the trees in the wooded areas kept the ground cool, and typically a bit moist, but not now.

Beside him, Prudence sighed. "These woods feel more like fairy tale woods than anything we have in Minnesota."

"What are the woods like there?"

She shrugged and then smiled. "Different. Depends on which direction you go. Towards the west, nothing. Just tall grasses and plains forever. Nearer to the lakes, evergreens. But it isn't just the types of trees, it's the undergrowth and the birdsongs and the smell." She took an inhale of the sweet summer air. "It just smells different."

"Sweeter?" Leo suggested, feeling rather poetic himself at the moment.

"Only when you're here," she quipped.

He barked out a laugh, which she seemed to be proud that she managed to elicit. Dear God, he *liked* her. They made it through the path in the woods, and Leo found the path to Hooper's Hill with no trouble. His memory of this place was pristine. But they said that memories made under duress were sometimes the most heavily drawn for that very reason. And these trees had borne witness to some black deeds.

Having Prudence at his side seemed to wipe the place clean, as if it were new, and none of his life before her mattered. She was the carbolic acid that cleaned out every bit of unsavory detail.

"Race you to the top?" Prudence suggested.

Before Leo could respond, she took off at a dead run. He was impressed, she was fast. But he thought he could hold his own. On her heels, he pumped harder, pulling ahead as they reached the hill. But that was where she excelled. He couldn't keep up, while she kept her pace easily. He dropped back farther and farther while she bounded up the side like a red deer.

As he crested Hooper's Hill, huffing and puffing like an old man, she stood, laughing at the sky, arms raised. There was no amount of words he could ever use to explain how he felt right then. This beauty, full of joy and passion and light, radiating it for the world, as if she powered the electricity of the world's largest city. His chest felt full and expanding, as if he could encompass that joy himself, as if he too may turn into that person full of light and passion just by being near her.

The sun slung low on the horizon, creating watercolor-like swaths of pink and blue and lavender. He sat down in the ankle-high grass and pulled her down into his lap. She wasn't a small woman, not so easily pushed and pulled, but he didn't mind. They were good together—complementary fits of their personal puzzles. She leaned her back against his chest and they matched their breathing, moving as one organism, one person. It was here that Leo felt complete and whole for the first time in his life.

Not an ounce was missing.

⇶⇷

IT WAS FULLY dark when they ambled back to the cottage. Without a candle to light their way, Prudence hung onto Leo's hand as he guided them through the dark woods and then out to the meadow, where the grass was already dampening with the evening dew. At least there they could see by the quarter moon and stars.

The cottage windows were dark. Neither of them had thought to leave a candle lit or bring the lantern, but Prudence remembered where she'd left the matchbox. It was fun to live simply again—without the hum of electric lights or the initial *whoosh* of gas moving through the lines that braided throughout some house walls. Most of America did not have electricity or gas in their homes, but much of London seemed to. She'd lived so long in luxury that she'd forgotten the extra steps it took to live in other places. To live as she once had with her family. It made her suddenly homesick to think of that life. Of snuggling young Adelaide when she was scared, or rocking Samantha in the chair in the middle of the night while her mother nursed the infant Benjamin.

She hadn't seen any member of her family for two years—since she left America after she settled Gregory's estate. She'd inherited most of it, and could show that it was her that owned the shares of the railway companies, and that they were not eligible to be taken by Gregory's nephews. They'd been kind to her, for which she was grateful. That was not always the case with moneyed individuals. Besides, she and Gregory's nephews were more of an age, and she'd had a sneaking suspicion that one of them had wanted to marry her himself.

"I know right where the matches are," Prudence whispered to Leo.

"Why are we whispering?" he asked.

"Because there is something about darkness that makes me feel like I must be quiet," Prudence insisted. "As if there is an unruly baby somewhere, fighting sleep."

"No babies here," he said in his normal voice, which was loud enough to make her startle.

"Good ta' hear it," said a man, stepping out of the shadows in front of the cottage.

Both Leo and Prudence jumped. Leo had automatically put a protective arm out, shoving Prudence behind him. The man had an accent unlike any she'd heard before, but the voice was low and rough.

"You Lenny Morgan?" the man asked.

"Go inside," Leo said to her, his voice low and even. He was calm, or at least pretending to be so. But his shoulders were as tense as they'd ever been in London, and his imperious veneer was growing over him like a quick-spreading moss.

"I—" Prudence didn't mean to object, she was scared. She was scared of the dark, of the man, of what might be lurking in the cottage.

Leo's voice came even softer, but more insistent. "Go. Inside."

Prudence shuffled in the dirt behind him, not willing to leave his side.

"Please," he added.

Prudence reached her arm out to feel for the low stone wall that ran around the perimeter of the house. Then she found the short wooden gate and unlatched it, wondering if she was walking into a fresh hell, or leaving Leo stranded in the wind with a highwayman.

"Who's asking?" Leo responded to the man. It was dark enough that she couldn't make out the man's features, and the shadows played tricks with her eyes, not letting her see how big he was. But she heard a horse snuffle in the distance, so she knew there was a horse tied to a tree somewhere. She wasn't sure why, but that gave her comfort.

"Lenny Morgan was a friend," the man said.

Leo snorted. "Of course he was."

There was a thick silence as they waited for Prudence to fumble her way inside the cottage. She would get the lantern lit, and they could have a look at this scoundrel who was causing them so much unnecessary fear.

"And you would be?" Leo asked, his voice so sharp it could slice bread.

"Like I said, an old friend of Lenny Morgan's."

"Did this Lenny Morgan make a habit of having friends with no names?"

Prudence's hands fumbled over every object within reach until she finally got a hold of the matchbox. Outside, there was the sound of a man spitting.

"If Lenny were ta know me, I'd be Granson."

There was a silence. Prudence struck the match, and it flared to life. She caught a momentary glance of the man before he put his arm up, shielding his eyes. Tearing her eyes from the scene in front of her was difficult. The man had looked younger than either Leo or her, but the harshness of his voice didn't sound young at all. He wore a dark hat, with a brim wide enough that it hid his face. He was shorter than Leo but much stouter. He looked like the Scots she knew back in Minnesota, built like plow horses, wide and stocky, strong as two oxen put together.

Leo put his hand out to shake the man's hand, and after a moment, the other man took it. Prudence frantically looked for either the lantern or a candle. She found a candle and lit it, rushing to hold up the light source and check behind her in the cottage. A quick scan revealed no one.

"No one by that name here, friend," Leo said. "Good evening."

And then, as if this had not been a fraught situation, as if Prudence's heart had not been slamming painfully in her chest for several minutes, Leo turned and showed his back to the stranger.

"Reggie sends his regards," the stranger called before he shuffled back into the darkness. Leo stilled, his eyes downcast, but he didn't turn or say anything. Prudence listened to the sounds of a horse being untied and mounted. Only after the hooves beat into the dirt did Leo enter the cottage.

"What was that about?" Prudence asked as Leo joined her inside.

Leo smiled, finding another candle and touching its wick to her flame. "Just as you saw."

"Someone asking for Lenny Morgan," Prudence said.

"Indeed. Lenny Morgan owns the cottage. No doubt word got out that someone was staying here." Leo seemed at ease again, the pomp of his London exterior receded. He opened the half-full bottle of Burgundy wine that sat on the table. He poured two glasses.

"I was nervous for us." Prudence needed to talk about this. She'd been afraid for his life, and he was acting as if this was merely a continuation of their romantic sunset stroll.

"Undoubtedly." Leo sipped. "But all is well."

Prudence held a candle in one hand and a wine glass in the other. She sipped her wine. If Leo was fine with the encounter, then she supposed she had to be as well. But that night, as he stripped off his shirt and got into bed with her, she traced the scars on his torso. The ones that had become the invisible plane of his chest. The cuts and tracings that just *were*. And now she wondered, between Granson and the bleached white stripes of those long-ago hurts, what was it that Leo hid from her? What was it that kept him quiet?

The next morning, Prudence was up early. She hadn't slept well, waking up repeatedly over every noise. Leo was still awake before her. He was returning with the hamper when she met him outside, in the sunshine.

"Good morning," he greeted her, clearly surprised at her consciousness.

Her stomach felt like a clenched fist, hard and aching. "Morning. I see you have our breakfast."

"Indeed." They settled at the outdoor chairs, each sipping at their own thermos of tea. Neither of them spoke as they watched the birds working through their mornings, finding food and moving from tree to tree. Both his sketchbook and his breakfast pie remained untouched. This was not the same as the quiet idyll they had the morning before. Tension simmered off him like waves of heat.

The sun rose higher, and Prudence thought about retrieving her parasol so that her neck wouldn't burn.

"I think we should return to London early," he said suddenly.

The words jostled her. "Why?"

"It's not like we are accomplishing anything being here."

She recapped her thermos and turned to stare at the man. "I wasn't aware we were at a purpose. I thought we came to enjoy each other's company."

"And we have," Leo insisted. "But my work is calling, and you have that party to prepare for."

It wasn't the words he used, it was the tone of voice. "That. Party." Prudence stared at him, as if he hadn't walked Bond Street with her all those weeks ago, getting prices and ideas, writing down every scrap of info to bring back to the Ladies' Alpine Society.

Leo looked at her face and had the decency to look sheepish.

"I'm sorry, I don't mean to belittle it. But we both have lives to return to."

She narrowed her eyes. This didn't seem right at all. "Does this have to do with the stranger who called on us last night?"

Leo shook his head, and if this had been two months ago, she would have believed him. But this was now, after four days of spending every waking moment together. She knew when he lied to make a joke, when he teased, when he exaggerated, when he felt overcome with emotion. And he was lying to her, and it wasn't for a joke. He was lying for some other reason.

"I don't believe you," she said, folding her arms.

"Prudence, if it makes you feel better to believe that I'm spooked by a stranger coming to our door asking for a stranger, then fine. But the truth is, this was already due to end in two more nights. Why not just go now?"

"Because we have two more nights," Prudence pointed out.

"And there are three hundred and sixty-five days in the year. It doesn't matter. Let's pack our trunks, and we can make the afternoon train. We'll be back in London by dinner."

"I don't want to be in London by dinner. I want to be here. With you." Prudence put her thermos down. "And I would wager that you would like the same, but for some reason, you feel the need to lie to me about that."

Leo shrugged his shoulders. "Why would I? Prudence, this is a business deal. We've had a lovely time together, our bodies clearly work together well, but it's time to go."

"A lovely time?" Prudence could barely see straight.

"I've had a lovely time," Leo said, drinking his scalding tea in a huge gulp, squirming as the liquid burned his mouth.

"You say that about garden parties and afternoon teas, not about having an intimate affair."

Leo swallowed with trouble. "My apologies. I did quite enjoy myself. I don't want you to think otherwise. But it's time."

"It's time?" Prudence asked, her vision narrowing. "Is this the end?"

"Of course not," Leo said, pausing a beat before asking, "Unless you want it to be over."

"I don't want to engage in something you don't enjoy."

"But I just said I enjoy it," he protested.

"But that it was time to leave a place where we could pursue it unfettered," she reminded him. "Which makes it sound on level with a mediocre jam sandwich."

It was then that Leo's façade slammed down. "Don't put words in my mouth."

"I'm trying to get words *out* of your mouth," she said. "I refuse to believe that this exodus to London has anything to do with our lovemaking. This is about the stranger from last night."

"You can believe what you like. I have no control over that." He stood abruptly, making Prudence pull back. "Stay if you want. I'll be taking the afternoon train to London."

He stomped back inside. Prudence sat in the sun, holding her thermos, absolutely stunned. What had just happened? She was at war with herself over what to do. Old Prudence would have sat meekly outside until she felt he'd cooled enough that she could go in and pack her own trunk. She would make nice to calm him down and return to London without another word.

This Prudence, however, did not appreciate being spoken to like that. This Prudence demanded more respect. He would just leave her alone in a cottage where some strange man—that made him nervous!—might return at any moment? And he would leave her there to fend for herself? She had a mind to do just that. She was handy with a rifle—she'd shot her share of pheasants and jackrabbits in her life—but she had no such weapon here.

She stood, put down her thermos, lest she throw it at him in a fit of pique, and followed him into the cottage.

"Why can't you tell me who that man is?" Prudence did her best to keep her tone even, her body calm.

Leo was throwing his clothes into his carpetbag, not bothering to keep anything tidy or folded. "Because I don't know."

"Why can you not tell me the truth?"

He looked up at her, his tongue sliding across his teeth, as if he were clearing something out of his mouth. "We don't really know each other, Prudence. How would you know if I was lying?"

"Because I do know you," Prudence said. "I know how you take your tea. I know that your sketches are exceptional. I know that you dislike your career, but you do it because you like knowing the financial secrets of your clients. I know you hate Lord Grabe, though I don't know why."

"Because he's a scoundrel," Leo bit out. "And a reprobate."

Now Prudence couldn't help but cross her arms. "And you aren't? Carrying on with a widow such as you are?"

"It's different." Leo went to the window ledge and rolled up his shaving supplies and his mirror.

"Different how? Because I'm a wealthy widow you aren't taking advantage of somehow? Despite the fact that you'd abandon her in a cottage far from anything she knows."

His jaw worked. "That's not what this is."

Prudence looked around. "Seems like it to me. I'm not ready to leave. We were having a wonderful time yesterday until that stranger showed up. Now you can't wait to leave. You're back to your extreme posture—"

"—My posture is not extreme."

"And you can't look at me. Not really."

He stalked up to her and stared her in the eye. "I look at you all the time, Prudence. The difference is, when you look at me, you don't see me. You see the show I put on."

It was her turn to bark out a laugh. "You aren't that good of an actor, Leo. And if I had to guess, given the remoteness of this cottage, your answers about Hooper's Hill, your ability to navigate a forest in the dark without getting lost, and meeting a man outside your home looking for a friend, I'd say that you are this Lenny character, and that this was your home at one point."

Leo's lips thinned until they disappeared. "I'm walking to town to get the tickets. I'll send a cart back for you and the luggage." Then he left. He turned his back to her and walked out the door, leaving Prudence staring after him.

She supposed she could be obstinate and stay in the cottage, though she didn't feel safe doing so. The nearby village likely had a room to let. She could stay there and ask around. But that felt strange and intrusive. She flopped onto the bed. What was she supposed to do? She'd gone from deliriously happy to feeling alone in the space of a day. This wasn't how adults behaved. Why was he shutting her out like this?

Georgie would not let her wallow like this. Nor would Eleanor or Ophelia or Justine. She might as well go back to London. There was a low ache in her belly. This was rejection. Not just being ignored or not explicitly valued. This was being evaluated, and found wanting. And somehow, this hurt worse. A tear slipped out of one eye, which she furiously wiped away. This Prudence didn't cry. This Prudence had bent railroad barons to her will. This Prudence made money out of nothing more than rotted timber and melted down Confederate cannons. This Prudence had buried her husband. This Prudence sailed across oceans.

This Prudence wouldn't miss Leo Moon's inability to be a decent human being.

Chapter Nine

Leo's mother flung open the door of his study. She'd been back for four days—he'd been back far longer than that. The heavy wooden door hit the wall behind it, no doubt scarring the wood.

Leo put down his pen and folded his hands. "Yes, Mother."

"Why isn't Mrs. Cabot coming?"

He smiled faintly, indulging her fury. "Coming where?"

"Here! What did you do? All was well when I left. Did you press her?" His mother, surprisingly, lifted her cane to point at him. He could see the woman from his childhood so clearly right now. Instead of the fluffy white-haired coif, her hair was a dark walnut brown, severely pulled back in a low bun. She'd been a housekeeper for years, after all. Some habits were hard to break. Her face had been clear and clean, the kind of neutral expression that years of service built into a person. Her punishments were swift and severe, but never given with malice.

Now that she was as close to a lady as she'd ever be, her anger could be aired. The lines and wrinkles of her face twisted and contorted, giving an almost cartoonish range of emotion. The two women were hardly recognizable as the same one.

"Press her about what, exactly?" Leo couldn't even guess. He was still muddled and incoherent himself. He'd sent dozens of notes. The ones with a postmark were returned. The notes from his footman were ignored. The only indignity he could muster was that she refused to end their business deal with civility and grace.

"You wouldn't," his mother now gasped. She tottered forward and sunk into a chair.

"I don't know what you are talking about." Leo picked up his pen again. "If you have something coherent to say, I'd be happy to discuss it. As it is, I've been accused of pressing her, and then a horror so unspeakable you could only gasp. If you have nothing more than exhalations for me, I'd like to get back to work."

"I *knew* it." His mother shook her head. "You *did* do something. I'll write to Mrs. Cabot right away. I'm sure I can smooth whatever this faux pas of yours is. I'll not lose a friend because you don't have the decency to practice social niceties."

His mother left, hooking the heavy door with her cane, slamming it behind her. He buried his head in his hands. What was he supposed to tell her? Granson knew him? That he'd gone back to Thornridge at all? That the very thing they'd worried about, he walked right into like some kind of fool?

Leo didn't know if it was his father or if it was Granson acting by himself. Either way, it was trouble. And now Leo had something to lose—he was no longer a boy yearning to protect a mother who could handle herself. Now he was a man who did need to protect his mother. And Prudence. And he wouldn't mind protecting his fortune either, while he was at it. He'd made a small life here in London, lost amongst another few million people. Reginald Morgan should never surface again because his son Lenny no longer existed. There was nothing left for Reggie.

>>><<<

"I'm so nervous," Eleanor said. They all stood in their shifts in Ophelia's dressing room. One last meal before they would be dressed and masked for the party.

Ophelia gave a tight nod of agreement. Prudence thought she

looked far calmer when they were descending Ben Nevis in gale-force winds, two members of their expedition missing, and all of them unable to feel their toes.

"But the tickets are sold out," Justine said, the calmest looking one out of all of them. "So as long as the auctions go well, we're in the clear. We're going to Switzerland."

Prudence felt like she was going to throw up. The stress of directing all the set up over the last week had taken its toll on her. Even Georgie had come and helped. She stayed not at the Strawbridge, but at Ophelia's house, as the guest of Lord and Lady Rascomb, which sounded very fancy, even if it only meant staying with friends.

The hotel was kind enough to forward her correspondence, but most of it she threw directly in the fire. There was a delightful missive from Mrs. Moon, full of snark and gossip, sounding exactly as she spoke. She missed the older woman, but she couldn't stand the idea of setting foot into Leo Moon's house. Not after he was so willing to abandon her out in the middle of the English countryside. She honestly had no idea where they were, and he would just *leave*? Even the thought of it now filled her with impotent anger.

He didn't even bother conversing with her. She'd tried to make him explain, speak to her—even when she revealed her beliefs—that he in fact was the Lenny Morgan the stranger was seeking. And while Leo didn't owe her his life story—after all, they weren't courting, though their business arrangement was far from strictly handshakes—he did owe her kindness. And he couldn't manage that. When she pushed back about leaving their paradise early, why had he been so cruel to her? So cold?

She wasn't having it. And that sacrifice also meant the friendship of Mrs. Moon, which was the real shame. There was something very comforting to Prudence about being with other widows. They understood marriage, and they understood the upheaval of having the man who ultimately controlled their every aspect vanish. No matter how good or poor of a wife a woman had been, it didn't matter, for then every man who'd ever breathed the same air as their husband found themselves entitled to the furniture you sat on, the bed you slept in, even the jewels that had adorned your breast. It made a person feel not just abandoned, but worthless. As if you were an afterthought to his life—a life that had ended. And if your husband were in the grave, what did that make you? Nothing. Invisible.

True, Prudence had her money—thank goodness for iron-clad contracts and sympathetic lawyers—and she had her freedom. But she was still adrift. That afterthought. The woman who could just be left alone in the countryside, because no one really cared what happened to her.

"Pru?" Justine said, putting a hand on her bare shoulder.

The touch shook her out of her reverie. She sighed. "Apologies. Thousand-mile stare."

Three sets of eyes turned to stare at her. "Pardon?" Ophelia said.

"It's just what you say when you stare off, not paying attention."

"We say 'woolgathering.'" Eleanor picked up a plate loaded with cheese and fruit and handed it to Prudence.

"Thank you, I'm not very hungry." Prudence waved her away. "And why woolgathering?"

The women all exchanged looks, waiting for the others to talk. "Because gathering wool is boring?" Justine suggested.

"Never gathered wool, so I'll take your word for it. We had cattle." Prudence stood, stretching her back. "Is there anything stronger than tea to drink?"

"Sherry already?" Ophelia asked, looking positively scandalized.

"Oh, no, I meant instead of tea. Have you coffee?" Prudence shook her hands out, as if she were readying to climb a rope. She felt both jittery and lethargic. Leo might come tonight. The idea of seeing him made her feel like her stomach was going to come up and exit her mouth.

"Have you not been sleeping well?" Eleanor asked.

"No, I mean, well, the sleep is fine. I'm just nervous about tonight is all." Prudence walked away from them, hiding her face as she went to inspect their costumes. Their dresses all matched the shades of blue of the banners that now hung from the ceiling of Ophelia's ballroom.

Justine's was the lightest color, as she begged to be the surface, since that's what everyone thought of her as anyway, she said. Eleanor was the darkest blue, nearly black, the depths of the sea, unable to freeze. Ophelia was the color closest to Justine, and Prudence was the darker color, closer to Eleanor's. It was a pretty color—almost a cobalt.

And she didn't want to wear blue. She wanted to wear red, the color of a widow on the hunt for a lover. Because that's what she wanted to be.

"We've sold all the tickets, haven't we?" Prudence asked, careful to keep her tone even and light.

"Yes," Ophelia said, sounding puzzled. They had discussed this many times over the past week. "Should be quite the crush."

There was a scratching at the door before it swung open. The cadre of maids entered, Georgie among them, ready to begin the preparations. Hair would take the longest, and while Georgie was useless with it, she would be good with her needle and thread, as well as providing an extra pair of hands.

The day was here. The day that ended all excuses to see Leo Moon. And she wasn't seeing him anyway, so this was an easy bookend to that adventure. Her attempt at having a lover. A lump formed in her throat, but she swallowed it down.

"Prudence, you haven't eaten a thing. If you keep that up, you'll either be drunk by eight or pass out at nine." Justine held out the platter of food for her. "You can go last. Try to get something in there, please?"

Justine was not prone to fits of mothering or overprotection. So if she was insisting, the situation was dire.

"Fine," Prudence said, accepting the plate. She picked at the summer strawberries and the soft brie. Ophelia was seated at the vanity table first, surrounded by the army of maids. It would take a great deal of engineering to fit them with the eighteenth-century-style wigs they'd ordered.

⋙⋘

"Why aren't you dressed?" his mother asked him, bursting into his study again.

"Mother!" He threw down his papers. "I am working. I am putting food in our mouths, do you mind?"

She thumped her cane on the floor. "Don't speak to me that way. Go get dressed this instant."

"I have no intention of going anywhere." He picked up the paper he'd just thrown—it was a short note from Eyeball. He skimmed it, finding the man was asking for his next lesson. Eyeball wasn't stupid, so that was fortunate, but he was still tiresome. At the bottom, he scrawled a sentence about seeing him at the charity ball. He could only mean this one. There were barely any parties now that the weather had turned and people were starting to leave for the countryside ahead of the Michaelmas break in Parliament.

"You had better go. If nothing else, then to see our influence in action." His mother waved him out of the room, which didn't work, since he was still sitting at his desk.

Mrs. Cabot says your mother assisted with the decorations. I have always enjoyed your mother and look forward to seeing her there to pay my respects.

Eyeball's respects made it hard to swallow. He didn't want the man anywhere near his mother. And what was he doing talking to Prudence? He tossed the missive to the desk and saw the stubborn defiance in his mother's expression. He came by his own, naturally. But there was a time to fight and a time to bend.

"I'll be ready in fifteen minutes. Please wait for me." Leo stood, and his mother smiled in triumph. But it wasn't her insistence. It was Eyeball's.

>>><<<

PRUDENCE WAS UNRECOGNIZABLE. She wore skirts that ballooned sideways instead of bell-shape. Her bejeweled mask revealed only her lips, which were rouged a bright scarlet. The wig pinned on her head must have weighed five pounds, piled high with powdered hair and an absurd cutout featuring the gentle slope of the Ben Nevis peak, crusted in paste jewels, as if it had been covered in a blanket of fresh snow.

Ophelia had the pleasure of wearing Mount Everest, Eleanor sported Mount Fuji, and Justine wore Mount Kilimanjaro. They all wore masks identical to Prudence's, leaving only lips and chin visible. To Prudence's eye, they looked strange, but Lady Rascomb clapped her hands when she saw them descend the stairs.

Each dress was a different shade of blue and cut slightly differently to accent each woman's natural shape. Justine's was the most true to the older fashion, a light ice-blue gown with a square neckline and sleeves ending in white lace at her elbows, showing off her ample cleavage and small waist. Ophelia's was the shade darker, and was cut with a high cream-colored lace collar that framed her perfect jawline and then plunged low to a deep vee. Prudence thought Ophelia looked the most regal. Like the portraits of haughty Queen Elizabeth, only far more beautiful.

Prudence looked nothing like Justine or Ophelia or Eleanor, and had several inches on all three women. Prudence's dress was cobalt, and of the four was by far the most fashionable because of her bare shoulders. The silver embroidery along the bodice stood out, the sinuous curves mimicking the shapes of waves. Eleanor was last, wearing a gown so blue it was almost purple. The silver embroidery was not just on her bodice, but stretched from skirt hem to her sleeves. The collar was high and elegant, as befitted a married woman, but it didn't look prudish at all. She was covered, but she appeared sleek and graceful.

"Marvelous! You all look beautiful." Lady Rascomb held her hands clasped in front of her, as if she were doing her utmost to remember the moment. Prudence felt a stab of homesickness for her own mother. What would Jane Foster think of this event? She could only picture her mother shaking her head, the indulgent hint of a smile on her face as she went back to her mending. With eight children, there was always something to mend.

Ophelia's father, Lord Rascomb, entered the foyer from the passageway that led to his study, dressed in Germanic lederhosen. His plain black mask was in his hand, the black ribbons dangling freely. "You all look incredible. And those mountains are recognizable from here!"

Tristan Bridewell, Ophelia's brother and Eleanor's husband, was walking while trying to affix his minimal white lace mask. He clearly could tell which one was his wife, and openly stared, jaw dropped.

"Close your mouth," Ophelia scolded her brother.

"Close yours," he countered. "That's my wife, and she is stunning."

Prudence glanced back at Eleanor, whose neck was flushed pink, and her lips were curved into a smile.

The evening was to commence with the women of the Ladies' Alpine Society posed around the ballroom. After the first half-hour, they would change position, taking the opportunity to dance with members of the ballroom, and then go to their next position. So they would rotate, dancing more and posing less, until the culmination at midnight, when the auction to reveal their identities would take place.

Prudence couldn't imagine they would raise much money, but she looked forward to taking off the mask and the wig. She didn't feel in her element here—she much preferred being out of doors, in the prairie or the woods. Like when she was at the Thornridge cottage. She cringed. She shouldn't think of Leo now.

It wasn't helpful.

"Last chance for a nibble or a drink," Lady Rascomb said as Prudence and her friends filed past her.

She'd barely eaten. But she couldn't manage another bite. She was glad for the mask now—she'd keep her expression hidden.

The arrivals were slow. But their entrances brought joy. Each couple announced by the majordomo gasped as they entered the Rascomb ballroom. The embroidered ombre banners made the room shimmer with otherworldliness. The small orchestra played older pieces before the dancing commenced, which helped with the strangeness, because their world was familiar and different all at the same time. Beeswax candles were everywhere, which did give a lovely aroma to the room.

The Matterhorn construction at the deepest end of the ballroom was surprisingly well-done. Prudence hadn't much hope, but the sculptor they'd found did an accurate job. Standing at ten feet tall, the replica had the same iconic scooped-out peak that anyone would recognize. It was painted in the same shades as the banners and their dresses, glittering with silver accents. There was a rope affixed (by Eleanor, so they knew it was safe and secure) to the top, allowing any would-be adventurer to wrap the looped end around their waist and attempt the climb.

Dinner was prepared in the next room, and the stockpile of ice in the kitchen was brought in by the wagon full. Everything was as lovely as it could be. All the hard work and planning was complete, and Ophelia had instructed them all to bask in the glory of their work. But Prudence felt empty. She could fake her satisfaction, of course. It wasn't the first time any woman had thought that, she mused as she took her place on a dais set up opposite the banners.

Ophelia, of course, began the evening at the Matterhorn peak. It was only right, since she was the leader of their expedition. Justine was nearest to the entrance, opposite of Prudence, and Eleanor was against the mirrored end wall, opposite of Ophelia.

In the end, they'd opted for simplicity, and Prudence was glad of it, as it lessened the complications of the evening by quite a bit. This had been done on a budget, and they were well under, thanks to the advice of Mrs. Moon.

Prudence wished for Mrs. Moon to appear. She missed the older woman as well. How had her life been so upended by those two people?

The crowd swelled, and the chatter became quick enough that she could no longer hear the majordomo announcing the guests. But without a doubt, she spotted Lord Grabe. His enormous shoulders were a dead giveaway. Perhaps she could be distracted by him this evening, if she could make him part with the throng of married women who followed him about.

His mask was half blue and half green, accenting his different eye colors. Prudence almost laughed. He was so vain, but if she were that beautiful and unusual, perhaps she would be as well.

A gong crashed from the orchestra, the cue for the dancing to begin. The women descended from their heights, ignoring all attempts at chatter, and headed to the dance floor. They opened the dancing with a minuet.

Ophelia danced with her father, Justine with her brother Francis, Eleanor with her husband Tristan, and Prudence was paired with the eldest Rascomb son, Arthur, the baron Berringbone, who clearly wished he was dancing with Lady Emily rather than Prudence, given the longing glances he cast the woman's way.

Prudence didn't mind. She hadn't found anyone she thought could be Leo, and no older woman with a cane had yet hobbled through the entrance. The dance finished, and Prudence wobbled under the weight of her wig as she curtsied to Arthur, Lord Berringbone. As she maneuvered to her position at the mirrored end of the ballroom, she purposely walked by Lord Grabe, giving him a daring wink as she passed. He stopped mid-sentence and grinned back at her.

At least that was something. She climbed up the black dais

and posed. She was Ben Nevis. The feared, mercurial Scottish mountain. Which she didn't feel akin to at all. As the ballroom filled out with latecomers, people filed past staring at her, whispering. Prudence wasn't sure if they were whispering about her dress, her wig mountain, or her identity. It didn't matter. She felt nothing. In this ice-themed ballroom, Prudence could blend in.

The next bell sounded, and Prudence descended. This time, Lord Grabe was on hand.

"I'd like the next dance, Miss Ben Nevis," he said, offering his arm. She looked up at him the best she could, the wig dangerously toppling back. She nodded as well as could be expected and smiled. "Will you not talk with me?"

She pursed her lips and shook her head no. They'd agree not to speak while in mountain costume. After all, mountains were silent, and besides, Prudence's American accent was a dead giveaway.

"A mountain full of mystery, I see," Lord Grabe said, his voice light and flirtatious. They made their way through the crowd, people staring as they passed.

Were they watching her or him? She was a spectacle—staring was the point—but Lord Grabe was handsome, wearing trousers that tightened at his powerful thighs and a coat cut to accent his broad shoulders. His duo-toned mask was barely a mask, which was likely so because the rest of him was so easily recognizable.

They took their place on the dance floor, and he smiled down at her. "You know, the one thing I can say for certain is that I've never kissed you."

The thoroughness of her mask made it impossible to reply, even with a facial expression.

"For I have not kissed any of the mountain girls. Not even Prudence Cabot, whom I had the pleasure of escorting to the opera." His hands were warm on her waist, and there was something comforting in him that made her want to put everything down and curl up next to him and cry.

"Perhaps you'll excuse my indelicacy, Miss Ben Nevis, but I can admit that while I was conversing with Mrs. Cabot at the opera, I got to know precisely how tall she was compared to my own size. She is a tall woman, something which I admire. My own height can make finding a companion of a reasonable size challenging." He gazed down at her, his different colored eyes making her almost dizzy.

He spun her in a circle. "Now why do I say all this? Because I have something very important to tell Mrs. Cabot, and I think you might be able to relay it to her, Miss Ben Nevis."

Prudence wished she could be in love with him, even if it were for only one night. To want to be taken into his arms full of passion. But she didn't feel that way. He was like a very lovely painting that she knew wasn't real.

"I'm not one made for love. But I know how to spot it. I'm very good at spotting it, since I've had my share of bed partners, and one thing I watch for is when she falls in love with me. That's when I realize I must end it gently. And this skill of noticing, of predicting, has allowed me to observe a great many things."

He paused their motion as the music died down, knowing it would once again swell. Her skirts swirled around his trousers, the shining fabric enveloping him.

"I know Mrs. Cabot is in love. Not with me, which admittedly, I did find somewhat insulting, even if I do not seek that admiration. But Mr. Leopold Moon is very much in love with Mrs. Cabot. So much so that he cannot see it himself."

Prudence shook her head. How wrong he was. If she could only explain what had happened at the cottage—that he thought to abandon her to the whims of a stranger instead of telling her anything about himself or the situation at hand.

"I do not know what happened, but I have seen the man in the last week, and he is broken. Not in the churlish way he had been, of course, prickly and surly as he normally is. No, he is bereft. And that, if I can add more to my own selfish story, is also something I know. Because that was my father, after my mother left him. I've seen heartbreak up close. And Leopold Moon is in the throes of it."

Prudence felt a swell of tears, but tamped it down. The idea that Leo missed her was too much for her to think of. As for love, she wanted that to be true.

"I've goaded him to arrive tonight. Perhaps too much, but I believe he'll show. We were childhood mates, and I admit I've enjoyed teasing him through the years. I know his temperament, and he believes he hates me, but he doesn't. He envies me sometimes, I think, but truthfully, I envy him. He's very smart. His mother would do anything for him—when we were children, she was a force of nature. She'd move all of London five miles north if it would help Leo."

Prudence laughed. She wished she could have known Mrs. Moon at that time. She must have been quite a sight to behold.

"He had a family, even if it was a family of one. He had his intelligence, his relentlessness. My God, that man wouldn't even need sleep!" Grabe shook his head, impressed with even the memory of Leo.

"What I am saying, Miss Ben Nevis, is please let Mrs. Cabot give him a chance to redeem himself. He is lost without her. He needs her, whether he'll admit it or not."

Prudence allowed herself a small nod. If he came. If he approached her. If, if, if. What a friend Lord Grabe was to advocate for him.

"Now that's over," Grabe said with a sigh and then a winning smile. "Let's talk about me."

⇶⇷

LEO WORE ALL black, because well, that's what he had. His black mask was barely a disguise, but he slicked back his hair with a pomade that made it seem a shade darker. He put on a crisp white cravat, and replaced the normal gold chain of his pocket watch with a white silk ribbon from his mother. His waistcoat was black, and he wore a formal cutaway dress coat.

"You look the very devil himself," his mother breathed as he came down the stairs. "Bravo, my child."

Leo raised his brows at his mother. "I wasn't aware you wanted your son to be the Prince of Darkness."

"If you're the prince, that makes me the queen," she remarked, taking his proffered arm. The footman handed them their overcoats and hats, and they clambered into the carriage to make a late entrance to what his mother had told him was the talk of the town.

They were late enough that the line of carriages was abating, though they were lined up and down the street, clogging the thoroughfare. The slow approach had Leo tapping his feet impatiently. His mother watched him without comment, but he could almost hear her thinking.

"Do you have something to say?" he demanded. Even his pulse beat faster in his temple. He hadn't realized what an impatient man he was.

His mother shook her head, giving him an imperious look. "Not at all."

Leo grunted. Finally, the carriage pulled up to the front of the house, and they were able to join the party already in progress. They handed off their overcoats and were ushered into the ballroom, announced in such a din that absolutely no one heard their arrival. There was a crush of people, and Leo escorted his mother to the chairs lining the room, finding some of her compatriots already ensconced in the gossip of the evening.

"You look quite dashing, Mr. Moon," said one of his mother's friends. Perhaps it was Mrs. Maybury? He couldn't remember. But the look she gave him was one of pure appreciation.

He nodded his appreciation and turned to look at the festivities. The crowd was full and the air already growing humid from the breath of so many in one space. Dancing occupied the far end of the ballroom. The music was lively, and the small orchestra was good. He would expect nothing less from a party thrown by Prudence.

"Shall I get you something to drink?" Leo asked his mother, having to raise his voice over the crowd.

She shook her head no, waving him off, clearly too busy for the likes of him. The music ended and people shuffled again, dancers coming off the floor, new partners being installed. Laughter and chatter now filled the air.

And that's when he saw the women ascend to the four ends of the room. They had to be the members of the Ladies' Alpine Society. Each was dressed in blue—the color of the banners he'd helped Prudence pick out on Bond Street all those months back. It had been a delightful day: he'd pretended his coldness, and she'd flirted back with her charming smile. His mother had been there, but ultimately stayed in the carriage, her knee bothering her as she had moved in and out of the vehicle too many times.

Those colors were imprinted in his mind. Each woman wore a towering, old-fashioned wig on her head, and a dark, stiff mask over her face. Given the different cuts of the gown and the heights of the daises, it was impossible to tell which woman was whom at a distance.

"There's an auction at midnight," Mrs. Maybury told his mother. "They'll reveal the girls then. I'm not certain it's proper, but then I'm not certain it isn't, either."

But Leo didn't want to wait until midnight to find Prudence. He wanted to talk to her, to understand why she wasn't corresponding with him. He understood that he'd behaved poorly at Thornridge. But the fear of Reggie walking back into his life, after all he'd done to build something in London for himself and his mother, was too much to bear. And how could anyone admit such a thing and be understood? *I'm afraid my father will destroy me and take all our money? I'm afraid I'll have to beg or con my way into a decent meal for my mother again?*

How does a person explain the misery of a father like Reggie to a woman who held her family so dear? The veneration in

Prudence's voice when she spoke of her childhood and her parents' dedication to each other was unmistakable. How could she look at him with any respect if he told her that he had long hoped his father was dead?

Even if Prudence no longer wanted to be his lover, it wasn't right to punish his mother for his behavior. But the word *lover* stuck in his throat. It wasn't as crass as all that. And the word *lover* was nowhere near as complete a meaning for what they were.

They were friends and companions, as well as intimates. Their time together was more than just bedsport. At least, for him. A few weeks ago, he would have wagered every farthing that was the same for her. But now. Now he didn't know.

He approached each woman, not too close, and tried to not be too overt. Men blended in the crowd far more than ladies, as every man was wearing a black coat. There were different cuts and different masks on each man's face, but from a distance, they all looked the same.

The first one, in an ice-blue gown, he immediately disqualified. Her proportions were all wrong. The second one, in a gown so dark it was almost black, he also dismissed. Her bright red lips were too full. They were the wrong shape. And her neck wasn't long and elegant as Prudence's was.

The next one he was almost certain was her. She wore a gown the color of an expensive sapphire. Her neck was long and elegant, and she had a small bust and a long waist. But it was also her posture, the way she carried herself. But he was a man of thoroughness, so he went to the fourth woman to make sure. It took some work to move through the crowd, but once there, he immediately congratulated himself on knowing Prudence. This woman was also not her. Closer to height, she was not as confident in her stance, but haughtier in her carriage. This lady had English aristocracy stamped all over her. This one was Miss Bridewell, of that he was certain.

He made his way back over to Prudence, but before he arrived, a chime went off and the women descended into the clamor of the crowd. He lost sight of her, and then, noticing the surge to the dance floor, he followed. And there, dancing with Prudence, was Eyeball.

Rage sizzled inside him. Of course Eyeball was there to swoop her away. He was always one for a rich widow, and it didn't hurt that Prudence was beautiful and smart and witty. Even if Eyeball were looking for a wife, Prudence would make a decent prize. With a title, Eyeball didn't require connections, he required capital, which Prudence could supply in spades.

Disgusted, he made his way back to his mother. He couldn't stand to watch Eyeball work his charms on Prudence. It made him physically ill to think that Prudence might actually fall for one of his ridiculous eye colors.

"Whoever wins the bid at midnight escorts them in to dine," a woman said in the crowd.

Ah, that was the rub with the auction, then. He was unwilling to make a scene trying to gain her attention as she descended from her perch, and it appeared they only danced a single set before moving back up to their posing daises. Fine. He could find the card room until the clock struck midnight.

He always did well at cards. Finding the room swimming with easy marks, he settled in at a table and raised a finger at a footman to bring him a drink. Time ticked by pleasantly enough. He managed to get through two sets of table mates before the hour grew late enough. He took his leave, his winnings, and his wine and headed to the ballroom.

The crowd had shifted again. The dancing was through, and men were attempting to climb the faux Matterhorn at the front of the room. The slick soft soles of the formal shoes proved to be a challenge for the brave men who tried their best.

"Looks awfully difficult," a man said near him.

"I beg your pardon, sir," the woman said as Leo jostled past.

He was sick of hearing about adventure and mountains, of ambitions and luxury. He was sick of this ball and watching men proving themselves on a stupid fake mountain. He was sick of newspaper reports celebrating some asinine explorer, as if there weren't plenty of people in the world who struggled daily for food and clothes and shelter. How dare they flaunt themselves when others had to push and struggle for their barest needs? What was he even doing here?

Through some hidden stair, Tristan Bridewell appeared at the peak of the faux Matterhorn. He'd removed his mask, and his open, golden good looks irritated Leo even further. He didn't consider himself an envious man, but suddenly, tonight, he found himself soured through and through.

"Ladies and gentlemen," Tristan Bridewell said, trying to quiet the crowd down. "Thank you so much for coming to this late-in-the-Season celebration. As you know, we are raising money for a majority women's expedition up to the Matterhorn next summer. I will also be joining the group, as an aid and companion—"

"You mean you'll be climbing it, and they'll be getting the credit!" a man yelled from the crowd. Leo fairly growled at the man, standing somewhere in front of him.

"No, sir, I'm afraid I will be bringing up the rear. My sister, Miss Ophelia Bridewell, is the leader of our expedition, and is scheduled to be the first woman ever to step foot on the Matterhorn's vaunted peak."

There was a hush over the crowd. Everyone knew what had happened to the crew that had successfully ascended the mountain three years ago—they'd ended up dying on the way down. Or at least, half of them did. Including the British aristocrat. It was hard not to see the parallels for Miss Bridewell.

"But to ensure we have the best equipment and the best local guides, we need your help. Tonight, we auction off the identity of our four intrepid adventuresses! The highest bid unveils the lady from her disguise, and allows that person to escort the lady into dinner before all other guests." Mr. Bridewell gestured to the door leading to the dining room, where the partygoers would eat in shifts, if they ate at all.

"Because both my wife and my sister will be up for auction this evening, please be aware that I'm watching you." Bridewell winked at the crowd after giving his menacing glare. He turned, reached down behind him, and he grasped the hand of a young lady in the ice-white skirts.

"Let us start the evening at the surface ice, shall we? Miss Kilimanjaro."

The crowd stared blankly at first. Whichever climber this was, she was stunning. Bridewell looked out at them, bemused.

"She does have that effect on people. Shall we start the bidding at ten pounds?"

A man shouted for ten over the sound of several other voices. The fee quickly escalated to one hundred pounds. The average worker's wage for two years. More shouting, and at one point, it looked as if a fistfight might occur.

A triumph was finally held by one man, holding his banknotes over his head. "Five hundred pounds!"

Tristan pointed at the bidder. Leo craned his neck around to see the absolutely crazed look on the man's face. "Five hundred! Any other bidders?"

People murmured, but no one else waved any banknotes.

"You win, sir! Come forward, and my father, Lord Rascomb will collect your notes, and you may collect Miss Kilimanjaro. But not before we learn her identity!"

The musicians played a lively jig while two women appeared on the platform, removing the wig carefully. Then Miss Kilimanjaro untied her mask, revealing herself to be Miss Justine Brewer. The winning bidder's face brightened and his chest puffed out. He'd clearly hoped it would be her. Leo suddenly thought that he was not the only man here who had set about trying to discern which lady was which.

Everyone clapped and laughed as Miss Brewer gave an elegant curtsy. She descended the mountain and disappeared from Leo's sight.

"Next we have Miss Everest. The tallest mountain in the

known world, the unconquerable peak, the challenge of future mountaineers!"

"Get on with it!" someone yelled.

Bridewell gave a scowl to the crowd. "Do I have ten pounds?"

The bidding was not quite as anxious as Miss Brewer's round was, but there was a restrained and respectable debate between some older men in the crowd. A few younger men made their attempts, but ultimately, it settled at three hundred and fifty pounds to a Mr. Grainger of the London Alpine Society.

Lewd jests rippled through the crowd of Grainger finally climbing a mountain. Miss Everest's wig was removed, revealing a pile of golden blonde curls. The woman untied her mask and proved herself to be Miss Ophelia Bridewell, the daughter of their host, and the leader of their expedition. The rude comments ceased immediately.

"Next is Miss Ben Nevis!" The woman climbed up to join Bridewell on the platform. That cobalt blue dress that accented her beautifully long neck bared her strong, sculpted shoulders, and the embroidered silver bodice adorned her trim torso that he knew so well.

"I would like to make sure it is known that the Ladies' Alpine Society successfully ascended the Scottish peak last summer. We came in under budget, under time, and I managed to realize that I needed a wife. If that's not the Ladies' Alpine Society producing miracles, I don't know what is."

Laughter rolled through the crowd. Yes, yes, Tristan was an unserious man, and marriage somehow made him less so. Leo's stomach tightened in anticipation. But the idiot kept talking. Leo pushed his way further up. He wanted to see her better. Mostly, he wanted her to see him when he won, and they could speak freely as he escorted her in for their midnight supper.

"Get on with it!" Leo was about to yell when someone else beat him to it.

"Do I bore you?" Bridewell asked with some venom.

"Yes!" came the emphatic reply.

"I'm insulted," he said, though his jovial manner belied that he was not, in fact, anything of the sort. "Fine, onto beautiful ladies, if that's what you want. Miss Ben Nevis! Let's start at ten pounds!"

Leo didn't have time for this. "One hundred pounds!"

Without so much as a hesitation came "Two hundred!" from further in the crowd.

Incensed, Leo responded with "Three hundred." He made his way nearer to the other bidder, who had now increased the wager to four hundred.

"Five," yelled Leo, finally picking his way over to none other than Eyeball.

Eyeball looked in him straight in the face and yelled, "Six!"

"Six hundred pounds, so far the highest bid," Bridewell said. "Do I hear seven?"

"Seven!" Leo said, turning his attention to the front, to Prudence. She stared down at him. Did she see him? Did she understand and know why he bid on her so outlandishly? Surely, she had to know that his ardor for her had not cooled—not one ounce.

"Eight!" Eyeball shouted.

"You great fool," Leo spat. "You don't have that kind of money."

Eyeball gave him a lazy grin. "You've been teaching me how to invest, Leo. Of course I have this kind of money. Are you willing to spend yours?"

"Nine!" Leo yelled.

"I would like to remind the gentlemen here that you must be able to submit your funds to my father within two days' time."

"One. Thousand. Pounds." Eyeball announced, staring Leo dead in the eye.

It was a ridiculous sum of money. It was all of his liquid assets. Yes, his investments would be fine, and they would be able to pay their household without issue at the quarterly, but one thousand pounds to merely speak to Prudence?

There was a gripping in his bowels, his stomach, and he began to sweat. The feeling of not having enough money—the one emotion that had been his constant until only a few years ago—swallowed him whole. His peripheral vision began to blacken, as if great theatre curtains were slowly closing. He blinked, wanting to shout *eleven hundred!* He wanted to be her hero. The man who would do whatever it took.

But he realized then that every man has his price. And while his was not eleven hundred pounds, it was never wanting to feel that desperation ever again. He couldn't force his mother into a restricted existence, not even in thought.

Leo looked up at Prudence, feeling her stare on him from her great height. How he wanted her to understand, to accept, to love. But he couldn't explain, so she would never realize what tonight had cost him.

Leo shook his head.

"One thousand pounds, to the large gentleman the size of a tree. Thank you." Bridewell was clearly unsettled by the bidding war.

Eyeball came over and stood next to Leo, leaning over to whisper to him. "You shouldn't have given up."

"Fuck off, you absolute entitled shit," Leo ground out.

"If you were willing to fight for her, she'd go to you. As it is, she'll settle for me. At least I know I can get her to come round to my charm eventually." Eyeball strode off with confidence, reaching into the internal breast pocket of his coat to dig out his banknotes.

Leo had never hated anyone more in that moment. Not even Reggie, who'd never done anything good in the world. But he couldn't turn away from the spectacle. Prudence's wig was removed, and unlike the other two ladies, her hair pins loosened, and that honey-colored hair tumbled down around her bare shoulders.

It was like a knife in the gut. She undid her black mask, revealing that straight nose and high cheekbones. She looked straight at him, and he could almost feel her silky hair threaded between his fingers. The taste of the morning tea and biscuits at the cottage on her lips as he casually grazed them with his own. The smell of summer grass and blue skies. The happiness that he'd cut short, fearing that his past was catching up to him, threatening all that he held dear.

Then she turned away, descending the mountain to meet Eyeball, who would sit by her as she ate. Talk to her of the party, of whatever stupid thing came into his distractingly limited mind. Leo turned then, making his way back to collect his mother, as Bridewell announced the final woman, Miss Fuji.

The bidding was low, as everyone knew this was Bridewell's wife. But Leo didn't care about any of it. He had to go—he couldn't be among this wealth, this luxury, these people.

When he returned to his mother, she almost protested that she wasn't ready until she saw his face. Then she stood without a word, bid goodnight to her friends, and they went home. Leo was glad she didn't speak. Once home, she ordered the footman to serve Leo brandy in his study and a hot toddy to her in her room.

It was a small gesture of caretaking, and one Leo noticed and appreciated. Loved her even more for understanding.

Chapter Ten

THE MEMBERS OF the Ladies' Alpine Society stayed at the Rascomb residence overnight, arising in the morning to seek each other out in their bedrooms in their nightshifts and dressing gowns in the morning.

Eventually, they all ended up in Ophelia's room, in her giant bed, with a tray full of leftover fruits and cheeses and a hot pot of chocolate.

"I almost died when I heard—" Justine puffed up her chest and dropped her voice into a gravelly bass "—One. Thousand. Pounds."

Prudence shook her head, tearing a bread roll into even smaller pieces. She was embarrassed to have had that kind of attention. Mostly because it ended up being Lord Grabe on her arm, and not Leo. She had a lump in her throat for the rest of the night, despite the viscount's attentions. The man had given up championing Leo, and set about championing himself in Prudence's eyes.

Why he would waste time with her, she didn't know. Wasn't he supposed to marry some blue-blood girl barely out of the schoolroom? Still, he was handsome, and that didn't make for a difficult way to pass the time, even if she wished he were someone else.

"I never thought we'd make that much money at all," Ophelia confessed. "Not even close."

"It was because Justine set the mood with the army of suitors bidding right at the beginning." Prudence was happy to set the attention on Justine, who always seemed to have an army of suitors at the ready.

Justine stuck out her tongue, which only made her cheek dimple. Cute as a button. "They are all useless."

"Not to us," Eleanor said. "That five hundred pounds will do nicely to get us comfortable train tickets."

"Fine," Justine allowed. "Their money isn't useless. But the men are twits. I can't stand them."

"How much did we total?" Eleanor asked Prudence.

"Two thousand and fifty pounds." Prudence looked each woman in the face as they broke out in brilliant smiles. They sat silent for a moment as the huge sum echoed in the air, as if it had weight of its own.

"We have plenty," Ophelia said.

"We'll get the best ropes!" Eleanor said, barely containing a squeal.

"And the best guides," Prudence added.

"And the best sleeping cars," Justine added with a mischievous grin.

"We're going to climb the Matterhorn," Ophelia whispered.

The realization sunk in for all of them. It was no longer an "if" plan. There were no more hurdles. There was only training and packing. Tears welled up in Eleanor's eyes, and if Prudence didn't know better, she would have thought she saw them shining in Ophelia's as well.

Justine wiggled with excitement, causing the cheese plate to tip over onto the bed. "Oh blast," she said, picking up the pieces.

It was later that evening when Prudence drug herself back to the hotel. Georgie met her there and helped her with her trunk and ran her a bath. Prudence gave her a report of the dancing and the bidding as she soaked in lavender-scented bubbles.

Georgie gave her head a nice massage when Prudence told her how Leo had bid and bid, until he'd given up on her. Without meaning to, Prudence might have let it be known that it was so very disappointing.

She ordered dinner for both of them, asking for a simple American dish of scrambled eggs, only to find that when they came they were wet and filled with cream. She stared down the dish, the toast completely cold beside it, and a serving of stewed mushrooms whose water started to mix with the absolutely sopping eggs. "I can't," Prudence said.

It was the look of utter sympathy on Georgie's face that made Prudence begin to cry. At one point, Prudence even questioned why tears were continuing to form and fall from her face, only to have Georgie utter a motherly cluck, which caused Prudence to sob all the more.

Georgie put her to bed. It wasn't even seven in the evening. Prudence wept, feeling silly and small and unlovable. She didn't know when she stopped weeping and fell into a dark sleep.

The next morning, feeling somewhat refreshed, slightly puffy, and now, quite hungry, Prudence rose to face a new day. It was strange to have the ball behind her. And no Leo. And no Mrs. Moon to visit.

But she needn't have worried. Her foyer table was thick with cards and notes, from strangers and friends alike. She ordered a pot of coffee to be brought up, and rang down for Georgie. They shared the pot and went through the correspondence. Prudence had never felt the sudden reversal of emotions so severe. Where last night she felt awful and unloved, all these notes and letters made it clear she was sought after and appreciated. There was even a letter from her sister and her mother in the stack—always a beloved piece of her week—and a strange note left with the front desk.

Mrs. Cabot,

Please forgive my forwardness. I believe you know the whereabouts of someone very dear to me. Please meet me at a place of your choosing. I need only a moment of your time. I will check back in tomorrow morning at eight a.m. for your answer.

Kindest regards,
Mr. Reginald Morgan

Normally she wouldn't think of meeting a stranger anywhere. But Morgan was the last name. And the stranger at the cottage had asked for Lenny Morgan, and now here was a Reginald Morgan, looking for someone. Hadn't that stranger said something about a Reggie? Did they believe she knew where Lenny Morgan was? What would she find out if she met with Mr. Morgan?

"Georgie, I think I'm about to make a terrible decision." Prudence looked over to her companion. Georgie didn't even look up.

"What time?" was all she asked.

"Eight a.m. tomorrow."

"I'll be ready at seven thirty," she said, tossing aside another card.

At a quarter to eight, both women were in the lobby of the hotel. Prudence had delivered a message to the bellhop the night before, telling the man where to meet them in the afternoon, should his appearance prove unsettling.

But instead of a highwayman, a well-dressed man appeared exactly at eight, ringing the bell for service. His coat was of a slightly older style, but given the salt-and-pepper hair and the fact that he likely lived in the country, Prudence was willing to overlook it as a sign of something untoward. He was tall and slim, a build that Prudence couldn't help but notice was much like Leo's, and drummed his fingers with impatience at the counter.

Prudence looked at Georgie.

"I've got a derringer in my reticule," Georgie whispered.

"Do you really?" Prudence asked, surprised.

Georgie just gave her a reassuring nod. Prudence returned the gesture and stood.

"Mr. Morgan, I presume?" Prudence approached him, extending her hand as an American businessman would. Old habits died hard.

He looked at her in surprised pleasure. "Mrs. Cabot?"

She nodded, and he took her hand, giving it a less than enthusiastic squeeze. She dropped her hand. "Lovely to meet you."

"Likewise," he said. His eyes were very blue, and despite his age, he was handsome. One side of his face did appear to droop slightly, but it did little to damage his good looks. "I do apologize for being so forward."

"If it is for a good cause, I certainly don't mind. This is my companion, Miss Georgina Pendansky, she'll be going with us. There is a teashop around the corner that opens quite early. We could go there, if you like."

"What suits you, suits me, Mrs. Cabot." Mr. Morgan swept into a gallant bow, a gesture that strangely reminded her of Lord Grabe's theatrics.

"This way, then," Prudence said, unsure of what to do.

The trio found themselves at a workingman's café, where they were clearly out of place. They served tea in heavy ceramic mugs and heavy, crumbling scones the size of her fist. It wasn't refined, and Prudence loved it. Somehow, it made her feel less homesick.

"Now, Mr. Morgan," Prudence said after they'd found a high table with stools. It was not where a lady might sit, but then, she and Georgie were Americans, and it took far more to ruffle her. Mr. Morgan likewise didn't look askance at their surroundings. She found that interesting too. Based on his clothing, she thought him maybe a country gentleman, who might be aghast at eating with the working classes. "What brings you to my door?"

"That is just the thing, Mrs. Cabot," he said. His accent struck her ear oddly. It was a cultured accent like Ophelia's and her family's, but there was something else there that she couldn't put her finger on. A native speaker could easily suss it out, she was sure. There was something about this man that felt false. But she couldn't say why. "I believe you came to my door first."

"Oh?" she asked.

"I don't mean to be indelicate, but I believe you rented a cottage on my property."

Prudence blinked. Leo had said once, quite by accident, that he owned Thornridge, but then he said Lenny Morgan owned it. Could it actually belong to this man?

She was not about to get into a land dispute between two men. Especially when one of them was Leo, who clearly didn't value her enough to win her time. Was eleven hundred pounds an unreasonable sum? Yes, of course. But she knew he had it. He'd looked straight at her and given up. It had hurt worse than she ever could have realized.

"Hm. And were you not paid for the rental of this space?" she asked, sipping her tea, letting the pieces of this strange puzzle fit where they may.

"That is just it, my dear. When I checked on it, the caretakers, lovely people, insisted it had been paid for. But I simply didn't receive the rent. I believe my son did."

A piece of scone stuck in her throat. She coughed and swallowed some more tea. "And who is your son?"

"That's just it. When I sent my man for him, the couple renting the cottage up and left. Very odd."

"And you think I am the woman from the cottage," Prudence asked.

Mr. Mason nodded. "A pretty American heiress makes a stir in a small town. Even in a big town. Your name and likeness was all over the papers the last day or so."

The charity ball had made quite an impression. With so very little left in the social season, their grand event took over the gossip columns.

Prudence was glad Georgie had a derringer at the ready, just in case. There was something about this man that discomfited her. Put her on edge. "You never told me who your son would be? Since that is the person you are truly looking for?"

"It is. His birth name is Leonard Morgan. I have every reason to believe he thinks me dead. I did, some years ago, have a devastating health issue, an apoplexy that left me paralyzed for some time. I was away, and no doubt they'd heard I had not survived. My wife and child were gone by the time I got back. Broke my heart. Couldn't find them anywhere."

Again, somehow Prudence didn't fully believe him. The droop of Mr. Morgan's face was a clear enough sign of apoplexy—Gregory had suffered episodes as well, causing him paralysis of one entire side of his body. It had been the harbinger of the end.

"Outside of your acquaintance, I'm sorry to say that I know of no Mr. Morgan," Prudence said, which was the utter truth. Georgie had put both of her hands under the table and was no longer pretending to sip her mug of tea.

"I'm not sure why, perhaps there were creditors—none surfaced when I returned, of course—but I believe he changed his name. He might still go by his first name. I always called him 'Leo' for short. My little lion. He was such a cute boy. I've missed him so." Mr. Morgan put a hand to his chest, as if he was pining for the boy of the past.

It was a theatric again. And Prudence had no doubt in her mind that she was looking at Leopold Moon's birth father. The tall, slim build was an echo of Leo's, as were the high cheekbones. Instead of gray eyes that glinted like steel, this Mr. Morgan had blue eyes that no doubt charmed many a young lady in his youth.

"Tell you what, Mr. Morgan. I will seek out my acquaintances and tell them you've arrived in London, wanting an introduction. I will not make a big deal of your possible relation, in case I don't have the correct man in mind. You could check back with me at the end of the week, and I'll be happy to inform you of all I've found."

"Bless you, young lady. My old heart beats with hope once again." Mr. Morgan stared her down, no doubt hoping to use his blue eyes to their full effect. But Prudence didn't swoon at the sight of blue eyes. Not when she had been taken by the cool strength of gray ones.

None of them finished their repast. Prudence stood, and Georgie echoed her movement, hand sliding out of her reticule. "Good day, Mr. Morgan. I'll speak with you soon."

※≫≪※

GEORGIE AND PRUDENCE returned to the hotel, not speaking until they were in Prudence's suite, safe from listening ears. They stared at each other.

"I should have used my derringer," Georgie said, putting her reticule on the long thin foyer table.

"I can't have you arrested for murder in England, Georgie," Prudence tsked. "Far too much paperwork, and I bore easily."

A smile cracked Georgie's normally very placid face. "I'd claim that it went off accidentally. Silly me."

"You don't sound convincing." Prudence paced. Mr. Morgan didn't *feel* right. She and Gregory had analyzed men like him before, when trying to judge which investments to make. Who was a confidence man and who was a legitimate businessman who wouldn't take their money and run?

Mr. Morgan had some elements of the trademark shiftiness— an overly formal, obsequious way of speaking. But was that just part of being English in a way she didn't understand? He had acted as if he could only hope for her help, rather than showing triumph when she agreed to make contact in the future. She couldn't see how he would benefit, but that was the way with confidence men. They tried to make it seem like they wouldn't gain anything, to pull you into the scheme all the more.

"I hate to make you uncomfortable, Mrs. Cabot, but I will be accompanying you on your outings today." Georgie was a solid girl. A farm girl. One of those from mixed-up bloodline families that had helped birth a calf when the calf was bigger than she was. Prudence admired her.

"Will you be bringing the derringer along as well?" Prudence asked.

"It is," Georgie said, solemn as a funeral, "in my professional opinion, the best chaperone in the world."

"I'd like to wait and call upon Mrs. Moon at proper visiting hours," Prudence said, the clock dinging once as it struck thirty minutes past nine. "But I'm so knotted up over this, I don't think I can."

"Then we'll walk slow," Georgie suggested, as if that wasn't what she did every day of the week.

They ambled, taking the long ways, winding through side streets Prudence had never bothered to explore. Still, Prudence was so anxious, she couldn't match Georgie's plodding gait.

It seemed like it took ages to arrive at the Moon residence. Prudence's stomach turned flips as she composed herself. Georgie stared at her.

"What? Do I have something on my face?" Prudence gave a quick wipe of her cheek with her glove.

Georgie shook her head. "Just wondering what you're waiting for."

Prudence huffed. "I feel like I'm out of breath."

"Take your time," Georgie said. Which seemed to be the girl's entire life view.

Prudence took another steadying breath and knocked on the door. The footman opened it, surprised to see young ladies at the doorstep at this early hour.

"Mrs. Cabot," he greeted. "Mrs. Moon is not available yet this morning."

Prudence smiled, hating herself on the inside for harrying an old woman. "I understand. But I have a most urgent matter. Perhaps I could come in and wait?"

"Come in, come in," Leo's irritated voice echoed through the hallway. "Jeffrey, are you honestly going to make them stand on the doorstep like beggars?"

The footman flung the door open and admitted them both.

But after closing the door, he just stood there.

"Take their hats, please, Jeffrey," Leo said through gritted teeth.

It was so good to just look at Leo. It felt like the ball—only two days prior—had been weeks ago. And she'd not seen him between then and the train platform after the cottage. Her chest ached as she noticed his freshly shaven cheek, knowing what he smelled like, what kind of soap he used, even the feel of the bristles from his shaving brush. Suddenly she felt hollowed out. Must he be so gruff?

"Mrs. Cabot, and Miss er—" Leo trailed off, not remembering Georgie's last name.

"Miss Pendanski, sir," Georgie said.

"Delighted. Yes. Perhaps we can talk in my study until my mother is up and about? Jeffrey, fetch us a tray, thank you." Leo ushered them into the room where Prudence had first met him. Had first let him put his hands on her. Had first felt the rush of pleasure from him.

Instead of going round to his desk, he led them to the sitting area. It was warm enough that there was no fire in the small hearth, and indeed, it had been swept clean for the season. Soon it would be cold enough to require a fire, even for Leo, who seemed impervious to heat or cold.

"Pardon me for being so forward," Leo said, sitting stiffly on the edge of a chair as Prudence and Georgie sank onto the sofa, where Prudence had once flung her legs open for him to see her in reckless abandon. "But what brings you here at such an early hour?"

"A Mr. Reginald Morgan tracked me down at my hotel." Prudence watched as Leo recoiled.

His eyes went wide and his gaze immediately went to the door. "Did he follow you?"

"Would he do such a thing?" Prudence asked. It seemed very rude. "I told him to return to my hotel on Friday and I would let him know then if I had found his son."

"Is that what he said he was doing? Looking for his son?" Leo pressed.

"Well, yes, he said that he was owed money for the cottage rental, and there had been some confusion with the son and some property rights, and—"

Leo was on his feet. "That bastard. Property rights, my arse." He went to his desk and rummaged around in the drawers. Not finding what he wanted, he headed to the door, nearly running into Jeffrey, who carried a tray with a teapot and toasted oatcakes.

"Where are you going?" Prudence snapped.

"I have to tell my mother. She needs to leave as soon as possible. Miss Pendansky, how do you feel about France?"

"Why France?" Prudence asked, just as Georgie was saying, "Never been."

But Leo was out the door. Prudence had half a mind to go trailing after him, as she'd never seen him in a panic. Or a hurry. Or anything but completely in control of himself. Well, not *always*.

"Should I pour?" Georgie asked.

"Please." Prudence couldn't think about tea or oatcakes or anything at the moment. Why did Leo care so much about this Mr. Morgan. Was he actually Leo's father? He certainly looked the part. That was something she didn't doubt.

She sighed after the footman left the room. "He'd better get back here quick. I have too many questions."

"You're mad at him." Georgie plopped a bit of sugar and milk in her teacup, but left Prudence's untouched.

"Yes." Prudence straightened her shoulders. She'd forgotten that because she'd been so busy puzzling over the strange connection. Her anger was subsiding. He'd wanted them both gone from that cottage, for whatever it was that connected him to Mr. Morgan. She wished for Gregory once again. Not as a husband, but as a people watcher. He was so good at getting at what men wanted, the whisper of truth that crawled beneath their words.

The only time she'd ever known Gregory to be wrong was about himself. He'd said that he wanted Prudence to be his wife, but he didn't. Not really. Or if he did, it was that he couldn't get over his shame of wanting her. Prudence didn't know which. And she'd finally grown weary of wondering about an answer she'd never get.

Leo returned, his gait quick and purposeful. "Ladies. My mother has questions for you; she's making her way to the drawing room." The muscle in his jaw worked and flexed.

"Mr. Moon," Prudence said, still maintaining their formal distance since Georgie was in the room. "What is going on? What is the urgency?"

Leo shook his head, his face a kaleidoscope of emotion as his expression morphed through difficult thoughts. "Mr. Reginald Morgan is a dangerous man."

Prudence nodded, but saw the rest of his answer spelled out across his angular face. The face that looked so much like Mr. Morgan's, who spoke of a son named Leo. "But is he your father? Biologically speaking?"

Leo winced. "Yes."

"So you are Leonard Morgan, not Leopold Moon?" Prudence pressed. She didn't even know the name of the man she had let into her bed. How had she become so reckless with herself?

"No. I was born Leonard Morgan, and I have legally changed it to Leopold Moon. There is nothing underhanded or shameful in what I did. If anyone cared to look, it has all been there in plain sight. I've not hidden a thing."

Prudence tried not to feel a sting of betrayal. This was the loose thread of his secret. The secret so big that he would not share it with her—that she was not trusted enough to be party to. She had trusted him so quickly, letting him see all of her messy self, telling him about Gregory and their marriage bed. Her cheeks burned with shame. How foolish she was. So desperate to be wanted that she let this man, whatever his name was, worm his way into her heart. Leo went back and rummaged through his desk drawers again.

"But I would guess you did so in London, not in your home county?" Prudence had to keep her mind focused on the facts of what lay before her, lest he affect her judgement again.

"Yes," Leo said, brandishing a small brass key.

"So the paperwork is here in London, which is not somewhere your father could get to, in order to find you," Prudence guessed.

Leo turned to a lower cabinet in the great built-in shelves that sat behind his desk. He flung open the cabinet door to reveal a second, keyed door, which he unlocked.

"You never expected him to find you," Prudence said.

"I hoped he was dead. I believed him dead, when he didn't come and didn't come." The door revealed a safe, which he deftly opened. There was a stack of banknotes that Leo removed and set on his desk. Prudence's stomach clenched. There was more than enough sitting on his desk for him to win a bid for her against Lord Grabe. But she hadn't been worth it. Not worth the secrets, not worth the money.

"What is that for?" Prudence asked, trying not to let anger and disappointment flood her voice.

"That old bastard just wants money, that's all. He wants to bleed me dry until nothing is left."

"So you're going to buy him off?"

"No, I'm getting all of us out of here. We're running."

"Why?" Prudence asked. This was absurd. Leo had more than enough to keep everyone for blocks in comfort, let alone one old man.

"You don't know how dangerous he is. How devious."

"I saw him not two hours ago. The man is old and frail, and half of his face barely works."

"Doesn't matter."

Prudence sat quietly, trying to parse out what exactly made the old man with salt-and-pepper hair and bright blue eyes dangerous. He certainly seemed mortal enough. As for danger, honestly, if she pitted Georgie against Mr. Morgan, she would bet on Georgie every time.

But this wasn't her fight. It wasn't her father, it wasn't even her country. This was a property dispute between two men, a Mr. Morgan and a Mr. Moon. No, this was Leo showing her exactly how little she mattered to him.

"He liked to seem like he was more than he was," Leo finally volunteered. "That's how he got my mother. Pretending to be a lord, titled and rich, handsome, all that. Everything a woman could want. I don't know how he knew she had a tidy sum squirreled away, enough for her to live on as an old maid, because that's what housekeepers generally became. They married their job, not a man."

Mrs. Moon appeared in the doorway, looking regal and striking. "That—" she interrupted with an imperious command, "—is not your story to tell."

"Mama," Leo started.

"Put the money away, Leo," she said, her tone stern and warning. "We are in London. In our home. We are safe here."

Prudence saw his youth, suddenly, there under the surface of the man he was. The way he'd been mistreated and unmoored, the fear and panic never completely gone. There were some ghosts that haunted, no matter how much time had passed.

Leo tapped the stacks of paper. Prudence could see his hands shaking. But then he acquiesced and put the money back in the safe, locking it away for some other emergency.

"Miss Pendansky, is it?" Mrs. Moon hobbled over, bearing her weight on her cane, as if her knee bothered her more than usual. "Please pour me a cup, if you wouldn't mind. No cream."

Georgie did as she was told, and both Mrs. Moon and Leo joined them at the sitting area. Prudence glanced from mother to son and back again, waiting for someone to explain, but neither spoke. She had missed her friendship with Mrs. Moon. The woman was incisive and sharp, and had a good mind for a funny quip. Perhaps one day Prudence could be friends with her again, but the rejection from Leo burned her from the inside out.

Prudence picked up her own teacup. "Leo once said that he held secrets that he would tell no one, not even me. I assume the identity of Mr. Morgan is at the root of that."

Mrs. Moon took her cup from Georgie's outstretched hand and looked over at Leo, who slouched in the chair next to her. "Well?" she prodded.

"Yes. My father was—is—a bad man." Leo spat it out, as if it tasted bad to even speak it.

"He still gave me you," Mrs. Moon said into her cup.

Prudence looked at the woman—truly looked. Leo had said she was a housekeeper? So she was in service, never expecting to marry. And then she ended up with a husband and a child, not to mention a beautiful house and social standing. That was quite a whiplash from her expectations.

"May I ask how you became a housekeeper?" Prudence didn't want to be rude, but this was a story she didn't want to miss. If this were the last time she would be able to visit Mrs. Moon, she wanted every juicy morsel from this woman.

"The way many young girls did. I went into service around the age of seven, scrubbing pots. Then I was a maid, and while I was young to be a housekeeper, it wasn't that unusual, as more and more girls were leaving the countryside to go to the cities to work in factories, or find a man who worked in one. I was proud of myself for obtaining the position at such a young age."

"As you should be," Georgie said.

"Thank you," Mrs. Moon replied.

Leo's leg shook with nervous anticipation. He was so out of sorts. Prudence stared at him. He was like a completely different man—one she'd never known at all. Who was it that she'd known? A carefully curated disguise, and this was the real person underneath it all? Or was it the other way around?

"Perhaps you should go look out a window, make sure there are no lowlifes lurking about," Prudence suggested. Mrs. Moon looked at her aghast.

But Leo was up in a flash, as if he could not bear to sit a moment longer. His mother watched him as he patrolled window by window, finally exiting the study to make a circuit of the house.

"It's really quite unnecessary." Mrs. Moon shook her head. "But let me continue the story. I haven't been able to tell anyone, and I do adore a rapt audience."

Georgie poured herself another cup of tea and grabbed an oatcake before settling back into the sofa, ready for a story, as if she were a child.

"I was a young housekeeper. Plain sort of looks, I think, but I ran a tight ship. The house was always clean, the larder stocked, and the butler and I worked well together. And then one day the master of the house brought home a guest."

"Mr. Morgan?" Prudence guessed.

Mrs. Moon smiled. "Yes, but he styled himself Lord Lovelace at the time. He played on the strained connection to Lord Byron, thinking it made him seem more romantic. Not that he needed it. The man was beyond handsome. All the ladies of the county were taken with him. And all the maids, too. I had to issue a special warning to each of them to not be caught alone in a room with him, or else they'd get sacked."

"You wouldn't be so draconian!" Prudence said, shocked at the rule.

"I had to be," Mrs. Moon said. "A pregnant woman cannot be a maid. The work is back-breaking, and the hours long. I couldn't be constantly searching for replacement maids because of one pretty face."

Georgie cracked a wide grin. "But you did, didn't you?"

Mrs. Moon shook her head with fond exasperation. "I confess I was a hypocrite. There was little seduction involved. He'd been there for a week or so, always polite, the very image of a gentleman." She sighed. "Which is how I should have known. Real gentlemen don't notice the staff. Real gentlemen are class conscious. Looking back, I think he'd realized that none of the young ladies of the county had enough of a dowry, or had fathers too smart to be duped by the likes of him for the length of time it took to get to the altar. But a romantic housekeeper like myself? I was such a fool."

"You were in love," Prudence felt as if she were shriveling up as they spoke, a plucked flower crisped in the hot afternoon sun. Love only worked if both parties felt the same. The shame of learning you were the only one who cared was world shattering. "You weren't a fool."

"Same thing, in the end, I'm afraid," Mrs. Moon said, still smiling. "We were caught by his valet, who I came to realize was his partner in crime. He told the butler, and I was sacked that afternoon. I had to go to the bank to retrieve some funds to pay for a boarding house. I think he saw the bank slip, for I'd asked for my account balance. And there it was. He asked me to marry him."

"Just like that?" Georgie asked.

"Oh, he was a beautiful man. But yes, just so. We applied for special license, given the circumstances, and were married a fortnight later. Leo came nine months later." Mrs. Moon smiled. "And he became my light."

Prudence cocked her head. "Your light?"

Mrs. Moon set her teacup down on the table. "My time with Mr. Morgan—who turned out not to be Lord Lovelace, as you know—grew very dark. He was not exactly an unkind man, but he did so hate to be bored. And poverty is so very boring. He drank up every cent we had, and when we ran out, he would threaten to leave me penniless in the streets with my child."

"Why didn't he?" Prudence asked.

Mrs. Moon smiled. "It's a bit silly."

"I would desperately like to know." Prudence wanted to know how any woman navigated a world set up for a man. Crucial bits of information were needed, could be shared, could be used for greater good.

"When you live in a small village, everyone knows everyone. My father had once saved the bank manager from drowning. It was when they were boys, but my father had jumped into the lake, where the boy's ankle was trapped or something of the sort, and pulled him out. When Mr. Morgan would go into the bank run by the bank manager who knew me and was indebted to my deceased father, there would always be some problem. As a married woman, he was entitled to my funds, but only if they could ever be verified to exist. Mr. Morgan could never manage to get all of my savings all in one go."

"So they knew?" Prudence asked. "The people of the village knew that Mr. Morgan was . . . bad?" Using Leo's word felt strange.

"'Bad' seems to me an overstatement. Giving Reggie more forethought than he possessed," Mrs. Moon said. "But the villagers didn't trust him. They saw him sleeping off a bender in the public square. They knew about the extended credit with the grocer, noticed how threadbare our clothes were. One can only mend a child's shirt so many times."

Mrs. Moon's brow furrowed, the memories catching up to her speech. "When Leo got older, Mr. Morgan took him along to help with his schemes. I hated it, but what could I do? Leo idolized his father, and then feared him. And then began to believe it was his duty to go."

"Oh," Prudence whispered. She thought of the scars she'd traced on his torso. The circular burn. All the other smaller nicks and pale marks that lived on his skin. The experiences that could never be forgotten.

"One day, amid a long stretch of Reggie's prolonged absence, I forged his signature on the bank card. Miraculously, the bank manager was able to find all the remaining money in the account that day and gave it to me. I whisked my son to London. I worked, sent him to the best school, because he was a smart boy, oh, he was smart. Chip on his shoulder as wide as Britain itself, but smart."

"When did you change your name?" Prudence asked.

"As soon as we arrived." Mrs. Moon looked down. "It's not

that I was ashamed. It was that I was scared. I kept the same initials, since I'd monogrammed everything over the years. But I altered a certificate of marriage to show I was married to a Mr. Moon, not Morgan, and changed our names. It wasn't hard, really, if you had enough ready money."

"And you had enough?" Prudence asked. Leo acted as if they had been starving, so which was it? The moment the specter of his father loomed, Leo had become a different man.

Mrs. Moon winced. "Yes and no. I was in debt, but Leo was so good with numbers. So very good. And once I finally told him of our predicament, he solved it straightaway."

"His schoolmates. They had money. And he did their work for them." Prudence started fitting the pieces together.

"I'm not proud of myself for leaning on a young boy for financial help. But the world was not made for a woman to work and support herself and a child. It was difficult. And that was with both of us having a decent education."

"You should be proud of yourself," Georgie said again. "You've done well."

"Only because of Leo," she smiled.

And then there was a knock at the front door.

⋙⋘

LEO'S PULSE HAMMERED like he was about to enter the worst fight of his life. In fact, he was ready for one. He'd pictured this day so many times over the years. What he would say, what he would do. Sometimes there would be a scathing monologue, but typically he'd envisioned throwing fists before even letting the man over the threshold.

How could his mother be so calm? This man had ruined her life. Every bit of it. He'd taken her independence, her money, her dignity. He still sometimes had nightmares of the thinness of her arms, how bulbous her wrists looked in comparison, as she had slowly starved so that he could eat.

But the money had belonged to Reggie and what he did with it was his business. Regardless if his wife and child starved in front of his eyes. Sometimes Leo believed Reggie drank all their money out of spite. He wasn't a man to raise his fists, but he wanted to punish his mother for not being the mark he'd believed her to be. She was stronger and calmer and smarter than Reggie, which was the most heinous sin she could have committed in Reggie's eyes.

There was nothing that made Reggie Morgan madder than someone who truly was better than him.

When Leo grew big enough, he'd tried to help his father make more money, in the hopes his father would be satisfied. But there wasn't enough gold in the world to satisfy Reggie Morgan. Because it wasn't only the money, it was prestige. All the things a low birth prevented. Odd, then, that somehow, despite Reggie Morgan, Leo had managed to garner that wealth and status Reggie had craved. Leo and his mother attended London balls and rubbed elbows with titled men and women. As the man of the house, Leo had done what his father could not.

And since Leo was the man of this house, he could protect its occupants how he liked. Leo could defend his territory, his women. His hands shook as if he were still that hungry child.

The knock at the door startled him. His blood thrummed. Jeffrey looked at him; he was tall and handsome as all footmen were somehow required to be, but he was an idiot. Leo pulled at his clothes, smoothing any wrinkles. "I'll be in my study," he told Jeffrey, nodding at the door.

Jeffrey thankfully was smart enough to wait until Leo had gone past the threshold of his room before he opened the door.

Leo heard the voice. He knew that voice even after the fifteen-odd years since he'd heard it last. It was raspier than it had been. Not as threatening and full. Still subtly slurring his words. Leo made his way to his desk, aware that the women all watched him. His mother appeared at ease, but he could see the strain in her jaw as she clenched it. How her posture went falsely rigid—

the way a person braces for the impact of a blow. He hated seeing it. The woman he'd remembered her as—gaunt, eyes made larger from lack of flesh—overlaid the plump older woman who sat before him.

Prudence stared at him, her gray eyes wide in surprise and wariness. God, she was pretty. He'd mucked the whole thing up, and after this business with his father was sorted, he'd make things up to her. He wanted her around. He liked having her around. More than anything, he wanted to have time at Thornridge, the two of them sipping morning tea in the sunshine, making love with a cool afternoon breeze wafting in through the open window. He'd give anything to go back in time and outbid Eyeball. He'd happily pay well more than eleven hundred pounds now. This was a nightmare to have her embroiled in the debacle that was Reggie.

"A Mister Reginald Morgan, sir." Jefferey bowed as he admitted Leo's father. It was completely unnecessary for Jeffrey to bow, but it did make the impact on Reggie Morgan, who looked around the room, no doubt assessing the value of every piece in it.

His father looked *old*. It was hard to miss the left-sided limp. The droop to his face. The left arm that was smaller than the right, and curled up in a tight slender fist, as if it might never unclench again. "You've done well for yourself, Len."

"Leo," he corrected. While his father and those men called him Len or Lenny, it was his mother who'd always addressed him as Leo. Her lion. And he meant to live up to his name.

"Of course. My mistake. Ah, and Mrs. Cabot and Miss Pendansky, lovely to see you again so soon." Reggie turned to address them, and again, Leo had the opportunity to see how the man's body had diminished. Reggie was in an old man's body. But Reggie had never had an old man's mind. He couldn't let his father prey on any of them. He wouldn't allow it.

"I thought you called him Leo," Prudence said softly. "Your little lion."

Reggie's head bobbed this way and that. "Leo, Len, does it matter? He can be both."

Leo stood, his heart wrenching when he realized that Reggie had already begun lying, but also realizing his father would never make it all the way across the room without assistance. The white-knuckled fist of his diminished hand looked painfully contracted.

"And there she is," Reggie said, grabbing his chest in over-dramatic theatrics, and ignoring any censure from Prudence. "The love of my life. My heart, my reason for living."

"Good morning, Reggie," Leo's mother said. Her voice betrayed nothing. No fear, no apprehension. Calm and cool and collected, as she'd always been.

"Morning, Lena." Reggie gave her a wide, lopsided smile. Leo came around the side of the sofa quickly enough that he saw his father attempt his seducer's smile. The one that had bewitched her.

Glancing at his mother, he was terrified she might succumb to this man that she'd once loved—for she had loved him, hadn't she? Had she used that word about him? He couldn't remember now. But his mother's placid expression still held.

"Won't you have a seat?" Mrs. Moon said. "It is a relief, is it not, to let our old bones rest a bit?"

Was she baiting him? Leo's pulse leapt at the thought, terrified that he'd have to make the seven-foot distance between them if his father was upset. But no.

Reggie Morgan sank gratefully into the chair next to his mother. "You've called it correctly, love. The things we used to do aren't so easy now, are they?" He winked at her, and his double-entendre made Leo's stomach churn.

For her part, Mrs. Moon tittered. Like a schoolgirl. Damn it, he was going to have to bodily haul his father out of this house before his mother fell to his charms again. "Reggie, if I believed for an instant you could still do that, I wouldn't have let you in the house."

Leo's mind felt like a curdled milk. His mother was dealing with Reggie far better than he was. How could she forgive him like this? How could she wipe away the neglect and hurt?

"Might I have a bit of tea? Always helps." Reggie looked at the ladies, no doubt noticing the extra cup waiting on the tray. The cup that was meant for Leo. Miss Pendansky leaned forward and poured. "I do better in the mornings. It's after I've walked a bit, my hip stiffens up and I have a bit of a go." Miss Pendansky handed him the teacup and saucer, which Reggie took with obvious relief. "Cheers, love."

His mother, for her part, put down hers and folded her hands into her lap. "Reggie. After all this time. What precisely is your aim in visiting us?"

Reggie had time to take a sip and make innocent calf eyes at her before he was forced to respond. The man had the audacity to look at Leo. "Can I not catch up with my very successful son? Take pride in his accomplishments?"

"So you need money?" His mother's tone was crisp, but not terse.

"Lena," Reggie cooed, drawing out her name.

"I want to be clear about why you've come."

Reggie reached his hand out, and Leo was up like lightning. The hand that was about to touch his mother's knee never made it to its destination. Reggie's teacup rattled on his lap and spilled onto his trousers.

"Don't touch my mother," Leo growled.

"What's this?" Reggie said, irritated, brushing the beaded liquid off his trousers. "How do you think you got made in the first place?"

Behind him, Prudence coughed politely into her hand, reminding them that there was an audience for this family drama. Leo was embarrassed that she had to witness this. All of the worst of him on display for her to judge.

"Thank you for the tea, Mrs. Moon. I very much appreciate seeing you again," Prudence said, getting to her feet.

"Mrs. Moon?" Reggie echoed, then moaned in a playful tone. Leo could see all of Reggie's clumsy manipulations laid bare. "Not you, too, love."

For the first time since Reggie walked in, his mother looked down. Her fingers clenched together, making strange shapes in her lap, her knuckles going white with the pressure. "I assumed you didn't mind, since you had set up housekeeping in the next county over. What was her name? Tabitha? Tara? Talia?"

Reggie's mouth gaped open, as it always had when he was called on the carpet for his own wrongdoings. He shook his head, making unintelligible noises. "You moved to London without me. What was I supposed to do?"

"That was long before London, Reggie," his mother said. "There was a boy, wasn't there? I'd say he would be about twenty-five now?"

Leo was shocked. This was new information. He suddenly felt like a child, being coddled and isolated. Why wasn't he allowed to know? Why couldn't he have a family? Why was he left out of the lives of all these people? Shame coursed through him, hot and liquid, that Prudence knew dirty secrets about his family that even he hadn't known.

Reggie looked grim and serious. "He was Reginald Morgan Junior. And he died of a fever when he was about ten. So."

His mother didn't look at Reggie with pity. "So."

Prudence stood stock still, as did Miss Pendansky. Leo had to admit, he would have no idea how to exit this room either. There was absolutely no graceful way to watch a train derail.

"And your daughter?" Lena asked, still polite.

"Daughter?" Leo asked.

Reggie cocked his head to the side as if he were being put upon. "She's gone as well. I'm not sure what it was. Some kind of sickness in the last few years."

"I liked her, if that is any consolation." His mother's voice was calm and kind, which Leo didn't know how she managed.

"You met her?" Leo asked. He didn't realize he had any siblings, let alone two of them. And those were just the ones Reggie had admitted to having. The ones his mother knew about. He suddenly felt his world turn upside down. Since childhood, he'd believed that he had protected and cared for his mother, not realizing how different her perspective had been. How much information she'd had.

If he'd ever admitted to his mother how terrified he'd been that his father would find them again, would she have told him that he'd carried on with a new family the next county over?

"Of course, that's where Granson came from." His mother let loose all her knowledge with such casual indifference. "The boy's real name is William, I believe?"

"You've an excellent memory, Lena," Reggie said. "I liked having a grandson. Couldn't stop bragging about him, so the name stuck."

Leo felt another stab of betrayal. He was not that much older than Granson. He'd been prouder of his grandson than his actual son. This grifter, this thief. How could Leo feel so hurt by a man who valued nothing?

Prudence let out a low huff of a laugh. "Granson. Because he is your actual Grand. Son." Leo felt as if he'd accepted an invitation from Eyeball to go a few rounds in a boxing ring. He wanted some of Prudence's sweet Kentucky bourbon, and then he wanted to go to bed. Preferably with Prudence snug in there with him so he could smell her and be comforted by the warm weight of her body next to his. But she'd never lie next to him again. He'd had hope before, but Reggie waltzed in and pulled the walls down.

"We should really be going," Prudence said.

"I would get up for you, but . . ." Reggie trailed off, gesturing to his tea-stained lap.

"Don't fret, Mr. Morgan," Prudence said. "We can see ourselves out, Mrs. Moon, Mr. Moon."

The two women hustled out of the room. Leo didn't blame them. This was no place for them to be. Leo watched them go, and wished they were staying. Or rather, he wished that Prudence were staying, as even her presence was a steadying force for him. Even if they were at odds.

"I am staying at a boarding house at the moment, with Granson. Since I came all the way to London to see you, I thought you wouldn't mind paying the bill, Len."

This was how it started. He shook his head because he knew he was going to agree against his better judgement.

"Of course, we could reunite the family, and we could move in here. Certainly looks like you've got the space. And a footman, too! I bet you've got an excellent staff. Ol' Lena wouldn't let anyone slide. Excepting herself, of course." Reggie winked at her.

"I'll pay the hotel bill, but nothing more. Please get out." Leo didn't have the energy to put a snap in his voice as he said it.

"Well, then there's the business of a hack," Reggie said.

"I'll pay that too," Leo said. "Just leave."

"Fine, fine. I can go. But I hope we can get reacquainted in the coming weeks. I'm an old man, and I don't know how much more I've got left in me. I'd like to make amends before I die."

Leo didn't believe him for one instant. He stalked into the hall, where Jeffrey stood by in the foyer, clearly unsure of what to do with himself.

"Mr. Morgan requires a hack. Flag one down, I'll pay for it. But get that old bugger out of here." Leo trudged up the stairs to his bedroom. Perhaps it was childish of him to not say goodbye. But he knew he hadn't seen the backside of Reggie Morgan.

Chapter Eleven

"THE ABSOLUTE NERVE!" Justine flung herself down in a flounce.

"I'm honestly not that upset about it," Prudence lied. Perhaps she should have kept the news of Leo's father's arrival to herself. She should have, she amended, but her friends saw her misery, despite her attempt to hide it. And out it spilled: her time with him, Thornridge, the rush to London, the auction where he'd given up on her, and then seeing stacks of money as he prepared to run from Reggie Morgan. Stacks of banknotes that sat, unmolested, in a safe. More than enough to outbid Lord Grabe.

"He's supposed to be gallant!" Justine protested, sitting up amongst petticoats and ruffles in a massive disarray. Her face was barely visible above the frippery. "What kind of arse does that to our Prudence?"

"You look ridiculous," Ophelia said to Justine.

Justine slapped her hands on the cushions, causing ruffles to flutter. "Of course I look ridiculous. Everything about the current fashion is ridiculous! The curls. The petticoats. The changing shapes of the cages. I hate it."

"You used to love it," Ophelia reminded her.

Prudence enjoyed watching the two best friends bicker. They loved each other and picked at each other. Ophelia was cool and composed, gliding purposeful towards a goal, while Justine bounced about like a puppy.

"Well, I've changed, haven't I? And that's your fault for making me enjoy hauling my carcass up a cold mountain. So you can sit and stew in that, Miss Ophelia Bridewell." Justine sat back against the couch, causing the wood to creak.

"It is perfectly normal to feel upset about Mr. Moon's behavior," Eleanor said, studying Prudence's face.

Prudence was full of turmoil thinking about him. His father. His mother. The revelations that came loose in his study that morning about his family and his father's lack of fidelity. But surely, that shouldn't have been a surprise. It seemed rarer that a truly handsome man kept faithful to one woman, as a handsome woman might keep faithful to one man. But then, the repercussions for a woman were much greater than for a man.

"Well, he's a glorified bookkeeper for us anyway," Ophelia said. "He isn't coming on the expedition, so he doesn't matter."

Prudence had to remind herself that there had been an article in one of the lesser papers about how women ought not to be climbing mountains. The article had not mentioned any of them by name, nor even the Ladies' Alpine Society, but it was so pointed in its venom, the targets could not be mistaken. This had riled up her friends, and the news of Leo's questionable conduct only piled on their already-frayed nerves.

Perhaps marrying Gregory had spoiled her for having a man in her life. True, their partnership had its deficiencies, but he'd encouraged her to learn his business. He recognized her intelligence and didn't stifle it. In fact, he never told her she couldn't do anything. He'd merely advised her on how to do it. But hearing stories like Mrs. Moon's made her realize that she was in the minority.

Everyone in this room was, in some way, beholden to a man. The only exception was Prudence, and it was only through death and wealth she had gained her freedom.

"Can we please stop all the fussing and planning and talking and just go for our run?" Justine asked.

"Are you asking to train more?" Prudence asked.

"I feel like I am crawling out of my skin. And if I do that, what am I? A bit of muck and a pile of bones. I'll not have any suitors at all."

Ophelia laughed. "I'm in for a run. You ladies?"

Prudence nodded, as did Eleanor. Sometimes there was too much internal turmoil, and the best solution was to take to the gardens.

Sadly, a stout run didn't help Prudence, even if it helped Justine. Prudence returned to her Strawbridge room, hungry but not wanting to eat. Georgie was waiting for her. "You've another note from Mr. Moon."

"Put it in the fire, Georgie." Prudence pulled off the hat and gloves. She'd bathed after the run at Ophelia's house, and wore borrowed clothing to take her exercise, but her skin felt sticky and too hot. She couldn't bear to read a letter from Leo. Not now.

"I don't want to overstep, but I think you should at least read them."

Prudence threw down her accessories and took to the nearest chair to take off her walking boots. "I don't want to talk to him."

"He needs to talk to you, though."

"Why? He lived an entire life without me. He certainly doesn't need me now." She yanked off one boot and then the other.

"You were present, as was I, for some family secrets we had no business hearing." Georgie stood and followed Prudence into the bedroom.

"Then you read the letters. You talk to him."

"I did read this letter," Georgie said. It should have been a shameful confession, but Georgie wasn't capable of it.

"That's quite the overstep, don't you think?" Prudence said, whirling around on her. "That was my correspondence."

Georgie didn't even bother to frown. "It was the fire's correspondence. There was just a longer time in my hands before, is all. And you should read it. He needs someone who might understand."

Prudence laughed. "There's no reason I would. My father is lovely. Nothing like Mr. Morgan."

"It would be a decent thing to do, is all." Georgie sighed. "Want me to undo your dress?"

It would be quicker than using her buttonholer. "Yes, please. But do I have to read the letter?"

"Yes," Georgie said placidly, moving in her slow and steady pace across the floor. But soon, her fingers were on the back buttons of Prudence's dress, deftly peeling open the fabric.

She had a point. Continuing her embargo of all things Leo Moon was childish. They were mature adults, and she could at least read his correspondence.

Prudence put on a more comfortable day dress, and there was a knock at the door. A bellman delivered a note—from Lord Grabe, who was waiting downstairs.

Leo's letter would have to wait.

⇶⇷

"SHE'S AVOIDING YOU," his mother said, sawing away at her lump of meat.

Leo hadn't tasted his dinner for well over a week now. His father had come by every day, sometimes long visits, sometimes short. Always asking for pocket change for this or that. Which Leo always paid, not begrudging the money, begrudging the *time*. There was no reason to believe that Reggie Morgan wanted anything to do with them, he only wanted Leo's money. Despite Reggie's very vocal protestations that he was lonely and wanted to spend them with his wife and son, Leo knew the truth: his father wanted coin.

"She isn't avoiding me." Leo chewed his food. He swallowed it, not tasting, not caring, just knowing he had to eat. His clothes were getting too loose, and he'd hate to have the added worry of tailoring his entire wardrobe all over again.

"She's been seen out with Lord Grabe again." His mother liked to drop bombshells.

This one didn't detonate. It just dropped and smothered him beneath its weight. "He is quite the catch." Each word hurt leaving his mouth, but he was glad for it. He wanted something to hurt right now. His world had been upended—first by the joy of Prudence, and now at her utter absence and his father's presence. Nothing felt right. Nothing felt *correct*.

So he'd poured himself into his ledgers. He increased his correspondence with the men on the floor of the stock market, using their observations to gauge the feelings of the traders. And then he invested, for himself, for his clients. And he made money. That was his daily life, like a mill grinding wheat into flour. Interrupted, of course, by disturbing paternal interludes that emptied his pockets.

But Parliament had ended for the year. Most of his clients had vacated London for their country estates, to hole up and enjoy the winter with their families. Cold had seeped in, and while it had not snowed, the morning frost crusted over shallow puddles, only to break free in the meager afternoon warmth.

His mother kept dabbing her nose with a handkerchief. He'd double the coal order to keep her warm. He hadn't noticed the chill himself. There was very little he had noticed.

"Lord Grabe has all but announced he's looking for a wife. Do you think he would dare marry a widowed American?" His mother was incessant.

Leo put down his cutlery. "Is there something you'd like to say, Mama?"

She stared at him a moment, then put down hers as well, giving him absolute attention. "I'm trying to spur you to action."

"By giving me the latest gossip on Lord Grabe? What action would I have, other than buying the man a celebratory drink?"

"I'm your mother, Leo. I see you in ways you cannot fathom. And I am trying to see if you harbor feelings for Mrs. Cabot. She's a good woman. And I like her." It was a ringing endorsement for marriage, coming from her.

"I'm shocked," Leo said. "I thought there was no woman on earth who you would encourage me to pursue." Because that's what this had been. A pursuit without point. The leaden feeling in his limbs worsened. What a fool he had been. Why had he continued to write her, begging her to see him, when she never wrote him back?

His mother leveled a warning look at him. But then the footman interrupted dinner. Jeffrey bent to whisper in his ear: "Your father is here to see you."

"We are at dinner!" Leo whispered back.

"He begs his forgiveness. Something about the cold?" The young man's face creased with apprehension.

Leo threw his napkin on the table. "We have a guest, apparently. And not a welcome one."

His father stood in the foyer, this time with Granson. In all the days before, Granson had not entered the house. This evening, as the young man doffed his cap, Leo saw how he'd lost a great deal of his bulk. He was no longer wide, likely the result of hard labor found in the village.

"What are doing here?" Leo asked, his voice cold, but he didn't care. He was sick of his father's games.

"Can a man not drop in on his son for a chat whenever he wishes?" Reggie asked.

"We've chatted already today. And I believe I gave you two pounds sterling while I was at it."

"Which I was very grateful for, you are a good boy," Reggie said.

"We're freezin'," Granson said, his country accent wide and broad, sounding nothing like Reggie.

"Does your boarding house not supply you with enough coal?" Leo asked. Fine, he'd give him a coal allowance too.

"There's been a development of sorts there," Reggie said, gesturing with his good hand, the other one tightly fisted and almost bone white.

Granson turned his face and Leo caught sight of his swollen and bruised face. "They took our money and turned us out."

"Good heavens!" came his mother's voice behind him. "Jeffrey, have Cook fill some water bottles for the Mr. Morgans, and have Daisy stoke the fire in the drawing room and ready two beds in the guest room."

Leo rounded on her. "What?" If Reggie slept here, he would embed like a tick. They would never be free of his wheedling, weaseling schemes.

His mother gave him a firm look. "I'll not allow them to freeze to death in the streets."

"He would have done me!" Leo protested.

His mother looked over at Reggie, who had the temerity to look ashamed of himself. "Yes well, we aren't him, are we? Compassion is a worthy trait. While we are at it, send for a physician to look over Granson. Make sure there's nothing worse than a blackened eye."

Granson, yes, he was willing to help the man who was his half-nephew, who he'd known since he was small. They were near in age, Granson being only a handful of years younger than Leo. He had nowhere to go than to be with Reggie. But Reggie? Leo couldn't hide his disdain.

His mother gripped his arm, leaning on him instead of her cane. "Look at him, Leo. Really look. He isn't the man you knew. This one is old, lame, and has no use of his left arm. What would you have me do?"

"Find a better hotel," Leo spat.

But his mother kept her level gaze on him, using that old trick every mother had likely performed on their child since the beginning of time. The silent command. She was not asking, she was telling. And Leo had no choice in the matter.

Leo pulled his coat and hat out of the closet where Jeffrey stored them. "I'll fetch a healer of some sort."

⇶⇷

IT TOOK PRUDENCE some time before she mustered the courage to knock on Leo's door. Indeed, the last time she'd been here, it had been a warm day. Now, the snow crunched under her boots as she descended from the hired hack. When the door swung open, she was informed Leo wasn't at home. He was out with his *family*—his father, his mother, and his nephew.

She left her calling card, but it smarted somehow. There had been drives in the park with Lord Grabe, training with the Ladies' Alpine Society, and then Lord Berringbone invited them all out to the country for the holidays. They'd stay the month, and Ophelia said that the family suspected he would announce his engagement to Lady Emily.

All the while, she had expected Leo to be there for her, waiting. It was the height of selfishness. And shame consumed her as she dismissed the hack, choosing instead to walk back to the Strawbridge. Leo had a family now. A bigger one, strained as it was. And she had her own busy life.

The cold seeped through her boots. More fashion than comfort for these ones. If she were being honest with herself, she'd dressed well today, to see Leo. Not sure what she wanted to have happen. Admittedly, she missed him. Every time Justine gave another wild outburst, she wanted to be able to share her friend's antics with Leo, and let him shake his head in fondness for her.

It was silly of her to try any further relationship with Leo Moon. She could see that now. They'd both asked for a summer dalliance, and that's what they'd gotten. A quiet, subtle love affair that never reached the ears of London's gossip pages. She should be very satisfied with herself.

But she wasn't. Since she dressed for fashion, and not the sudden winter chill that descended upon London, she ducked into a nearby chocolate shop to warm up. The hot chocolate was delicious, but the package of French-style chocolates that she tucked under her arm would manage her for the next few days. Until she left for the Berringbone country house.

>>><<<

GRANSON WAS AN excellent carriage driver. Even with unmatched horses, he guided the vehicle with absolute ease. "I'd like to be a hack driver, I think," the man announced. "I like being outside."

Within a few weeks of Reggie and Granson's arrival at his home, they'd burrowed in. But Leo found he didn't mind. Granson sought honest work, and his father stopped talking so damn much. Indeed, his mother and father sat in the drawing room, taking turns reading to one another in the late morning, when the sun shone its brightest.

With Granson occupied, and his father content, Leo was free to spend his days working again, which he did. And with the holidays soon, his father was pressing about decorating the house—which they'd never done. His mother seemed happy to do it, so he gave them an allowance, wondering what would happen with the two of them together.

But it seemed to work, somehow. They never touched or were physically affectionate with each other. Now that his basic needs were met, Reggie no longer attempted his flirtatious seductions. Which was a relief.

Jeffrey told him that Mrs. Cabot had called while they were out purchasing the holiday decorations. Granson drove the carriage for the practice, with Leo up top giving him scarcely needed directions. The parents were inside, snug with fur blankets and hot water bottles to keep warm.

But then winter truly descended, and the temperatures plummeted. He couldn't abandon his elderly parents and Granson to go see Prudence. He had obligations here. Indeed, his mother told him that under no circumstance was he escaping hanging the boughs of holly they'd liberated from the Covent

Garden stalls that morning.

The bell rang for dinner—the first time it had been needed in ages. And he joined his family at the table, listening to his parents' ideas for the month ahead, answering when Granson asked advice on routes around London, and discussing the needs of the household for the impending cold.

After dinner, instead of retiring with a snifter of spiced brandy, Leo *decorated*.

"A little to the right!" his mother called from below.

Leo stood on his tiptoes then, on the first floor, next to the stairs, hanging the pine boughs. Granson was behind him, affixing the bright red holly berries where the bough touched the ceiling.

"No, your left!" Reggie called.

Leo rolled his eyes and did as his mother directed. He drove a nail into the wood and hung the bough.

"Bravo!" His mother clapped when he finished the draping of the garland. "The silver bells next, don't you think, Reggie?"

"Absolutely." His parents hobbled across the foyer where the boxes sat. "Lena, did you remember the red ribbons?"

"Of course I did. Oh, but they are up in the drawing room. Leo, would you mind fetching the bag of red ribbons? It's on top of the mending basket."

Leo grumbled his assent, but he couldn't help but feel dumbstruck in this domesticity. He had a real mother and real father. And there weren't any schemes or desperate measures being discussed. No scrounging, no excessive drinking; was this what other people had gotten in their childhoods? No wonder there was a term "domestic bliss."

The only thing Leo thought could be better was if Prudence were there. He wanted her to see them, his parents, this way. He wanted her to chat with Granson, tell him about America and Minnesota and the railways. She was the only thing missing.

He ran to his study and jotted a note. He had to catch her before this sudden snowstorm became too much for the streets of London. "I'll be out for a moment," he told his mother as he pulled on a jacket.

Granson was by his side in a second. "I'll do it."

"Not at all, I can manage," Leo assured him.

The sheer pleading in his nephew's gray eyes, which he was surprised to notice looked exactly like his own, made Leo soften. "Fine then. Take this to the Strawbridge hotel. Leave it with the front desk and come home straightaway. The weather will be getting worse as night falls."

Granson reached past Leo to grab his overcoat and popped his hat on, tipping the brim to him with an off-kilter smile, revealing chipped teeth. Again, it was the first time Leo had noticed them, and he wondered how Reggie had treated him during his childhood. Leo gave Granson the note.

"Hunker down if you need to, but do try to return quickly," Leo said, listening to the wind picking up outside.

"Obliged." Granson wound a woolen scarf around his neck and stepped out.

THE TRAIN RIDE down to Berringbone was enjoyable, and traveling in style made everything more enjoyable. She hadn't heard from Leo before they boarded the train, and she wondered if she should have written him to let him know that she would be in the country for the entire month of December. In the end, with the snowstorm and the freezing temperatures, she didn't send a note, not wanting to force someone to deliver the letter in hazardous circumstances.

"My brother tells me he's planning on a holiday ball," Ophelia said in the carriage, snug under the fur blanket with Justine. Prudence and Eleanor were on the opposite side, just as tucked in. The coach ran smoothly on the snowy road, as if the ruts were filled in.

"Who will be on the guest list?" Eleanor asked, thoroughly

ensconced in the blankets.

"Essentially the same guests as last year," Ophelia said.

Prudence's heart leapt. Leo and his mother had attended last year. If invited, surely they would venture here.

"But there is concern about traveling if the weather keeps up as is now."

They all looked out the windows where fat, fluffy snowflakes fell in a slow, dizzyingly innocent descent.

But it did continue. After a fortnight, Berringbone cancelled the ball. It was a reckless proposition, as not only was it a perilous journey for his guests, but also the extra servants that would be required to bring in and prepare the food and the house. It was still a jolly holiday with the Bridewells and Prudence's friends. The Pipers came out to be with Eleanor and her new husband, and Georgie seemed content with listening to Mrs. Piper's chronic ailments.

But the days were slow for Prudence. They hiked in the snow with heavy woolen jackets on, allowing them a better idea of the conditions on the Matterhorn. She waited for the post to come, and when it did, was always disappointed when nothing came from Leo.

Until the day the post finally arrived, practically overflowing with letters for everyone.

"The weather," Ophelia said as way of an explanation. The piles were sorted, and Prudence's mail had been forwarded from the hotel. It contained two letters for Georgie, and a delicious stack for Prudence from her family. But as she flipped through the pile, one unsealed missive caught her attention.

Leo's handwriting was clear and precise. His words simple and lacking any subtext of scandal. But Prudence was convinced she knew what it meant. She read between his *sorry I missed you*, and his *deeply regret not being available*. The feelings could be of her own invention, but perhaps they weren't.

Clutching her remaining letters, she stood, looked at Georgie and said, "I have to go to London."

"What, now?" Justine asked, looking at the window outside where even more snow fell.

Prudence followed her gaze to the weather, the dark, the difficulty such a journey would entail.

"For Mr. Moon?" Eleanor asked quietly.

Prudence nodded, afraid that if she spoke aloud, tears might start to trail down her cheeks. There was so much emotion that she hadn't allowed herself to feel, all struggling to get out all at once.

The rest of the women were on their feet immediately.

"I'll help you pack," Georgie said, moving uncharacteristically quickly.

"I'll arrange a carriage to the train, and find the schedule. Father has all of that." Ophelia strode off to her father's study. If anyone could make her logistics smoother, it was their leader.

"I'll get you a basket prepped downstairs. Still a journey, and you'll need some tea and sandwiches." Justine grabbed Eleanor.

"I'll get the warm bricks," Eleanor said. "I know what to do, Justine. No need to prompt."

The room emptied, and Prudence's eyes glassed over with tears at the support from her friends. She couldn't live without them, it seemed. They were a new family here in England, since her birth family was so very far away. She clutched their letters to her breast and headed up to her room to get changed.

She caught up to Georgie on the stairs.

"I think I might stay here for this," Georgie said, her wide face scrunching up in question.

"That would be—" Prudence hadn't thought this through. "—that would probably be for the best."

In her bedroom, Prudence changed into her heaviest wool frock, with thick woolen underthings. Georgie was halfway through packing when Ophelia knocked and entered.

"Father is going with you," she said. "He'll wire ahead to make sure you have a carriage there waiting for you. It's too cold to take chances."

Prudence nodded, but doubt suddenly struck. Was she making something out of nothing? Was Leo only being polite in response to her visit? She had to put that thought out of her mind before she lost her courage.

※※※

JEFFREY APPEARED IN the drawing room with a silver tray. "A telegram, sir."

It was nearly Christmas, and the room was filled with a sensory delight Leo had never known. Between his mother and father, the room looked and smelled like the very definition of cozy. The scents of cinnamon and clove wafted above the aroma of beeswax candles, and the garlands of pine gave a whimsical touch and a heady smell of forest. They were all there together in this beautiful room, the silver bells glinting in the firelight. His body felt loose from the spiced wine and the brandy that had followed dinner.

Jeffrey brought the platter over, and Leo snatched the paper up. She was coming. In the cold and the snow. He looked at the clock in the corner. They had an hour before the train arrived. Enough time to prepare the carriage, and gather up extra blankets. Would he take her back to her Strawbridge, or would he bring her here?

He looked up, panic clutching his chest. "Granson, would you be willing to drive me to the train station?"

"What, now?" he asked, his gaze going to the dark window, where they could see fat snowflakes wafting to the ground.

"We need to meet the next train in an hour." Leo caught the exchanged glance between his mother and father. "Don't look at each other like that."

His mother ignored his comment. "Would this be a telegram from Mrs. Cabot, by any chance?"

"No," he said, if only to prove her wrong, even if she was

right in spirit. "But she is arriving on the next train."

A smile cracked his mother's face, and his father hid his grin, knowing it would only irritate Leo.

"That pretty bird you had with you at the cottage?" Granson asked. When Leo gave him a harsh look, he added, "She seemed very nice."

"Will you drive?" Leo repeated, getting to his feet. There was so much to do, but he couldn't figure out what he needed to happen first.

"I'll get the horses ready and bring the carriage around front." Granson put his snifter down. As he was leaving the room, he put a hand on Leo's shoulder. "I'm glad. You look a proper man with her by your side."

"I'll alert the cook to warm up something for a meal. She'll no doubt need something to fortify her after a cold journey," his mother said, accepting the cane that Reggie handed to her.

"I'll find Daisy and let her know to remake my bed. I'll bunk in with Granson tonight." Reggie stood and then gave that old mischievous grin. "Unless Mrs. Cabot will be bunking with you, that is."

His mother, now on her feet, hit him with her cane. "Don't be presumptuous, Reggie. That was always your problem."

"According to you, I've had a great deal of problems," he grumbled.

"Obviously." His mother sniffed. "And how fortunate for you that you'll finally listen to me and fix them."

"I'll tell Daisy and then move my things," Reggie said, still smothering a grin.

Leo bolted from the room, changing into warmer clothes and shouting down to his mother to have Cook prep warm bricks, a hot water bottle, and to alert Jeffrey to find all the heavy carriage blankets and put them inside after Granson brought it around front.

>>>><<<<

THE WIND HOWLED through the train station. Despite her woolen ensemble from head to toe, Prudence shivered. Her toes were hard chunks of ice crammed in her boots, and she flexed her fingers to keep them warm. She held a carpetbag, while her trunk had been loaded onto the next train and delivered to the hotel.

She put her head down to move through the cold, until she heard her name. Snapping up to see who shouted for her over the howl of the winter winds in the practically deserted station, she staggered when she saw Leo.

He hurried to her, taking her carpetbag and swooping her toward the exit. She moved with him, staring up at him. They didn't speak. He locked eyes with her, and she felt a surge of comfort and safety. Of *rightness*.

The carriage was ready, and the driver tipped his cap to her beneath his mountain of blankets. She climbed in and immediately relaxed. It was warm—hot bricks sat in the foot warmer position, and there was a hot water bottle wrapped in soft cotton, meant for her to hold, which she did gratefully.

Leo arranged a blanket over her and hit the carriage to spur it on. They stared at each other. Prudence didn't know what to say. Her chest felt tight. Seeing his face, with its cutting cheekbones and his steel-gray eyes, made her jaw clench in wanting.

"Prudence." His voice was hoarse and so welcome to hear.

"Leo." His name was like music, as if she were singing to him when she said his name.

"You came." His body was rigid, coiled, as if he were going to spring forward. She wanted him to—just to be nearer. If she were going to read his expression, she thought he was happy to see her. "Why?"

Her stomach dropped. Perhaps he hadn't missed her the way she had missed him. The months apart had been a slow, quiet agony. The drives in Hyde Park with Lord Grabe were tedious, the endless hours of training with her friends had been distractions, pouring herself into a physical world so that she didn't have to feel the weight of his absence. Her eyes dropped away from him, and unbidden a shivering gasp came out of her.

"Prudence," he whispered. "I missed you."

She looked up at him again, desperate now for any kind word.

"I wrote you letter after letter, everything from long-form desperation, to short notes begging to see you. Why now?" The mask he wore for everyone else was gone. She looked at his vulnerable self. The one who had begged for her.

She closed her eyes, not wanting to admit her pettiness, her selfishness. "I—" She couldn't manage it. "—I only just got your last note."

He looked pained, as if what she said wasn't enough. It wasn't a lie, but it wasn't the whole truth, which was a truth she couldn't admit: that his unwillingness to get the highest bid at the ball hurt her. That his attempt to abandon her in a strange countryside in a foreign country felt like a betrayal of the most basic kind.

But she wanted to hear his side. His absence felt worse than any of these. All of those words clogged in her throat, the emotions spinning out of control.

"I'm glad you're here." Leo looked out the window. "Things have changed since the last we spoke."

Again the panic that swam in the brackish pond of her feelings rose to the surface. The carriage lurched to a stop. Had he met someone else?

"My mother is happy that you came as well," Leo assured her, getting out first to help her down.

The chill bit into her, and those steps into the house were almost painful on her toes that had only begun to thaw. They entered the house, the familiar foyer, and the boyish footman helped her with her hat and gloves as Mrs. Moon leaned over the first-floor railing.

"Mrs. Cabot!" She looked happier than last Prudence had

seen her. There was a blush to her cheeks and a surprising new ease to the way she moved. Behind her came Mr. Morgan.

Prudence startled and looked to Leo.

"Part of the changes," Leo admitted. But he didn't look stressed by the man's presence, only chagrined.

"Come up to the drawing room and warm up, once you have all those sodden layers off you." Mrs. Moon turned away, leaning on her cane. "Come along, Reggie," she said to Mr. Morgan, as if he weren't waiting for her.

Clearly something had changed if Mrs. Moon bossed Mr. Morgan around as if he were her lapdog. She looked to Leo again, and he smiled. "Let's get you upstairs next to the fire. Cook has prepared a tray for you."

After Prudence had finally doffed her fur hat and woolen everything else, she noticed the décor. Aside from a shop, she'd never seen a place so festive for the holidays. Pine boughs punctuated with red holly berries and silver bells accentuated every architectural detail. Even the string of red wooden balls lent a festive air, coiled in a large glass bowl, with preserved feathers instead of hothouse flowers.

"This is beautiful," she said, peering at all the efforts.

"I'd save your praise for the drawing room." Leo offered his arm to her, and she took it.

Now devoid of so many other layers of fabric, his arm felt like a dose of laudanum. It was pleasure and honey-sweet drunkenness all at once. They ascended the staircase, and the pleasant aroma of cinnamon and cloves, of beeswax and lemon polish, all came floating in around her. Her past homes had never smelled so pleasing, but somehow, this was the most she'd ever felt "at home."

It was as if the feeling of taking off her shoes and stockings became a scent. The feeling of taking all the pins from her hair, and the corset from her body, and changing out a linen shift damp from the sweat of her body, it was here, embodied in different senses.

And then they entered the drawing room, the epicenter of this harmony. Draped again in pine boughs and silver bells, the spiced scent stronger here, with the crackling fire to warm her, a tray of food, and the welcoming smile of her dear friend, Mrs. Moon.

"Sit here, darling," Mrs. Moon said, gesturing to the chair next to the fire on one side, and Mrs. Moon on the other.

It didn't escape Prudence's notice that Mrs. Moon called her darling. Other than the Spanish Doña who had called everyone darling, no one had felt her dear enough to call her so. It felt extravagant.

Prudence's toes weren't the only bits thawing. Her heart ached to belong here, to stay here, to revel in this welcome. Gratefully, she sank into the chair and Leo took up the one nearest to her. *He wanted to be next to her!*

"It is lovely to see you again, Mrs. Cabot," Mr. Morgan said from across the small table that held her tray.

"And you, Mr. Morgan." Prudence smiled, her cheeks hurting with the thawing of her skin. It seemed all had been patched up in the weeks she'd missed Leo. She was happy for them—they seemed complete somehow, more relaxed than she'd ever seen Mrs. Moon. And Mr. Morgan seemed like an altogether gentler person than he had when he'd first met her in her hotel lobby.

"Mr. Morgan is responsible for the decoration you see," Mrs. Moon said, gesturing to the garlands and bells.

"I beg your pardon," Leo said with mock indignation.

Prudence couldn't help but giggle at his teasing tone. They seemed like a family!

"Leo hung it all," Mr. Morgan admitted.

"Why not have help from your footman?"

Mrs. Moon again waved her hand. "This was a family affair, and needed to be done by the family."

"They say that, knowing that I was the only one tall enough in this family to do so," Leo said wryly, but not without affection.

"Tuck in, dear. You must be famished." Mrs. Moon looked

pointedly at the plate in front of Prudence.

As they bickered, Prudence ate the pork with a cranberry sauce, the chunks of seared potatoes, and the thick slice of bread with butter and honey. Her stomach was full and her heart content. She wanted to forget any misgivings she'd ever had about Leo, about their affair, all of it, and mindlessly reenter the times they had in the spring. She had missed him far more than she'd been willing to admit.

But then another man walked into the room. He was welcomed and admitted not as a servant but as one of their own. Prudence stared as Leo introduced Granson Morgan.

He was the stout man that had been asking for Lenny Morgan at the cottage. Prudence went cold. The one that made Leo willing to abandon her in the countryside because he'd appeared. And now he was, by the looks of it, living here?

Prudence glanced between the happy faces of her hosts and hostess. None of them felt his presence was amiss. Alarm bells clanged in her head. Her heart began to hurt—the reminder of Leo's dismissal of her safety roaring to the surface.

"I am feeling a little overwhelmed," Prudence said to no one in particular. "I think I might need to retire early."

Leo sprang to his feet. "I can show you to your room."

Prudence looked around to see if anyone else could—but Mrs. Moon had her cane, Mr. Morgan would be just as inappropriate, and like hell she was going anywhere with Granson Morgan.

Leo walked her down the hallway, but while he waited for her to speak, her mind whirled like a top.

"Prudence, I don't know why—"

They reached her door. "I'm really very tired, Leo." Prudence put her hand on the doorknob. "Let's talk tomorrow."

He nodded, his expression strangely open to her. She was able to read his confusion and disappointment and hope that had all flickered across the sharp lines and steel-gray eyes. "Tomorrow."

Prudence slunk gratefully into the guest room. She took off her boots by the fire that was already warming the room, and then began to cry. There was no true reason for it—not just one anyway. She cried because she was exhausted. She cried because she was lonely. She cried because Leo had wanted to abandon her because of the man who now lived in his house. She cried because she was still scared that this man was in the house and she didn't know how he came to be there, only that he was some kind of relation.

She cried because she wanted to be with her friends, but at the same time was glad she came. She cried because she missed the steady presence of Gregory, even if he hadn't been the husband that she'd wanted. She cried because she was a young widow and she didn't get to have the lives that Ophelia and Justine got to have. And she sobbed because she was so lucky, and yet not.

Chapter Twelve

L EO WAS UP at dawn. He was normally an early riser, but not usually this early. He'd slept poorly, anticipating his talk with Prudence. She'd seemed so happy to arrive last night, and he was sure that she felt... what, exactly? She'd traveled through a snowstorm to see him. Clearly she felt something positive.

And what was he asking for? His training as a broker reared up. He needed to be clear about what he wanted before he could make any demands of her. They certainly couldn't be so cavalier as to fall into bed together without making sure feelings were known. Even though he'd missed her so much. The knowledge that she slept in under his roof made it difficult to think straight. The memory of her taste, of her feel, the swell of her calves as they melted into the back of her knee, and the rise of her strong thighs... he needed to not think that way. He was getting hard, and that made thinking impossible.

Leo worked in his study, and when he heard stirrings of others in the house, he took the daily newspapers into the breakfast room. He felt as if he were lying in wait for Prudence. And in some ways, he was. But not as one might ambush an enemy, more as a man impatient for the woman he liked very much.

His mother would not be down for breakfast—she had always taken a tray in her room. Reggie would sometimes take a tray and sometimes come down. "Jeffrey," Leo said as the footman came in with his coffee, "would you be so good as to make Mr. Morgan a tray? He should take breakfast in his room."

Granson appeared, filled his plate and sat down. His mouth full of jammy toast, he asked, "What?"

Leo shook his head, as if he weren't wishing Granson gone with all of his being. Then Prudence appeared. She looked lovely. Her dark-green day dress was embroidered with white and pale-green botanical designs, and Leo barely managed to keep himself from sighing as she swished across the room.

Granson watched Leo watching Prudence. He swallowed his toast hard and picked up his plate. "Excuse me, I have somewhere to be." He scurried out of the room, for which, if he noticed correctly, both he and Prudence were glad.

Leo said nothing as Prudence fixed her plate. Jeffrey asked if she would prefer tea or coffee, and Leo was gratified when she answered coffee, just like him. "Good morning," he said to her as she sat down next to him.

She gave him a tentative smile, which confused him. Prudence was known for her embarrassingly large American smiles. He frowned as she returned his greeting in a small voice.

Then he noticed the puffy redness about her eyes. She'd been crying. He didn't know what to say, so he put his hand on the table, palm up, inviting her to hold his hand.

She looked at it, as if she were debating the wisdom of touching him, but then slid her hand into his. Even that small contact felt so good to have.

"May I ask what has you out of sorts?" Leo curled his fingers around her hand.

She looked away. Leo didn't blame her, speaking of discomfort was against his upbringing as well. But they had to find some way through the thornbush in their relationship. She withdrew her hand as Jeffrey entered and placed a coffee pot between them. He poured Prudence a cup.

"Jeffrey, please excuse us. I'll ring for you when we are finished." Leo dismissed him, once again taking the room for the two of them.

Prudence sipped at her cup with both hands, clearly fortifying herself. Leo could do nothing, say nothing. He was at an utter loss.

"Who is Granson?" she asked after she cleared her throat.

Leo started. "He is my father's grandson and aide-de-camp. Why?"

"*Who* is he? Was he the man that appeared at the cottage last summer? The menacing stranger?" Her eyes finally met his, but he saw no warmth there. This must be how she was when she did business. Cool, polite, detached. Her bearing was confident but not aggressive. Like encountering a wall of smooth concrete.

"He was, yes."

"The one asking for Lenny Morgan."

"Yes."

"Which was you, at one point."

"Correct." Leo felt like he was being interrogated. "What is this about?"

Prudence squeezed her eyes shut. When she opened them again, she took another big sip of coffee with both hands. "Do you remember that morning at the cottage?"

"Of course I do. I remember every moment at that cottage." Leo had never dreamed it could have been so good between them. When he'd bought it outright in his own name years ago as an investment, he'd never thought to use it as a vacation home for his... what was Prudence to him? Mistress sounded so wrong.

"Then you'll remember your panic over Granson's appearance there."

"Yes. And at the time, based on what I knew of my father and his previous activities, it was warranted. I was unwilling to risk an encounter with my father while you were at my side."

She cocked her head to the side, and her expression wasn't a smile, nor was it exactly a grimace. Leo did not like what it meant. "If that fear was about me, why did you tell me that you would leave me there?"

"I certainly did not say that," Leo protested. Did he say that? It didn't seem like he would.

"You, in fact, did. I refused to leave without knowing more about what had you spooked, and instead of explaining or even looking at me directly, you told me in no uncertain terms that you were leaving and I could stay if I liked."

"I was only trying to get you to come with me," Leo protested. Now that she put it like that, he did remember saying it. But he hadn't meant it. Not in so many words. It was an ultimatum employed to get her to do the right thing.

"Can you look at that scenario from my point of view? I'm an American in the English countryside, and the man with whom I'm having a scandalous affair threatens to leave me in the middle of nowhere when an unknown man who scares him shows up?"

Leo frowned. "But I wouldn't have left you there."

"But you said you would."

"Yes, but I didn't *mean* it."

Prudence sat back in her chair. He could see the muscle in her jaw ticking. "And now that very man who scared you lives in this house. The man who frightened you enough to abandon me slept under the same roof as both of us last night."

"You were there when my father arrived," Leo said. Prudence was twisting things around. Granson was helpful and mild. Really, he was a wonderful man, needing only a bit of direction now that he was in London. "You saw how convoluted and messy everything was between us."

Prudence looked away, and Leo could see tears shining in her eyes.

"Prudence, I didn't mean to hurt you. I don't want to hurt you. Is that why you stopped reading my letters?"

A giant tear rolled down her cheek, and Leo realized then and there that he'd rather be punched in the face by Granson than witness this. Prudence nodded her head. So that had been his error: threatening to abandon her to a man that he'd convinced her was dangerous. Oh, that made him feel very bad. Very bad indeed.

"But I didn't know. If you'd told me, I could have—"

"—Explained?" she interrupted. "I asked for that explanation, and you refused to give it. Not there in the cottage, not on the train. You made it very clear, Leo. I existed for fucking, not for talking."

Her vulgarity made him draw back. He couldn't even speak. That's what she thought of him? Was that the American brazenness coming to bear in their conversation? "That is not—"

"I know you'd never say it aloud, Leo." Prudence leveled him with a gaze that he'd never seen before on anyone. The malice there. "Because you're too polite. But was that not our initial agreement? No relationship, just bedsport? Well, we did that." She looked out the window.

Leo still couldn't speak. The world had upended itself, and he hadn't a clue what was happening.

"The weather has cleared up. I'll take a hack to the hotel and be out of your hair." Prudence stood, drank the rest of the coffee, and left the room. Leo stared at her untouched plate of food. He felt as if an explosive had been set off in the room, and he sat there dumbfounded, ears ringing.

He was still sitting there when he heard the front door slam. She'd left. How had everything gone so horribly, horribly wrong? She had seemed so happy last night, dazzled by the holiday décor, by the friendly chatter of his parents. It was the sight of Granson that changed her. Reminded her of the perceived injustice, for honestly, who in their right mind would leave a woman alone in the countryside to be discovered by undesirables? He certainly would not do so.

But he had said he would, and why would she not believe him?

It was too early for scotch. Besides, he found that he liked the sweet molasses taste of Kentucky bourbon.

>>><<<

When Prudence arrived at the hotel, she discovered they'd rented out her suite. She knew this was a possibility, and all of her extra trunks were packed and stowed in the basement of the hotel. She was, after all, planning to be gone for at least a month.

According to Mr. Brown, the red-cheeked manager with brown hair and red whiskers on his face, a minor German aristocrat arrived and needed a place befitting their rank. They were perhaps related to Prince Albert? Or had met him once? Or perhaps they were to be the new ambassadors? Mr. Brown was unclear and wheezing, making it very difficult to follow the very long and apologetic explanation. This same aristocrat had likewise filled the rest of the rooms with his extensive entourage, and there was no place for Prudence to stay there.

Still, she collected her mail that had not yet been forwarded to the countryside and left.

With no room at the inn, which Prudence tried to find humor in during this holiday time, she was at a loss of where to go. She most decidedly did not want to return to Berringbone's estate where there were games planned and jolly times to be had. She needed a place to hole up and lick her wounds, like a stray cat. She went the only place she could think of: the in-town home of Ophelia's family.

A year ago, if someone told Prudence that she would be imposing upon a viscount during the month of December, she would have been appalled. But their friendships had grown deeper, and she knew the staff wouldn't turn her away. She stopped and sent a note to Lord Rascomb regarding her hopes to stay until her hotel suite became available, and after a nibble at the café where she'd met with Mr. Morgan, she went to the Rascomb townhome, weary and in need of solace.

The housekeeper, the solid Mrs. Murty, knew to expect her arrival, and while Lord Rascomb had gone out, and would be gone until late, Prudence was welcome to stay and avail herself of anything he had to offer, including access to his private cellar. Prudence was grateful for the hospitality, almost bursting into tears to have access to the indoor plumbing of the residence, and the cold cheese and fruit tray with excellent Madeira port.

Under normal circumstances, Prudence would not be someone to drink to excess. But tonight, after her hot bath that left her pale skin red like a lobster, it seemed not only a good idea, but the best possible one. She paced in her room, drinking from her glass, railing against Leo. She redrew her words from earlier that morning, making them more elegant, more pointed, more biting.

And then she went into the other things that he'd done to hurt her. About how he didn't win her at the ball. About how he kept himself so apart from her with the exception of when they were in bed together.

She drank until she started to laugh. Then she finished off the plate of hard, salty cheese and fell asleep.

The next morning came without remorse. Days did not have any compunction when dealing with the brokenhearted. Her body felt stiff and her eyes felt dry, but she felt calmer than she had the day before. Having no plan for the day, and no company—not that she would be fit for it anyway—Prudence spent longer brushing her hair and massaging lotion into her dry hands.

Without prompting, Mrs. Murty brought up a tea tray in the midafternoon, noting no doubt that Prudence had not eaten yet, nor come out of her rooms.

"I wanted to make you aware that you will be having company this evening, and that dinner has been ordered," the housekeeper said as she placed the tray on the table near the fireplace.

Prudence felt her cheeks heat. Had her one-sided argument grown too loud last night? Had they noted how much wine she'd drunk? Embarrassment flooded her. "Thank you, Mrs. Murty."

"Mr. Sellers has sent over for your trunks at the hotel. Perhaps there is a gown from there we can ready for you?"

It was then that Prudence realized she had left her day dress out and had managed to spill wine on it last night in her pacing. Mrs. Murty had no doubt noticed that. And noted her lack of luggage.

"Thank you. Yes, if you have someone to spare for me, I would be very grateful."

"Of course. I shall send a maid up once the trunk arrives." Mrs. Murty left, perfunctory and thorough, as a housekeeper must be.

It made Prudence think of Mrs. Moon, and her background as a housekeeper. The thought of Mrs. Moon was the first pierce of that day's armor, and it wasn't long until Prudence was back in the bed, wishing she could sleep through the fact that her chest felt as if it might cave in. She should have wondered what company was coming, but she didn't care. Nothing mattered.

She must have slept, because the scratching at the door woke her. In crept a maid with one of Prudence's dinner gowns in her arms. And not far behind her was Justine, followed by Eleanor, and then Ophelia running down the hallway to keep up.

"You're here!" Justine crowed.

"And awake!" Eleanor added. Eleanor was wearing house slippers and shucked them off and climbed into Prudence's bed.

Ophelia flounced onto the end of the bed. "How did it go?"

Prudence sat up, and they all saw her face.

"Oh," Justine said, the response they all seemed to have as one. "That bad?"

Prudence flopped back down. "I can't."

"Of course not," Eleanor tutted, taking Prudence's hand. "Now, what can you not do?"

"Everything," Prudence groaned. "Anything. Be a reasonable person. Love another person. Forgive. Forget."

"Do we know what exactly Mr. Moon did that was so unforgivable?" Ophelia whispered to Justine.

"Do we want to know is the better question," Justine said.

"I'll tell you the details," Prudence said. "If you want."

Prudence opened up every secret to her friends, the bits she'd glossed over before. She ended her recital with yesterday morning's argument, and his inability to speak after she accused him of wanting her only for bedsport. She even admitted precisely what she'd said that shocked Leo so much. Even Justine was shocked.

Prudence lay back again, unsure of what to do with herself. She felt tired all over again. Eleanor left the bed, leaving a cold spot behind. But soon she returned with Mrs. Murty's tea tray. Eleanor poured a cup and made Prudence drink it.

"I don't really even like tea that much," Prudence protested, but the other three all gave her resoundingly cold glares. Eleanor poured a second cup after Prudence finished the first, and then insisted on Prudence eating the nibbles left on the tray.

"I wish we could just go now," Prudence said.

"Go where?" Ophelia asked.

"Switzerland. I want to go now."

Ophelia ducked away, almost as if Prudence had struck her. "There are far too many details to prep, Prudence. There is no way we could leave yet."

They sat in silence.

"But what about if Tristan and I went ahead with her?" Eleanor suggested. "We could keep her company, and perhaps we could stop in France for a bit before we set off?"

France! Yes, what a delightful side trip. Prudence looked to Ophelia. They still had much to look over to see if it was possible.

"We can ask my father tonight at dinner," Ophelia said. "Besides, it might be nice to have someone scout ahead."

"Excellent!" Eleanor clapped.

At dinner, Lord Rascomb expressed interest, and Lady Rascomb suggested she might go along as well, to keep company with Prudence since newlyweds could sometimes be too caught up in themselves.

Prudence couldn't taste the meal, but she drank her wine with enthusiasm, which made her queasy, and she excused herself from the drawing room after dinner.

When she awoke the next morning, she had a headache, but was pleased with herself for not crying. She took a quick, cold bath and changed into her day dress and went downstairs, suddenly famished. The hour was later than she thought, and the butler, Mr. Sellers, was directing the footmen in cleaning up the breakfast room. Prudence snagged a piece of toast and some coffee, which was all she really wanted anyway.

But after her coffee, Prudence couldn't find the other women all morning. It was as if they had all vanished. She wandered from room to room, but they were not in their bedrooms or out of doors, training in the snow. Nor were they keeping company with Lady Rascomb in the drawing room. Prudence found a spot in the library where she amused herself reading some Sir Walter Scott.

"There you are!" Eleanor cried from the doorway. "I've been looking for you all over."

Prudence looked up from her spot in the window and put her finger in the poetry book. "Me? I haven't been able to find you lot."

"Well, come with me now. We've made a plan, and I think you'll absolutely adore it."

⁂

After Prudence left, Leo sulked. And then he raged by taking long, cold walks around London. He drank some, with Granson, mostly. Then Eyeball came by for some year-end advice, which devolved into more drinking. Fortunately, no one mentioned Prudence.

Until his mother did. She entered with her usual flair, knocking his study door open at some ungodly early hour with her cane. The door hit the wall with a bang. "Granson, go to your room."

Granson was on his feet instantly, though he wobbled from the amount of scotch they'd put down the night before.

"Your Lordship," his mother said.

"Yes, Mrs. Moon," came a reply from the floor, as Eyeball struggled to his feet. When he gained his feet, he faltered only a little, catching the chair to steady himself. "Mrs. Moon. Good morning."

"It's well past noon now. I'm asking you very politely now, Lord Grabe, to please get out of my house."

"Yes, Mrs. Moon," he said, taking a step and gulping as his giant body heaved in revolt.

"Potted plant in the hallway will do nicely," she said as he made her way past her, and then Leo could hear the retching.

The sound did not bother him while he lay with his eyes closed. It was when he opened them that he could smell absolutely everything. Himself, the cushions, the scotch bottle that Lord Grabe had brought over to celebrate a new year.

When Leo sat up, his world spun and his stomach clenched.

"Water!" his mother called, and in came Jeffrey with an ewer. After Jeffrey left, his mother banged the study door closed with her cane.

"Your timing is impeccable," he said, his voice rasping against his dry throat. She sank down in a nearby chair and watched as he drank directly from the ewer, and then used its accompanying bowl to splash his face.

"Better?" she asked.

He nodded as his stomach flipped over. "Coffee?"

"It is on the way," she promised. "But first I need you to answer some questions."

He felt suddenly as if she were his captor, making promises in exchange for something she wanted. "Of course."

"Why have I received a letter from Prudence Cabot lamenting the end of our friendship?" She held up a letter. "It's postmarked from Paris."

He snatched it away from her, desperate for word from her.

He'd checked her hotel, but she wasn't there, and then the next time he'd gone by, even her luggage was gone. The manager would give no forwarding address. He'd debated going to the houses of her friends, of going straight to Lord Rascomb, but then he felt too desperate and wanted to wait until he could think straight again.

> My Dear Mrs. Moon,
>
> I write to tell you how much I have valued your friendship, expertise, and strength during my time in London. You must know now that your son and I pursued a type of courtship that did not bloom as it could have. While I sincerely love our friendship, the tenor of my last conversation with Mr. Moon prevents me from continuing our acquaintance. It is too painful to consider the reminder, especially in light of what you shared with me regarding your past. One must value the relationships that protect and strengthen, not threaten and abandon.
>
> I am now on my travels to Switzerland, and I ask you to watch the newspapers come June and July for reports of our successful ascent. The path will be grueling, but I know that I am capable of enduring hardship.
>
> My sincere admiration,
> Prudence Cabot

Leo let the letter drop into his lap. She was already gone. He felt hollowed out, as if his blood had been filled with ice and shattered. He looked up at his mother.

"What did she mean 'threaten and abandon?'" Mrs. Moon looked quite serious.

Leo shook his head. "I didn't threaten her."

She lifted her eyebrows, looked expectant.

"She is accusing me of something I didn't do," he tried again. The horrified look on his mother's face had him equally horrified when he realized what she thought. "No no no. No. Mama. Mother. I would never."

She frowned, but still said nothing.

He cleared his throat, wishing he had some coffee. "Last summer, while you were away, I also went away, with Mrs. Cabot. Prudence."

His mother canted her head when he said Prudence's given name. But he'd have to grit his way through his discomfort for his mother to think him a decent human being. His father had not given her the best mold of manhood, and he couldn't blame her for being skeptical.

"While we were away, in Thornridge, at the Garden Cottage—"

"You took her to Thornridge." She blinked rapidly.

"Yes, I did, I thought—"

"—and you thought you could show up anywhere near Thornridge and your father would not find out you were there?" She thumped her cane.

"I wanted to show Prudence something beautiful, something I knew."

His mother shook her head, and he knew she was thinking of him in disparaging ways. "And a few days in, Granson shows up at twilight, asking for a Lenny Morgan."

His mother looked unimpressed. "You say that as if you expect me to realize something important."

"It was very important! It made me uneasy. I am not typically aware of that particular sensation, and I wanted to get out of there as soon as I possibly could."

"And that's when you threatened her?"

"I did not threaten her. I never threatened her. I would never." Leo sighed. Where was the blasted coffee? "She wanted to know who Granson was, why I was frightened, and why I wanted to leave. She insisted that she would stay in the cottage if I didn't tell her everything, to which I agreed."

"You agreed to stay?"

"No. I agreed that she could stay. But that I would leave."

"So you said you would leave her to a stranger who frightened you?"

"It sounds terrible when you say it." Leo's head felt like it had been suddenly cleaved into two distinct halves. Both of which pounded. "And I only said it so that she would come with me."

His mother made a noise of understanding and rocked in her chair, thumping her cane.

"So you understand?" he asked, feeling very relieved that his mother was on his side.

"Of course I do. And that was the threatening part. I love you dearly, Leo, but I hope you have adequately apologized."

He sat back, stunned. "Well, I would have apologized."

Again her eyebrows went up. "Would have?"

"If she would have seen me. I felt that an apology had to be made in person. But for months, she ignored my notes. I couldn't help it if she didn't want to see me."

"Fair point, but you could have done some sort of gesture to let her know of your wish to speak with her."

"I did! I went to her ball. I was there at midnight and raised the bidding to an extravagant amount!" Leo was sweating, and it smelled like the garbage heaps in summer.

His mother once again cocked her head at him, and he knew in his bones that she would not be taking his side. "The ball I forced you to attend. And pray tell me, who won the bidding to escort Prudence into the dining room?"

"Eyeball."

They sat in silence. Jeffrey entered with a pot of coffee and a breakfast tray. The footman poured the cup, which Leo snatched up immediately. He drank it so quickly he scalded the roof of his mouth. The shame coursed through him. He hadn't wanted to spend the money. The money that kept them fed and warm.

The money that had seemed so necessary and essential, because without it, Leo felt like he couldn't breathe properly. But now his father was here. Granson was here. And that fist that had lived, knotted in his stomach, had relaxed and released. He no longer worried his father might arrive and take it all. His father was here, and surprisingly, was very thrifty.

If only his father had arrived before the ball, Leo would have acted differently. He would have to let Eyeball raise the price to the sky, and he would have still outbid.

His mother waited, looking enormously displeased. "Leo. I am your mother, and that means I will always be your champion. But when you act in counterproductive ways, it makes it difficult to cheer you on. Therefore, I must ask you, do you wish to have an ongoing relationship with Prudence Cabot?"

He looked out the window, dull winter afternoon sunlight gilded the nude tree branches. Could he even say what he wanted aloud?

"Tell me the truth, Leo. Even if you are embarrassed to do so."

He closed his eyes, which was a terrible idea. The world spun until he opened them again. "Yes. I want more time with her. She—the time I spent—it was more—I mean, the happiness that—" He sighed and splashed the cold water from the ewer on the back of his neck.

"Very articulate, thank you. Do you think you might be in love with her?" His mother asked this question as if it were as simple as saying it.

"I don't know. What does that word even mean?"

"It means, do you think you've made a terrible mistake in letting her go to the Matterhorn without telling her how you feel?"

Leo stilled. "I beg your pardon?"

"The Matterhorn kills people. That company of women might very well die this summer. Are you willing to let Prudence Cabot fall to her death thinking that you don't care about her?"

"That's ridiculous! Of course she knows how I feel about her!" Leo's gut churned again. The Matterhorn was an abstract. The venture equally as mythical. But the letter said she'd already left for Switzerland. A panic started to rise in him, deep, as if manifesting from the earth beneath his feet.

"Does she?" his mother asked coolly. "Because you may be

too late. She is traveling, which means she had no address. We don't know where she's staying in Switzerland, so you cannot send her a letter expressing your affection."

"Are you trying to make me go to Switzerland?" he demanded.

"I'm asking if you want to go to Switzerland," she said, her voice barely above a whisper.

His eyes wandered to the window, again looking at the tree, looking dead in winter, knowing that in a few months it would spring to life once again.

"I'll leave you to think on it," his mother said, and hoisted herself out of her chair. "But be honest with yourself. I'll not have you moping around this house for nothing."

⟫⟫⟫⋇⟪⟪⟪

THE FERRY TO France was choppy, but settling into the south of France was lovely. Prudence enjoyed the warmer weather and the time to relax with Georgie, Eleanor, Tristan Bridewell, and Lady Rascomb. It was the aristocratic name that opened the doors for them, and Tristan Bridewell's arms that carried the luggage through them when a porter was not available. Georgie kept her mouth shut most of the time, not even conversing with Prudence. They stayed in little hotels along the way from Calais to Paris, from Paris down to Marseilles.

Not every hotel was equal. Some were as lavish as the hotel she'd stayed at in London, fit for a foreign aristocrat. But some were small and full of holes in the mortar, desperately poor, having never recovered from the Reign of Terror that ravaged France almost a century before. While they were extraordinarily generous with those inns, usually run by an elderly couple, they moved on quickly, as February was not a month one stayed in drafty rooms.

Over the trains and carriage rides, Prudence had gotten close with Lady Rascomb—Joanna—which she was grateful for. Eleanor and Tristan were a giggling mess most of the times they managed to leave their rooms. But Joanna regaled Eleanor with her climbs of this mountain or that mountain, and her wistful tone made it clear that she wished she were ascending the Matterhorn as well.

Prudence often wondered if Georgie listened to Joanna's tales as well, but it was impossible to tell, given the woman's constant placid demeanor and lack of facial expression. She always had a book open, and given how slowly she did everything, it was unclear if she was reading or listening.

But despite Joanna's stories and the beautiful snow-covered countryside that gradually melted into fallow southern French fields, Prudence was restless. She wanted to see the mountain, which she was gradually feeling ownership over. The Matterhorn was quickly becoming *her* mountain in her mind. The mountain she shared with Eleanor, Ophelia, and Justine. Their lives were so intertwined in this goal, living and breathing it, training, looking at maps and potential routes up the mountain, Ophelia scouring newspapers and journals for any mention of the next party attempting its ascent, how could they not feel close to it?

And now, she was in France, and she could see the French Alps. Joanna spoke of their ascent of Mont Blanc, where she'd injured her leg, how Tristan had carried her down the mountain after the avalanche had buried her. How she'd have died had it not been for her son there when she needed him. But Prudence didn't care about Mont Blanc.

Prudence needed to be at the Matterhorn. Waiting any longer was impossible. It had been a month since they left London, but it was only February. They had planned on taking the Strasbourg-Basel railway to pass the miles into Switzerland. But now, they were in the south, as far from Strasbourg as they could be and still be in France.

At the breakfast table one morning at a quaint inn fifteen miles outside of Marseilles, Joanna noticed. "Did you sleep well,

Prudence? It looks as if something is bothering you."

Prudence smiled her expected American smile. "I'm fine."

But Joanna, perhaps it was her experience as a mother, perhaps as a mountaineer, peered closer. "You are restless. Would you like to get on with it?"

"On with what?" Prudence asked, distracted momentarily by Eleanor's giggle—a noise that she only made when she was near her husband. Tristan was gallantly buttering her toast.

"Going to Switzerland. We could attempt the St. Cenis train around the Alps." Joanna's offer was considerate, but Prudence had to be equally considerate.

"But how will we get through the other passes in February? I'd be concerned about cave-ins and then the long journey through the mountains to get to Zermatt." Prudence didn't want to mention that traveling with Joanna, given her leg injury, would make things exponentially harder. As hale as Joanna was, she was twenty years older and had not been training as they had.

Still, the older woman grimaced, knowing that she was the slowest link the in the chain of their expedition. Well, Prudence considered, Georgie was not known for her speed either. "So we take the Strasbourg train as we'd planned."

Prudence nodded. The trip to get back to Strasbourg would take a week in the winter. But she would be one step closer to the Matterhorn.

"Tristan, Eleanor," Joanna called down the table. The couple looked up, red cheeked, as if they were naughty schoolchildren caught smearing mud on the walls. "We will be departing today for Strasbourg. Please see that your belongings are ready."

They both nodded and then hastily excused themselves from the table. Prudence wanted to roll her eyes. It wasn't that she begrudged them their happiness, it was that neither of them could acknowledge the world around them.

"Newlywed couples," Joanna said with a wistful smile. "I'm sure you once felt like that, too."

Prudence winced. She had, but not when she was newly wed.

Gregory had never been that entranced by her. They were at arm's length most of the time, if not further. They chatted as academics and polite acquaintances across his dinner table. They were proper and distant. And the nights were dark and perfunctory.

But she had felt that giggling effervescence with Leo. The day they'd shopped on Bond Street, pretending still to dislike each other. And those days in the cottage, just the two of them, before Granson had appeared and ruined it all. They had been so swept up in each other. She knew that her irritation with Eleanor and Tristan stemmed from not having that feeling herself.

But in her very marrow she knew that his threat to leave her in the English countryside alone was unforgiveable. If not unforgiveable, it would at least take a reasonable apology to forgive. Something he still had yet to offer.

And so they packed their trunks and boarded yet another carriage to get to the Marseilles train to Paris. It took two days to get there, given the weather, but upon arrival, the trains whisked them off in relative comfort. Until Strasbourg.

In Strasbourg, a warm week had melted the snow and, coupled with rain, flooded the city of canals. The bridge over the Rhine was imperiled, and the trains could not run underwater. Prudence and her group, like many other passengers, were turned away at the train station, with no idea when they could leave the flooded town.

They holed up at Strasbourg's "English" hotel, reassured that they would be comfortable there as they waited out the storms. Two days passed, with daily treks to the train station in the rain, checking once again on conditions. Finally, on the third day, they were reassured that the train would run the following morning, and told to return with their luggage.

Tristan didn't mind being the pack horse, and of course there were no complaints out of Georgie or Eleanor. Joanna bore the inconvenience with aplomb. It made Prudence feel surprisingly petulant. She was already out of sorts, and this delay had not made her feel any better.

The next morning, they trundled over to the train station early, hoping to get their first-class tickets. The station was already full of four days' worth of irritated passengers. Prudence made her way to the ticket line with Tristan, jostled by the sheer number of people. Once, in a flash, she could have sworn she saw Leo. It only added to what felt like the sheer mayhem of the morning.

They managed to prove their ticket purchase for first class seats, but the clerk told them they would be in second class. Tristan puffed up his chest, and Prudence swore he grew three feet taller as he protested on his mother's behalf. The clerk would only bend so far, and in the end, they were able to obtain three first class tickets. The rest would be in the second-class car.

"That's fine," Prudence said. She and Georgie could be in second class, and it wouldn't bother her a bit. At least they would be in Switzerland by the end of the day.

But boarding the train proved another feat. Strangers stepped on the hem of her dress, and Georgie, despite being quite a solid woman, was pushed into several times. A less sturdy person would have fallen.

"If you are a single passenger, please queue here," a clerk shouted between the cars. He shouted the same phrase in French and German, and then back in English again.

Prudence and Georgie boarded and found two seats together, settling in them with a feeling of finding safe harbor at last. Georgie, in rare form, looked disturbed by the experience.

"At least we got on the first train," Prudence said.

A clerk walked through the car, noting empty seats. One of the seats opposite theirs was empty. An older woman occupied the window seat, and she peered out of it, even though they were still inside the train station. She had white hair, pulled back into a severe bun and a black hat pinned into place.

"Pardon me, madame, do you have a companion with you?" Prudence asked. She certainly didn't want the clerk to get the wrong idea and give away a seat that was needed.

The woman peered at Prudence with watery blue eyes and blinked. "Kein Englisch."

Which Prudence took to mean that she didn't speak any English, and she gave up. The clerk who spoke German could sort it out. The meager words that Prudence had managed to learn in the last year were not enough to have a complex conversation. They were barely enough for a simple conversation.

A gentleman was ushered to sit down next to the older woman. He was round in every way—a round face, a round belly, and his fleshy palms round with short fingers that he curled over his kneecaps. "Guten Morgen," he said with utmost seriousness.

The old lady returned the greeting as uninterested as she had spoken to Prudence.

"Guten Morgen," Georgie returned, and Prudence shot her a glance. Georgie shrugged and whispered, "The German colony was the next town over from me."

Prudence shook her head and was relieved as the train lurched forward. Finally. Finally, she was on her way to the mountain. The one bright spot she had left. She stared out the window just as the old lady did. The train left the station, revealing gray clouds and flooded roads. Once outside of Strasbourg, the landscape was sodden and the rivers were bursting. Mud churned as they slid by on a surprisingly smooth track.

A flurry of German was spoken, but Prudence didn't bother trying to pay attention. And then Georgie elbowed her. She looked over as the round man stood and made way for another gentleman. A clerk was in the aisle as well.

"This man says he is a business acquaintance of yours?" the clerk asked in accented English.

Prudence looked at the seated man, who still wore his hat, and her heart flipped. It was as if the breath had been knocked out of her. Leo sat there, looking polished and fine and angular and capable.

"He is," she managed. The clerk looked pleased and shuffled off.

Leo stared at her, and she couldn't manage to break his gaze. Georgie elbowed her again.

"Switch seats," she whispered, standing. Prudence slid over, so that she now sat directly in front of Leo. Could touch him if she wished.

"What are you doing here?" Prudence asked.

He examined her, as if memorizing her face. "I came to apologize."

"You came to France to apologize?" She felt a grin coming unbidden to her face.

"I had never wanted to make an apology in writing. It felt too easy. I needed you to see my face so that I wouldn't use the wrong words to make things worse."

Prudence gobbled up the sight of him, the sound of him, but she bided her time. She needed sweet words at last. No one had ever said things like this aloud to her, and she was anxious for them as she was for her mountain. "I see you."

Leo swallowed, as if he were nervous, and it touched her.

"I have had time to think about us. About our months together. It was the happiest I've ever been in my life, Prudence. In fact, it might have been the first time in my life that I was happy. I have had successes, yes, but those were financial and social, but none of it made me happy. They made me and my mother comfortable, and that's different."

Prudence understood. She had been happy as a child, but not as an adult. Her accomplishments were satisfying, signing documents to purchase new railway systems, ordering new track to be built. Even ordering stock trades on behalf of the incapacitated Gregory. But she hadn't been *happy*.

"That week at the cottage was—" Leo broke off, looking down in his lap.

It had been transcendentally happy. "Sheer happiness," Prudence supplied.

Leo nodded. "To have you there, with the morning birds, and my sketchpad, it was new and different, and made me the man I want to be. And I'd thought, that night, coming down from the Hooper's Hill, I could be this man all the time if I wanted."

Prudence waited. She knew there was an exception coming.

"But when Granson showed up, and called me that name—that name who, as far as I'm concerned, belongs to a dead man. It all came flooding back—why I couldn't be that man in the garden with the sketchpad. Why breakfasting with you amongst flowers was impossible. Why London was the only place I could be. And I wanted you with me, still. But I wasn't willing to give you up. I shouldn't have said I would leave you. Because I wouldn't, Prudence. You have to know that I was desperate. All that helplessness I'd had with my mother in that place, it all came flooding back. And the idea of you knowing that weak and helpless starving boy—I snapped." Leo took a shaky breath. "I am so sorry for not explaining it to you. For not behaving better. For not being the man in the garden with the sketchpad. He would have held you and told you everything. He would have brought you along every step of the way as a partner, not as baggage to haul off and put on a train."

"Your sketches were rather good," Prudence said.

"I mean it, Prudence, more than you can imagine. When you showed up at the house in the snowstorm, I thought this was what I had waited for. I was waiting for you. What I didn't understand was that you were waiting for me to realize that I still hadn't found the man I was for those few days. And I desperately want to show you how my life has changed since this summer."

Her heart ached to forgive him. She wanted to forgive him so badly. But there was still more, and she felt so childish for wanting to know why he didn't outbid Lord Grabe at the auction. She squeezed her eyes shut, trying not to cry.

"I wanted to say all this to you the night of your ball. Which was beautiful, by the way. The room was stunning. You were stunning. But I couldn't get to you."

"But you could have," she whispered, cracking open her eyes. "You could have."

Leo hung his head. "I don't know how to explain this bit. There were times, when I was a child, that my mother starved so that I would have just a tiny morsel in my growing belly. She was so painfully thin that it hurt to look at her arms. So gaunt. Since then, I've been determined to always have enough money for us. I needed back-up accounts and hidden accounts, places that no one could find the money I kept on hand for us. I'm not proud of it. But the sum of eleven thousand pounds was too much for that part of me. The starving little boy, who was watching his mother reduce herself to a skeleton. I couldn't. And when you looked down at me, and I saw the disappointment in your eyes when I didn't bid, it undid me. I was wretched. And I thought, how can I explain this to her? How on earth could I make someone like you—who had a lovely childhood with lovely parents—how could I make you understand what it was like to have Reggie Morgan hounding my every move?"

Prudence swallowed hard. She'd never felt that instinctive need for money. The drive he described. But she could understand how a man like Reggie Morgan could make a boy feel like that.

"And then you saw him arrive in my house. You cannot know the embarrassment and shame I suffered that day, watching as everything unfolded in front of you. All the things I'd sought to keep away from you. All the nasty bits of my life and my family."

"All families have their own dynamics. No one's is perfect." Prudence knew this was true, and while hers had squabbles, she loved them all so much.

"Living with Reggie and Granson has changed me, Prudence. Because you are correct—my family is strange and odd. But Reggie is a different man now. No longer drinks, and is surprisingly frugal. How my mother bosses him around, it's really quite funny."

Prudence ducked her head, smiling, because she heard affection in his voice. "I've missed visiting your mother."

Leo smiled—he actually smiled! "It was your letter to her that made her beat me hard enough to get my head out of my arse."

Prudence reared back. She couldn't imagine.

"Metaphorically speaking," Leo said, holding up a hand. "I was full of whisky and keeping company with Granson and Eyeball every night. It wasn't a healthy choice."

"Eyeball?" Prudence asked, flipping through her memory, searching for the name.

"Lord Grabe. He's known how ardently I've regarded you for some time."

Prudence giggled, reminding herself of Eleanor. "Ardently regarded?"

"Most ardently," Leo assured her, scooting forward on his seat, so their knees touched. He removed his gloves and stowed them in his coat pocket. Then rested his hands on his knees, palm upward. "Prudence. I hadn't known the meaning of the word until I missed you so badly I didn't want to be in this world. I love you. The words scare me and compel me and make me drag myself across a very cold continent to find you. I love you. And I don't ask for anything in return. I would never be so presumptuous."

A warmth inside of her chest glowed brighter. As soon as he said the words, she felt them echo in herself as well. "I love you, too, Leo. I couldn't breathe for how much I loved you." She laid her gloved hands in his bare ones.

"Wunderbar!" cried the old lady next to Leo, clapping her hands. Even Georgie joined in, a smug look on her face.

"I doubt you'd be willing to kiss me in public, would you?" Leo asked.

"Would that not scandalize you? I'm an American, after all. I'm nothing but scandal." Prudence tightened her grip on his fingers, pulling him toward her.

"I'm willing to risk it."

He leaned forward, and she met him, the feel of his lips and the scent of him reeling her in to a place she hadn't even known she thought of as home. Her shoulders relaxed for the first time in weeks, and the rightness of it—of him, of the train, of the applause—felt the same as the hum of the wheels as they picked up speed.

Because there was a future there. A place they both belonged.

>>><<<

Leo did not remember the transfer from Basel to Zurich. Nor did he remember much of the long carriage ride from Zurich to Zermatt. They had to ride donkeys to get through the climb up to Zermatt, which was bumpy and uncomfortable, but all Leo could think of was getting Prudence to a room and making love to her. Showing her with his body all the ways that he loved her, cherished her, wanted her.

"They won't allow us to share a room, Leo. It isn't proper." Prudence had giggled as she'd whispered it, when their two donkeys narrowed the gap between them.

"Then marry me. Now. Tomorrow. As soon as possible. I don't care. Prudence, I love you. I will do anything to be with you."

Apparently, their conversation was nowhere near as quiet as they'd supposed. The cold mountain air and the snow let their voices travel.

"The town of Zermatt is mostly Roman Catholic," Joanna said, conversationally. "If you were to marry in a Catholic church, the Anglican church would still require yet another marriage license for England."

Leo frowned for a second, but then took her meaning. He wished he could take Prudence's hand. Give her a proper proposal. "Would you mind becoming Mrs. Moon earlier, without the fanfare?"

"Is not the room name already under Mrs. Cabot?" Prudence asked, teasing.

"If you want me to become Mr. Cabot, I absolutely will." He didn't mind changing his name. It wouldn't be the first time. Prudence giggled again, and Leo was finding the sound to be more and more erotic as the trip wore on. But then, everything about her was. Dear God, he wanted to lick up the expanse of her neck, from the high collar of her traveling cloak to her chin.

"I appreciate it, but I think I would rather become Mrs. Moon. Another connection to your very formidable mother." A serious expression darkened her face. "And I've already been married to Mr. Cabot. It wasn't bad, but I think it's time for a new chapter."

"Mrs. Moon it is," Leo pronounced. "And I notice you haven't said yes to marrying me."

"Very perceptive." Her lips glistened, and he was nearly felled when she bit her lip. "Let me think on it. I've been married before, you know."

"I'm well aware." Leo kissed her cheek, given the surrounding company of the crowded carriage. "But I will wait for you Prudence. For however long you require."

She put her hand to his cheek, and even through her glove, her touch lit a fire inside of him. "And I promise I won't make you wait a moment longer than you must."

<hr />

THE INN WAS a blur of luggage and blonde wooden boards lacquered and freshly built. It had taken ages to finally get the key, exchanging impatient pleasantries as Leo held her hand.

His anxiety to be alone matched hers. Finally, finally! The door to their perfunctory room with its large, unadorned bed, and simple white feather duvet, closed. Leo had tipped the broad-shouldered attendant who carried up their trunks, and it was he who closed the heavy wooden door.

"We're here," Prudence said. He was rumpled from the train and subsequent donkey ride. She had no idea how she looked—probably not dazzling. But the way he looked at her made her feel that perhaps she was.

"Here as in Zermatt, or here as in a private room together?" Leo asked, taking slow steps towards her.

All of it felt right to her. The Matterhorn loomed at the end of the valley, distant but yet so close. So forbidding, but yet familiar. They'd talked of it, planned routes up it, scoured maps of it for the past year.

Leo felt the same—exciting and new, but also familiar and beloved. She felt the magnetism of him, the nearness of him as he approached slowly. She wet her lips and watched his eyes dart to them.

"Both," she said. There was a flash in her mind of how she must smell of donkey, about feeling dirty from a long day's worth of travel. But she didn't care if Leo smelled of donkey and wool soaked in old sweat. It didn't matter. She loved him clean, and she loved him full of the hardships of the road.

"May I?" Leo asked, taking her hand, finally close enough to gently pull her to him.

Her breasts pressed flush against his hard chest, she swallowed. "Please do."

Slowly, too slowly, an ache flowing through her, he lowered his face to hers. Pressing his lips against hers, gentle, not presumptuous in the least. But Prudence was. She was presumptuous and needy and feeling not at all slow or gentle. She deepened their kiss, licking at the seam of his lips to make them open and admit her tongue. A low groan emitted from his chest that she felt ripple through her.

"Leo, I know that this fast but—" Prudence gasped between kisses. He tasted like everything she knew and wanted.

"Fast is fine," he said, ripping off his coat.

"Good," she said, kissing him again as she undid the buttons on her own. The four large silk-covered buttons slipped and skittered beneath her imprecise fingers, but she tore the garment from her shoulders.

He ripped off his neckcloth and collar and then helped her with the small pearl buttons on her shirtwaist. Enough were undone that he helped her pull it over her head. Pins from her coiffure pinged on the wooden floor. He pushed down his braces, letting them hang from his waist before pulling his own shirt off over his head. Finally. Skin.

She shivered in her corset and shift, despite the woolen stockings still in place. She worked the hook at the waist to her heavy woolen traveling skirt. He looked at her with hunger and need. She couldn't keep her focus. She stepped out of the skirt pooled on the ground and pulled his face to hers. It was as if she stopped kissing him, she would drown.

"I need you, Leo."

He picked her up. She squeaked in surprise, not realizing someone might *do* such a thing. He placed her on the bed, his steel-gray eyes strong and fully focused on her. "I need you too."

He kissed her, and they both rucked up her long shift, pulling off her boots and the woolen stockings and drawers. He unbuttoned his trousers and shucked off his shoes.

He dragged his hand from her jaw down her neck, across her still-cossetted breasts, down between her legs. His fingers gently swirled there, testing her, pleasing her. "I love you, Prudence. I do. I would do anything for you. I won't ever keep anything from you again."

"I know, I know," she said, her back arching as pleasure built. "And I won't stay away. You're stuck with me now." She gasped sharply as her climax shot through her, surprising her.

Leo shifted himself quickly, entering her as she was still in the throes of her pleasure. "I missed you." He thrusted into her, and she wrapped her legs around him, grabbing his arms, urging him into her, pulling him, begging him with her body. They needed to be closer. They needed to be one, together, united.

And finally they were. Leo bellowed as he came, and Prudence shuddered in pleasure as he did.

Afterwards, hastily cleaned by their own dirty garments, Prudence lay in his arms, one long leg draped over his. "You're stuck with me now, Mr. Moon. I hope you are prepared."

He snorted. "I'm the one with the scandalous and strange family. You should be worried about that, not the other way around."

"You haven't met my family yet," Prudence reminded him. But someday, she hoped he would. In fact, she looked forward to the quiet but strong handshake between her father and him. How her mother would tut and go to the kitchen to make him a plate of food.

He kissed her hair. "But I will. Let's hope they'll accept this London ne'er-do-well."

"I'm just glad your mother can accept an American."

"She's full of misguided sentiment. Just look at her husband."

Prudence gave him a playful bite on the arm and he chuckled. They were quiet for a moment. "Thank you for coming after me. I wouldn't have thought you wanted me otherwise."

"You are awfully hardheaded, like all Americans. But you are *my* hardheaded American."

"Go to sleep, you smelly redcoat."

Leo murmured, and soon they both drifted off, exhausted from travel and misunderstandings, heartbreak and resolve. The Matterhorn sat unmoving in the distance, unwavering and majestic, awaiting the future and what it might bring.

The End.

About the Author

Edie Cay writes steamy feminist historical romance. Her debut, A LADY'S REVENGE won the Golden Leaf Best First Book (2020), as well as the Indie Next Generation Book Award (2020). The second in her series, THE BOXER AND THE BLACKSMITH won the Hearts Through History Legends Award, A Man for All Reason in 2019 as an unpublished manuscript, and then went on to win the Best Indie Book Award (2021). The third book, A LADY'S FINDER was a finalist for a Lambda Award, the most prestigious LGBTQ+ literary award in the world. A VISCOUNT'S VENGEANCE garnered the Best Indie Book Award for Regency Romance as well in 2023.

Previously, she published short stories, poems, and non-fiction in small presses. She co-wrote and starred in several short films and documentaries from MadLaw Media, including "Big 5 Dive" about scuba diving in the Great Lakes, and "How to Be Sexy," a fictional short about confidence and self-worth.

She obtained dual BAs in Creative Writing and in Music from Cal State East Bay, and her MFA in Creative Writing from University of Alaska Anchorage. She has been a professional musician, bookstore employee, and a healthcare worker.

She has participated in several anthologies, including Unlocked, The Grand Mistletoe Assembly, and the upcoming Beneath the Midwinter Moon.

Her next series will be about Victorian women alpinists, out in August 2024 from Dragonblade Publishing.

She is a founding member of the historical fiction collective The Paper Lantern Writers, and helps edit and publish their anthologies. She gives presentations at conferences around the world on the history of women's boxing and other aspects of

Regency culture and writing.

In addition to fiction, Edie writes and reviews for the Historical Novel Society. You can keep up with her on her website, www.ediecay.com, or follow her on Instagram or Facebook @authorEdieCay.